The Gypsy Warned You!

CAROL PRIOR

To my sister Julie,
For all the laughs.

All characters appearing in this work are fictitious. Any resemblance to people, living or dead is purely coincidental.

Cover designed & created by Zara Prior

New edition September 2019
Copyright Carol Prior 2018
Winchelsea Publications

The Grim Reaper....

'Annabel Leggat?' the voice was young, enthusiastic, male... 'Annabel Leggat, this is your lucky day!' I heard murmured thanks and then footsteps running up the stairs. She was trembling slightly when she came back clutching a large pink envelope decorated with a smattering of hearts and diamonds with FIRST PRIZE in gold emblazoned across the front. I peered at her anxiously, my sticky iced bun poised temptingly somewhere between mouth and plate; 'I've won!' she gasped, 'I've actually won! I don't believe it! I've always wanted a Tarot reading, ever since I was really little when I used to see Madame Zelda down on the pier; she looked so... exotic, all floaty frocks and gold earrings... I can't wait! Will you come with me?'

I rolled my eyes; I couldn't believe I'd encouraged her to enter the competition in the first place and I didn't think for a minute that she would actually win a free reading from 'An Expert in the Art of Tarot'. It didn't bear thinking about; to say that she was gullible, not to mention easily influenced, was an understatement. Still, there was no going back now.

It was a crisp autumn morning when we turned up at a rather posh house in Ealing. There was nothing floaty about it though; no, this place was super tasteful with neutral linen blinds and Bay trees in pots on either side of the doorstep.

'Are you sure this is the right address?' I asked, 'Show me the voucher again.'

It was the right place, unfortunately. I squinted through the letter box; it looked gorgeous inside as well. There was an antique hall stand and a row of chairs for the clients, and a lovely polished oak floor. We rang the bell, one of those brass affairs where you pull it and it clangs inside with a deep melodious DING...!

An elderly lady opened the door; she reminded me a bit of the Queen with her grey perm and comfy blue twinset. 'Come in,' she said, 'Julia is ready for you, she's in here. Does your friend want to wait in the hall?'

'Would you like a cup of tea and a biscuit?' she asked me.

'Oh, yeah, great,' I said, 'yes, please.'

'I've changed my mind,' whispered Annabel, 'I don't think I want a Tarot reading after all.' She eyed the front door as if she was working out whether she could make a swift exit without anyone noticing, and then she gave a shudder and turned to me.

'You do it, Kate; please...' which is how it came to be me sitting in front of Madame Zelda instead of Annabel. Though, of course, this wasn't Madame Zelda; 'I'm Julia,' she said, and she smiled; she gave no further clue to her identity, but I could see that with her high-necked floral frock and Alice band she certainly wasn't a Madame anything.

'Shuffle please,' she instructed, and she handed me a deck of cards that were larger than the usual sort and felt soft and worn with use.

'You should try to touch every card as you shuffle, now spread them on the table in front of you and pass them to me one at a time, I will tell you when to stop. Choose carefully, now.'

So far there was nothing remotely creepy; apart from the card bearing a picture of the Grim Reaper that leapt out of the pack seemingly of its own volition.

'We'll keep that one,' said Julia, and a shiver ran down my back; someone must have been walking over my grave, as my Gran used to say.

'Now give me three more cards; choose them carefully, Annabel. Take your time.'

I was about to tell her that I was Katherine because Annabel had chickened out and was, at this very moment, sitting in the hall slurping my cup of tea and chomping on my biscuit but I decided to keep quiet; maybe I could pretend that this was her reading and not mine, at least I wouldn't believe it all, would I?

'These four cards represent your past which means they are a great influence on the present and on your future...'

The Grim Reaper glowered at me from the table top where it sat next to the Ten of Swords, the

6

Seven of Cups and the Hanged Man… they looked terrifying!

'…Oh, very interesting; first of all, Death, or the Grim Reaper,' she murmured, and I gulped; 'I always reassure people when this card pops up. It usually represents the end of a phase and a new beginning, but in this case, and I don't want to worry you, my dear, well you have to take the cards around it into account. Of course, it's all in the past but it seems that someone wanted something very valuable that was in your possession and they were prepared to, as they say, stab you in the back to obtain whatever it was. These four cards represent your past. Does any of this ring a bell with you? I mean, has your past been um… violent in any way? Any traumatic events, for instance…?'

I racked my brain; well I suppose Mum might have got a bit cross with me when I stretched her patience to the limit, but I couldn't recall any death and destruction, or having any possessions that anyone would really want.

'Of course, it could all be in your subconscious, maybe a past you are somehow unaware of…?'

I pointed to the Hanged Man, 'What does he mean then?' I asked.

'Oh, he's one from the Major Arcana and one of my favourite cards. In this case I would say that he's indicating a state of limbo; there's something unresolved, couldn't say how far back though. You must be very careful!'

I gulped again 'Let me see where we are at the moment, shall we? Give me four more cards and think carefully about your current situation when you choose them, thank you. Oo... had a few sleepless nights, have we, dear?'

She pointed to the Nine of Swords where a distraught woman was sitting up in bed with the aforementioned nine swords hanging perilously over her, '...and the Lovers; which can indicate meetings and partings, but in this context, I'd probably say partings. Have you had some kind of upset with your boyfriend... or your husband?'

She glanced down to see if I was wearing a ring, which I wasn't. 'Don't worry; this King of Wands is dashing into the fray, unless that is your partner, it's hard to tell sometimes but my intuition tells me that a new man is on the not too far distant horizon. Be careful, he may not be all he seems, and this one, this Seven of Swords, he's a tricky fellow. Hand me another card for clarification, thank you. Oh, the Moon, well, I'd say that you should be very careful, my love, don't be taken in by tall, dark and handsome men, they're all just after one thing really.'

Apart from the fact that I was extremely alarmed I was beginning to think that Julia was perhaps Madame Zelda in another guise. She must have done so well on the pier that she'd moved upmarket, I was almost expecting her to say 'cross my palms with silver, darlin'.

'Oh well, never mind, the last four cards will help us decide on the outcome.'

She shook visibly when I gave her the next card, and who could blame her? Eek... the Tower and it looked extremely grim even to my untrained eyes.

'There's no need for you to be alarmed, no need at all...' said Julia, rather unconvincingly I thought, 'The Tower simply indicates change, a bit like Death really,' she added, but I could tell she wasn't fooling herself, and she certainly wasn't fooling me.

'And, oh look, the next one's the Sun, that's much better, at last some good news. You see, it will all be fine, in the end, and you've got this nice Queen of Cups, must be your mum. She's looking after you, and finally, Justice, so lots of joy... in the end!'

Oh yeah, who's end, I thought but I kept quiet.

'What a very interesting reading, no less than seven from the Major Arcana!' She gazed at me with pale blue, slightly fishy eyes. 'You must be on your guard though, and beware of deception, and don't forget the choice is yours, the cards are but a warning.'

Then she smiled and went to open the door. 'Goodbye, Annabel; such a pretty name,' she narrowed her fishy eyes and gazed at me with a quizzical expression, 'but then I'm not sure it's really you at all! Do come again.'

When hell freezes over, said my brain, but my mouth said, 'Yes, thank you so much, Julia. It was... intriguing, and erm... very interesting.' I didn't mention that actually it was terrifying, and that I was nearly scared out of my wits.

I handed over the voucher and made a run for the front door. Annabel was quite surprised as she'd struck up a friendship with the Queen and they were having a girly chat about perms and where to buy the comfiest twin sets.

I grabbed her arm and dragged her out, past the twee little Bay trees in pots and onto the damp pavement. A breeze had got up and there were leaves blowing all over the place, so I took my black beanie out of my bag and pulled it onto my head until it covered my ears.

'Well, what did she tell you?' asked Annabel impatiently. 'Are you going to meet a dark stranger and travel across the sea? Coo, the minute you went in there I wished it was me. I just got cold feet, you should have made me!'

'Huh, if you really want to know it was all death, deception and destruction, the dreaded three Ds; and she kept going on about a Major Arcana somebody, whoever he is! Oh, and, this is really weird, I think she guessed that I wasn't you, plus, I don't know how, but she knew I'd broken up with Tom, and if she got that bit right, well my future looks grim, and my present, and my past. Oh yes, he was there as well, Grim...'

Annabel looked puzzled, 'Um... that would be Grim who? Is he a friend of the Major Arcana?'

'The Grim Reaper of course, he's the only Grim I've heard of!'

'Serves you right for living opposite that creepy old cemetery,' said Annabel. 'Coo... I'm really glad it was you and not me, I think I would have fainted if she'd said all that to me. I was having a really nice chat with Julia's auntie, and the biscuits were yum, homemade. She said they used to travel with the fairs, very lucrative. And anyway, none of it is true, not really, especially if you pay by voucher, she probably likes cash best.'

'Yeah, I should have crossed her palm with silver.'

'Eh? Come on; let's head down to the wine bar. I'll shout you lunch and a glass of vino then you'll feel much better!'

'Yes, I reckon you owe me that, at least!' I muttered.

CHAPTER 1

It was quite true; I did live opposite a creepy old cemetery.

'The dead centre', that's what my Mother called it when she saw our tiny flat at the top of a creaking flight of stairs on the wrong side of Highgate Cemetery.

'It's a bit… well, spooky, isn't it?' she added, and fair enough, it was rather Gothic with its ancient twisted chimneys and arched windows, not to mention the cemetery view; the rent was cheap though.

'Still, you've got Gran and Grandad over there. There's Karl Marx as well, and all those musicians and rock stars; everyone wants to get in there now, you know.'

I shuddered, 'Not sure I do, Mum, well not for a while anyway.'

She laughed, 'Oh, you are funny, Kate, it must be eerie at night though, especially now Tom's not around.'

I had to agree; the flat was great when Tom was there, when all the odd sounds in the night could easily be explained away. 'This place is over a hundred years old,' he'd say, 'so of course it creaks; it would be strange if it didn't.'

We met on our first day at university when we both signed up for the same teaching degree, along with Annabel, and Tom's new crush, the adoring, but definitely not adorable, Lorna. Annabel had stuck it out until the end then vowed never to enter a classroom again, which was doing everyone a favour in my opinion as she wasn't nearly as mature as some of the ten-year olds I'd taught. Now Lorna was working in the geography department at the same school as Tom, so she'd been hanging around him for years.

Mum droned on... 'I don't know why you had to break up with him, such a nice young man, lovely manners, and so good with children. And teachers are paid really well these days, and they get lovely long holidays!'

I'd heard it all before, 'He dumped me, Mum, but I don't mind at all, he was boring! If it hadn't been him it would have been me, eventually! And, anyway, I've decided to go to Venice; I thought it would be good to get away for a holiday, you know, a change of scenery. I'm flying out of Gatwick on Friday morning.'

I watched her face as it turned from surprise to alarm. 'But Katherine,' she stammered, 'you're not going on your own, surely; and what about your job?'

'I work for an agency, Mum; they call me when a teacher hasn't turned up, which is usually because they've been driven to distraction by unruly little monsters. I always end up with all the classes that no one else wants! I've saved up loads, and I need a break.'

She nodded but she still looked baffled, 'Well, that's understandable, I suppose. I know I wouldn't fancy it; but why are you going to Venice?'

Why Venice? That was the question I'd been asking myself, but I still didn't know why I'd decided on Venice. I can only say that I felt somehow compelled to go; as if a giant hand was beckoning me. I wasn't likely to tell her that though because she was already convinced I'd gone mad. I'd looked online and found a small apartment described as 'A part of the Villa Alatri, a fourteenth century palazzo with a canal view and a sunny courtyard - very close to St Mark's but away from the crowds', and there were photos of a sweet little terracotta sitting room and a double bedroom with a pretty window and a big ornate mirror. It gave the owner's name as Sofia Lazio and it said she lived in Verona during the week but was on hand to greet potential visitors. There was an email address, and a phone number underneath, and it sounded perfect, so I booked it there and then and instantly wondered why I had.

Annabel popped round that evening brandishing a bottle of Prosecco.

'Just thought I'd get you in the mood for Italy; I don't see why you'd want to go on your own though! You know, Kate, you've got very weird since Tom left but, well, it's probably for the best, you know, play the field for a bit. Maybe you'll be seduced by a hot-blooded gondolier with a sexy curling moustache, and he'll serenade you with operatic arias as you drift gently under the Bridge of Sighs,' she paused to take a quick gulp of air before continuing, 'I feel quite jealous, actually. Imagine, you could meet some gorgeous Italian waiter and come back in about three years' time with a couple of bambinos.'

Bambinos! Hot blooded gondoliers...? I checked to make sure the bottle was unopened; maybe she'd downed a couple of glasses before she left home?

'And why didn't you mention it before you booked, I would definitely have come with you, I could do with a holiday, away from the grind... er... where are the champagne glasses...?'

She was right; I'd never been away on my own before; what if I couldn't find my way from the airport to the hotel? I knew I was being ridiculous, if I could manage a class of thirty raucous adolescents, I could definitely find my way around an airport.

'Hellooo... are you even listening to me?' she asked, '...and, I've got no idea what he sees in that woman, she's got a huge nose and that weird blonde hair, and she comes over as really aggressive; she looks just like a Viking. In fact, she's got a face like an 'orse! An 'orse, Norse, get it?'

'Haha... very amusing,' I muttered unconvincingly.

'And...' she went on, 'I think she was stalking him, has been ever since second year at uni. Then she gets a job in the same school, very sus' if you ask me. Have you got any nibbles?'

I filled a couple of glasses with Prosecco and rummaged in the fridge for snacks while Annabel gazed through the window at the dark cemetery.

'I really don't know how you can stand living here. It's so... morbid, it gives me goose-pimples; I can just imagine them all lying there, under the ground.' She shivered, 'You don't think this Venice trip has got anything to do with that Tarot reading we had, do you, Kate? She did warn you and I agree, maybe you should be careful, after all, it is a bit sudden and that's not like you at all.'

'Huh, what do you mean, 'we had'? As I recall, it was me in the hot seat because you chickened out at the last minute! And, are you saying that I'm not spontaneous?'

'No, not that,' she shook her head, 'I mean... it's just that it's all rather unplanned, and you've never said that you wanted to go to Venice until now, so it doesn't make sense!'

She was beginning to sound just like my mother! I wondered if I should tell her about my dream, the repetitive and terrifying dream that haunted me and woke me up with a jolt, clutching my throat and screaming blue murder. Okay, so it had only happened three times, but that was three times too many as far as I was concerned!

I wanted to move but Tom had insisted it was just my over-active imagination. 'Everyone has vivid dreams sometimes,' he'd mutter impatiently, 'just try to forget it. It's only your brain sorting information, you don't have to go on and on about it!'

Right; I see, so nothing to do with living opposite a scary Victorian cemetery? Looking back, I'm not sure why I put up with him for so long; to say that he was lacking in empathy was an understatement! Anyway, now he was gone, and his departure had been so sudden and unexpected that I was left floundering and finding a new flat had been the last thing on my mind.

No, probably best not to mention the dream; Annabel would never be able to handle it, she'd tell Mum and then they would both fuss around me until I gave in and stayed at home.

'Look, I'm only going for a week,' I told her cheerfully, 'and if I really enjoy it we'll go back, okay? Here, I've found some bread and cheese; it will soak up the alcohol!'

'But what about the Tarot reading, you know, the death and destruction bit, and the deceit; aren't you worried?'

'No, of course not, it's all nonsense! I just fancy a few days away, no other reason, nothing sinister, so stop panicking!'

That night I had the dream again. It always began in the same way, in a narrow street, silent but for the clatter of footsteps on the cobbles that stopped when I glanced over my shoulder to see who was there. Someone was following me, getting closer, and closer, until they were almost stepping on the hem of my cloak as it trailed in the dust. I felt the blood pulsing in my throat as I tore down dark alleyways full of long shadows, and over tiny bridges where the reflection of the moon was a perfect circle in the still water.

A flight of stone steps leading up to a wooden door came into sight just ahead of me; if I could only reach them I knew I would be safe but they seemed to recede further into the distance even as I ran; then bony fingers reached out, winding tightly around my neck until I was gasping for air, and a scream rose from deep inside me filling my head and reverberating through the night... and then...

I woke up!

My heart was pumping so hard that it felt like it was trying to burst out of my chest and run around the room on its own, and for a long moment I couldn't remember where I was. I lay there for a while staring into the darkness but eventually it slowed down to something approaching a normal rhythm and I climbed shakily out of bed and turned on all the lights. Only four in the morning but there was no way I was going back to sleep. I filled the kettle, and threw a tea bag into a cup, and wondered again why I felt this compelling urge to return to Venice. Return... where had that come from? I hadn't even been to Italy before, let alone Venice. 'Something unresolved', according to Julia; could it be possible that I was expected to sort out something that had happened in the past, perhaps centuries before I was born; something that, even now, was influencing our lives? It seemed ridiculous, insane, but there was no doubt that something, or someone, was summoning me to Venice, an unwanted invitation that I couldn't refuse. It was completely illogical and yet I was actually going!

Annabel was right, I decided; I was going mad, I'd cancel first thing in the morning, and if I lost my money, so what... and then I'd call her, and we'd go to Ibiza instead, and I'd find somewhere else to live the minute I got home!

I suddenly felt much better, but I still wasn't brave enough to go back to bed, my dream had been far too vivid; I had to get away from the grave stones that were watching me, gleaming bone white in the moonlight like rows of crooked teeth. The bleak November night looked inviting by comparison and ten minutes later I was bundled up in my winter coat and scarf and heading towards Camden Town where I knew people would be about, even at this hour. Music filtered out of some of the houses, and lights shone from windows and I felt better straight away. There were cars whizzing along the dark streets, and shadowy figures on early shift heading down to the tube station. People, hooray! Living people! Then I was hurrying along the main road through Tufnell Park, and Kentish Town, on and on, to where people huddled in doorways on sheets of cardboard, wrapped in dirty blankets. I picked up pace and hurried on till I came to a café on the Camden Road. It was open, and the lights were on radiating an opaque yellow glow through steamed-up windows and promising warmth, and company. I pushed open the door, it was too warm and almost empty, and there was the distinct aroma of slightly stale fried food.

'What can I get you, love?' enquired a large woman in navy dungarees that grasped her huge circumference in a mummy-like grip. I grinned up at her maniacally with my pallid face and knotted hair, 'Eggs, bacon, toast and a cup of tea, please,' and she nodded and smiled sympathetically. She was probably used to odd customers demanding a cooked breakfast at half past four in the morning. She went behind the counter and I heard her cracking a couple of eggs, and the sound of bacon sizzling on the griddle and the smell made my mouth water. It was only then that I remembered my purse sitting all by itself on the kitchen table. I rifled through my coat pockets for change even though I already knew that they were empty; then I searched frantically through the pockets of my jeans, and there, at the very bottom of pocket number three, I found a folded ten-pound note! Whew... things were looking up; I wouldn't have to do a runner after all!

An old man was watching from a table near the window; he reminded me of my grandad. He smiled at me and winked, and I was somehow certain that he would have offered to pay if I'd been penniless; he probably thought I was a rough sleeper, one of the homeless, yep, I certainly looked the part. I smiled back, 'Panic over...' I said, 'look, found a tenner in my pocket!' and he nodded and grinned.

'You really are mad,' said Annabel when I called her the next morning, 'totally bonkers and round the bend. No way can you wander around London like that, and just because of a little nightmare, and on your own, in the middle of the night, in the dark. You could have been mugged; or worse they could have taken your phone!'

'I didn't take my bag; actually, I didn't even take my phone... and it was a big nightmare, not a little nightmare!'

Annabel gave a gasp of disbelief, 'What? You should always take your phone, Kate, it could be a lifeline! And who was this old guy who winked at you? You can't trust any old geezer just because they remind you of your grandad; honestly, you shouldn't be allowed out on your own!'

'I had to get out of the house,' I explained, 'and I'm going to move, as soon as possible!'

'I'm really sorry,' she said, 'it's my fault, I didn't mean to spook you about the cemetery, and the Tarot stuff; and, actually Kate, I think you're amazing going to Venice on your own, I wish I was as brave as you! Right, I've got to go to work now, it's nearly eight o'clock! Honestly, some of the people I work with, they're worse than kids, they do nothing but bitch about everyone behind their backs, really nasty! Maybe I should go back to teaching!'

'Oh no, don't do that, Annabel, please...' I began but she'd already gone. It rang again immediately though.

'Did we get cut off?' I asked.

'What... no, I don't think we did,' said a voice that I recognised as Barb from the Agency. 'Is that Katherine Elliot? I've got an urgent request for a stand in teacher down at St Job's near Paddington Station. Can you get down there, sharpish?'

'Um... well actually, I'm not available today,' I stuttered. The very thought of St Job's, better known as St Yob's in the trade, filled me with dread. 'I'm... I'm...' I wracked my brain for excuses, I'd been though most of them already; I gazed towards the cemetery hoping for heavenly inspiration, 'I'm going to a funeral...' I squeaked eventually, 'yes, very sad... so I'm not available, sorry!'

'Oh dear,' sighed Barb sympathetically, I could tell by her voice that she didn't believe a word of it.

'So many devoted teachers unavailable,' she continued sarcastically, 'all these ailments that prevent people working, not to mention births, deaths and funerals!'

'Lot of it about,' I agreed.

'Still, you'll be free next week, won't you?'

'No, sorry, I'm going away... to Venice, so I won't be available, and actually, Barb, I'll call you when I'm available again so byee...' and I cut her off before she could say any more.

Just because I said I was going to Venice, it didn't mean I had to go, I could just as easily go to Malaga, or Ibiza, with Annabel, and no one would know, or care; though with only two days to go it was probably too late to change my mind, and why did I have the uncomfortable feeling that I'd be somehow letting myself down if I cancelled. I was going; there was no getting away from it. The die was cast, as they say, and the mere thought made an icy chill run down my back that started at the top of my neck and shivered its way down to my knicker elastic.

It was no good, I couldn't stay another night on my own, I'd be a nervous wreck; even in broad daylight I was jumping at every sound and flinching at shadows. I considered staying at Mum's, but she would try to persuade me to move back home and I had to resist that, it would be far too comfortable, she'd do all my washing and cook my food, and I'd save loads on rent and I'd never move out. Still... and I'd almost persuaded myself that it wouldn't be so bad when I had a better idea, I'd ring Great Auntie Flo, Grandad's youngest sister, still alive and kicking, and living in Sussex, and only two train stops from the airport, brilliant; I wouldn't have to rush, it would be SO much easier.

Her phone rang and rang, and I was about to give up when a gruff voice answered. 'I might have rung the wrong number,' I said, 'but is Flo there?'

'Someone on the phone for you, Sweetie,' shouted the gruff voice nearly deafening me.

Sweetie! He didn't mean old Auntie Flo, surely?

'Of course, you can come,' enthused Flo, 'arriving today, yes, two nights. Oh, how nice, it will be lovely to see you, it's been ages!'

23

I went off to pack with a spring in my steps and a sunny summer smile on my face. Things were improving; it would be so much easier to get to the airport from Flo's, and I was wondering, who exactly was the friend with the deep voice?

CHAPTER 2

Auntie Flo's cottage is what estate agents refer to a 'desirable property in a typical English village with an easy commute to London'. It has a thatched roof and roses around the doorway, and a garden full of daffodils in the spring and hollyhocks in summer. Oh, and not forgetting, riders in fancy jackets and jodhpurs, clip-clopping past at all hours of the day; and it's worth a bomb! Mind you, she's been there for so long that she probably paid next to nothing for it!

She was waiting for me outside in the lane even though it was absolutely freezing, and she looked happier than I'd ever seen her.

'Wooo hooo...' I yelled, and waved, it was great to see her.

'Katherine, how wonderful, welcome!' she called as soon as I was within earshot, 'I wanted to catch you before you knocked, just to warn you,' she blushed a bright pink, 'you see my friend Jim has moved in and I haven't mentioned it to your father yet. He might think it's a bit scandalous.'

I laughed and gave her a hug, 'Honestly, Flo, everyone lives together these days, and no one takes any notice of it any more. I won't tell Dad though, I promise.'

'Well, come in, he can't wait to meet you! Jim, this is my niece, Katherine,' she said when an elderly man appeared at the door, well, I say elderly but in fact he was obviously quite a lot younger than Auntie Flo. Jim looked right at home already in his checked slippers and denim jeans, he was carrying a hammer and was bald on top with a comb over, and he had a pencil balanced over one ear; like those old fashioned workmen that you get in those black and white films from the nineteen fifties, 'Carry on up the Workers', that kind of thing.

'Pleased to meet you, Katherine,' he said. 'I'm just fixing the sink unit; the drawer keeps falling out!'

Well, no wonder Flo looked so happy. I would be too if I had a live-in handy man. Tom was always useless at that sort of stuff.

'Come upstairs,' she said, 'you can put your things in your room and I'll show you where the bathroom is. I've got roast lamb for dinner, you're not vegetarian or anything, are you; no allergies? Everyone is so sensitive these days; Jim reckons it's all the pesticides and genetic modification. He's big on genetic modification is Jim,' she winked at me and chuckled.

'Yum... Flo, it's one of my favourites; but actually, I'll eat almost anything, mmm... especially roast lamb...!' It made my mouth water just thinking about it.'

She nodded, 'That's just what Jim says! He's such good company, Katherine; a widower, very traumatic past...'

I smiled sympathetically, 'He's seems nice, I'm sure Mum and Dad would love to meet him.'

'Oh, do you really think so, dear? And you don't think they'll disapprove? After all, I've never been married so it's all new to me.'

Whoa, Flo, too much info... the mind boggled; after all she was seventy, at least! I nodded and smiled again, 'I'll be down in a minute,' I called as she went downstairs, 'do you need any help?'

'All done,' she called back, 'and dishing up in ten!'

I felt a bit guilty actually; I was there mainly because it was easy to get to the airport, and because it meant I wouldn't have to stay in the flat on my own, after Annabel had helpfully reminded me of the proximity of my deceased neighbours, not that I really needed reminding. I couldn't blame her entirely though because, as she had pointed out, it was my fault for living opposite a creepy cemetery in the first place, not to mention the weird dreams, I couldn't really blame her for those.

It was great to see Flo and I wished I'd been before. Next morning was sheer bliss, lying in bed with a cup of tea, surrounded by chintz; flowery chintz curtains, flowery chintz bedspread, flowery, almost chintz, carpet! It was all very comforting, especially as I'd slept soundly, untroubled by ghoulish pursuers. And then there was breakfast in bed, courtesy of Jim, and a very nice visit to a garden centre for tulip bulbs. I felt like I'd retired for the day! They certainly had a nice time, no biological clocks ticking away; they'd already ticked their last! And no career worries; they had everything they needed, and I resolved to either buy a good pension scheme or marry a millionaire. In fact, an old millionaire was what was needed; Annabel and I should start our quest pronto, I'd tell her as soon as I got back.

In the wink of an eye it was Friday and I was up at five, but Flo was up before me and raring to go. It was still dark but there was a thick frost icing the grass; it sparkled under the street lights, and I could see my breath in the cold air as I loaded my tiny case into the car.

'Wretched thing won't reverse, must be the gear box,' complained Flo, after she'd been grinding away for a good ten minutes, 'I'd better wake Jim.'

'There's not time; I'll have to walk! How far is it?' I asked. Oh goody, maybe I wouldn't have to go after all, the ultimate get-out; let down by a dodgy gear box through no fault of my own. I groaned inwardly when she added, 'Now don't you worry, Katherine, it's only about twenty minutes, I'll come with you and then you won't get lost. Quick let's get your things out of the car...' so I unloaded my wheelie reluctantly and we rattled through the streets to the station.

'My train...!' I yelled as the barrier went down, 'Sorry, too late,' said the ticket inspector with a smug half smile, 'can't let you through; regulations, more than me jobs worth!'

On the other side of the barrier I could see hordes of sleep-deprived people boarding a train that was less than a stone's throw away. Why were so many people up at this time of the morning?

I delved around in my bag, 'I've bought a ticket; really I have, it's in here... somewhere.'

'Don't worry, take your time,' whispered Flo reassuringly, 'there's another one in ten minutes; we're in the commuter belt. I'm off home but you have a lovely time; and send me a postcard.'

I found my ticket eventually and pushed onto the empty platform, along with a crowd of sullen teenagers who huddled silently in groups of three or four and eyed me suspiciously, but soon the platform was crowded again, with commuters mainly, all jostling for position as the train approached.

'Is this the right train for Gatwick?' I asked a girl in four-inch heels. I was impressed; wasn't she worried about breaking something? Like an ankle, or her neck; and where was she going that required her to be four inches taller than she really was? And why did everyone measure heels in inches and not centimetres?

She frowned at me as if she could read my insane thoughts, 'Yes, it's the right train, are you off somewhere nice?'

I nodded, 'Venice, it's my first visit so I hope it's nice.'

'You'll love it,' she replied, 'and not too crowded in November. It's like a rugby scrum in summer!' And then she disappeared into the anonymous crowd, lost in a sea of faces concealed behind newspapers or captivated by screens.

I breathed a sigh of relief when the train arrived at the airport; it had its own station so even I couldn't get off at the wrong stop. My Gate still hadn't opened so I went to one of the Terminal restaurants and had a dry sausage roll and a cup of weak tea. Eventually it came up on the board, Gate twenty-eight! Hooray, I'd done it, nothing could go wrong now! I clutched my boarding pass feverishly and waited for the announcement instructing us all to board the plane. The queue was long but at last I reached the counter where the crew were carrying out the final checks, feeling light headed with relief that I'd actually made it.

'This is Gate twenty seven, the twelve thirty flight to Milan!' said the attractive young man in a navy blazer, 'You need Gate twenty eight over there for Venice, but you'd better hurry, I think that flight was scheduled to leave at twelve fifteen, you might make it, if you're lucky; and yes, I know it is confusing Madam, there's not much space at this gate, just too many flights I'm afraid.'

I pushed back through the impatient mob; even people whose seats hadn't been announced were lined up; it wasn't as if the plane was going to leave without them, whereas mine might if I wasn't there at all when it took off. I felt like a right idiot, a 'nincompoop' Dad would have said if he'd seen me. I expect everyone in the queue thought I was as well as they parted reluctantly to let me through.

Then we waited, and waited, and waited.

'Makes you wonder why we bother,' complained one elderly gentleman, 'I never minded a week in Southend.'

'Have you tried getting to Southend these days?' said a second elderly gentleman, 'you wouldn't believe the traffic. Last year it took me ten hours to get from Ipswich to Clacton, not a word of a lie!'

'Overpopulation,' muttered an old girl in a striped top that was a size too small, 'overpopulation, alright if you've got a bit of money. The rest of us have to put up with this!'

I was about to pitch in with, 'it's nothing short of a miracle that we can get to Venice in three hours', but something stopped me. Of course, it could have been the fact that I'd already been in transit since five which was over ten hours ago, or equivalent to the long way round to Clacton; plus another five or so left to go, which made it almost fifteen hours in all.

Clacton was beginning to sound more attractive.

CHAPTER 3

Venice, at last...! I couldn't believe I'd actually made it! I turned left heading straight for the quay and the vaporetto stop; the Orange Line, according Mr Trip Advisor. The air was warm for November; I could smell the sea in the breeze and a few raindrops dampened my cheeks as I joined the end of a long line of tourists feeling lost and very alone in the midst of loud American voices mingled with rapid French and Italian.

'On your own?' enquired a welcome voice in English. He looked about thirty and he seemed really nice, though to be honest, by now anyone who spoke English would have seemed nice.

'Yes, my first visit; I'm heading to San Stae. Do you know if this is the right vaporetto? It's been a bit of a day.'

'Yeah, the flight was delayed, I saw you at the airport.'

Eek! He'd seen me at the airport!

'Yes, it was so embarrassing, I was at the wrong gate to start with and I nearly went to Milan instead of Venice.' I toyed with the idea of relating the whole sorry saga in detail but decided against it, he'd think I was completely hopeless, I'd just give him the short version, 'Of course, it didn't matter in the end because the plane was delayed for hours...! And I missed my train and...'

Stop..! I said to myself, he doesn't want your life story, let him get a word in!

'…and Flo's car wouldn't start so we had to run to the station…and…'

God…! It seemed that now that I'd found someone to talk to, I couldn't stop.

He laughed, 'Oh well, you're here now. I'm Adam, Adam Vicenza, we've been loads of times; I've got cousins here. I'll tell you where to get off, that's if we actually manage to get on this water bus. Louise went to the loo and she's not back and the boat is about to leave.'

The line was surging forward. It didn't look as if there would be enough room for so many people, but they were gradually disappearing down the steps and into the hold helped by one of the Italian crew.

'Andiamo… Andiamo…' he cried, 'Let's go! Allons-y Signorina…'

'You'd better go ahead,' said Adam as I was seized by the hand and practically dragged onto the vaporetto. I squashed myself into one of the few remaining seats between a man-spreading American in a crumpled grey suit and a skinny Frenchwoman. We were crammed in like sardines and I was sitting next to the largest sardine in the can!

I glanced out at my new friend Adam; he was waving frantically at a girl with long red hair and a green jacket who was running along the quay towards him.

'Hurry…' I heard him yell, 'come on, Lou, or we'll have to wait for the next one!'

Oh, good, Lou was back from the loo! I stared at her, she looked gorgeous! Just my luck, I thought, he's already got a girlfriend. Annabel would be really disappointed. Help, I was beginning to sound just like her, the last thing I needed was another man in my life, well, not for a while; still he did look attractive leaping up and down on the quay. Tom would probably have left me behind. I could just imagine it, 'Oh, I assumed you'd get the next one,' he would say. Ha ha… maybe I was being a bit unfair; and anyway, he was 'her' problem now, not mine, not any more.

Adam pointed at me as they came down the steps and Louise grinned and waved, and we shuffled along so that they could sit down. I could feel the skinny woman next to me getting skinnier by the second, while my extra-large neighbour on the other side was getting ever larger as he settled down comfortably into his spreading buttocks; and then, hooray… we were off!

The sky was a jigsaw of rosy pink and smoky greys as we bumped across the lagoon. Spray splashed and misted the windows and I craned my neck to see out in case I missed something. I'd been hoping to arrive in the afternoon so that I could get my bearings, instead it would be dark when I got to my stop and it gave me palpitations just thinking about it. Then the lagoon was behind us and we were in a narrow waterway heading into the heart of Venice. Tall multi-hued palazzos, with graceful arched windows, bordered the canal on both sides and reached down to dip their foundations into the slopping, velvety water, shimmering with green, orange and terracotta reflections in the fading light.

I was starting to nod off, lulled by the rocking motion of the boat, when I noticed Adam trying to attract my attention. 'Next stop…' he was saying, and I leapt to my feet and started to weave my way over legs and assorted luggage. Louise held out her hand to steady me, 'Here, take this,' she said as I passed them, 'it's my mobile number, if you get lonely call us, we'll have lunch.'

I was alone; the only one to disembark at the Church of San Stae. Its flat visage loomed on my left like a dark shadow and a maze of tiny streets lay ahead. I'd already programmed the address into my phone, so I switched it on; what could be easier, a row of small arrows directed me straight ahead. It was true then; there were no tourists in Venice in November, except what about the mob on the waterbus, day trippers? One thing was certain; they weren't staying in, or near, San Stae.

I walked on trying hard not to look down into the shadowy alleyways that wandered off into creepy half-light. Why am I doing this? I asked myself yet again, I must have lost the plot, there's no other explanation. We could have gone on holiday anywhere; instead I'm here, in Venice, on my own. I screamed as a cat ran across in front of me nearly tripping me up; it was all very well following a Google map if you didn't mind falling over small animals and banging into obstacles! I stopped for a moment and gazed around at the tall buildings that fenced me in and rose to meet a narrow ribbon of indigo sky. Footsteps! I glanced behind me; a dark figure came around the corner no more than a few steps away from where I stood; someone was following me!

'Hello,' called the figure, 'is someone there?'

It was a woman and her face was lit by an eerie glow as if from beneath, which, of course, it was; by the Google map she was following!

'Oh, hi,' she said in a cheerful voice. 'These phones are a godsend. I'd be completely lost otherwise! I've been here three days and I still can't find my way back to where I'm staying! Are you alright, not lost, are you?'

'Yes,' I stammered, 'No... I mean I'm fine, you just gave me a fright, it's so dark, and quiet!'

'Oh, sorry, luv, I didn't mean to scare you! How long are you here for?'

'I arrived tonight, just got off the water bus; I'm staying a week.'

'Oh, you'll love it, a bit pricey mind you, but it's Venice so only to be expected, and it's a fascinating place, shame it's got so busy.'

'Busy,' I gasped, 'actually, you're the first person I've seen since I got off the boat!'

'Well, it is November, so most people are indoors now, or in the main tourist areas like St Mark's, or in the restaurants. During the day it's chaotic. I've been coming here for nearly thirty years and every year it gets more crowded, even in the winter. Where are you heading, I'm down there too, according to this thing. I'm Shirley, by the way, known to all my friends as Shirl.'

'Hi, I'm Katherine er… Kate,' I said.

'I'm leaving on Sunday. Not sure if I'll come again, this could be my last visit, it's changed too much; all those giant cruise ships, too many people, and the natives are always ripping off the tourists. They know there'll be another batch along. Oh, look, you're here, Mr Google says it's just down that alley. Byee… have a nice time, enjoy Venice, I hope I haven't put you off?'

Talk about garrulous, she could even out-talk Annabel! I could hear her footsteps tapping away into the distance as I turned into the tiny alley looking for number eleven, the Villa Alatri. The blurb said that it had been a palace in the past, but I couldn't imagine how they'd have fitted a palace in this alley. It opened out slightly and turned abruptly at the end and facing me was a flight of five or six stone steps leading to an ancient wooden door.

CHAPTER 4

I should have turned and disappeared back the way I'd come, but I didn't. Instead I climbed the stone steps and peered through the metal grill into a moonlit courtyard where the shadowy outline of a stone lion sat in a flowerbed and an olive tree leaned crookedly against the wall. Then I heard the sound of a door opening somewhere in the darkness beyond the lion and a slender figure emerged and walked towards me.

'Welcome to the Villa Alatri,' she cried as she unbolted the gate, 'I'm Sofia, come in, come in, you found us at last, I've been waiting for you, I was getting worried. Here, it's this way, let me take your case, you must be worn out! Your apartment is upstairs, I'll let you in; I live down here, well, some of the time, when I'm not working in Verona. I've got one full time resident, an old lady, and she always switches off the courtyard light. I've told her so many times to leave it on but she's convinced she's saving electricity...' She turned and stared at me under the harsh landing light, and I stared back, I was unable to speak. Then she quickly unlocked the door and threw my suitcase inside.

'Come for coffee in the morning, we need to talk! Shall we say half past ten? Just bang on my door...' and she ran back down the stairs as if she couldn't wait to get away.

The apartment was very small. The narrow hall served as a dining area, with a small table and two chairs, and led to a bedroom at one end and a sitting room at the other. Directly in front of me a door opened onto a tiny kitchen with a minute sink next to a surprisingly modern refrigerator containing a carton of long-life milk and six eggs and, rather oddly, a box of tea bags, a jar of instant coffee and a loaf. There was no kettle, just an old saucepan so I filled it with water and put in on the stove to boil. It took several attempts before I managed to light the gas, but no way was I asking Sofia for help, I had some thinking to do before we met for coffee the following morning; and I had the feeling that she didn't want to see me either. The saucepan boiled after what seemed like an age and I made a cup of tea and carried it into the bedroom where I took off my coat and boots and collapsed exhausted onto the bed. It was a very soft bed and the room was warm and I was just considering why Sofia and I looked so alike when my eyes began to close and I sank into a deep untroubled sleep.

My phone woke me at nine, it was Mum. 'Katherine,' she said, 'is that you? Why didn't you answer your phone? It rang for ages! And you might have called last night, I was really worried, I thought the ship had gone down!'

I eyed my forgotten cup of tea from the night before and it gazed clammily back at me, 'Oh, hi Mum, sorry I was asleep, the phone woke me...' I checked the time, just gone eight in England so she must have been really worried, '…and, actually, I was only on a boat for less than an hour. If you recall, I came by plane and I'm here safe and sound so stop worrying about me, I'm twenty-eight for goodness sake.'

'You wait until you have children; you never stop worrying about them no matter how old they are! And planes aren't that reliable.'

'Mmmm…' I agreed; it was much easier, less tiring.

'Anyway, was going to say, Flo was so pleased to see you. She said you're very welcome to stay any time you're going to the airport… and Jim sounds nice, she said he liked you too… and…'

I put the phone on loudspeaker and got out of bed. My suitcase was lying in the hall where Sofia had thrown it when I arrived, so I wheeled it into the bedroom and put it on the bed. Mum was still having a long conversation, with herself mainly; though I did add the odd 'yes…' just to keep her happy.

A thought suddenly occurred to me, 'Um, Mum, sorry to interrupt but I'm just wondering, do you happen to know if we have any family here in Italy, distant cousins, or aged aunties, for instance?'

'Oh, funny you should say that, Kate! When I told your dad you were off to Italy he said the strangest thing. He reckons that an uncle lived over there, just after the war it would have been, around

40

the early nineteen fifties. Well, I said to him, I had no idea and why hadn't he mentioned it before.'

'Yes… and why was that,' I asked impatiently.

'He said it didn't interest him and they'd all lost contact with that side of the family after his grandad died, must have been years ago. Sad isn't it? Why are you asking, any particular reason?'

'Not sure yet, but I'll keep you informed. Got to go now, it's nearly half nine here, we're an hour ahead, speak later.'

Well, I thought, that might explain things, perhaps it's as simple as that, Sofia and I are distant cousins and we resemble each other because of some genetic quirk; a latent gene in my DNA, easy, nothing sinister at all. I searched through my suitcase for my battery charger and it buzzed as I was plugging it in; a text, I glanced at the screen, Annabel of course.

'Are you there yet, Kate? Hope your ship didn't go down!'

What was all this nonsense about ships going down? She must have been talking to my mother!

'I just wanted to tell you about my research on the Tarot but far too much to text so I'll call you! Plus, I've decided to go back to teaching! Wooo… hooo!!!! Speak soon, Abel (smiley emojis) xxxxx'

I messaged back;

'Hi Abel, Arrived safe and all well, lots to tell you too, but later, I have a date at half ten!'

I realised my mistake as soon as the phone rang.

'What's all this about a date? Coo... that was quick work!'

'Hi Abel,' I said, 'it's just a figure of speech, not necessarily a man.'

'Whoa, you mean a woman? News to me, I thought you really liked men...'

'A date doesn't mean... a date necessarily... Oh, I give up! What I mean is, I'm having coffee with the owner of my apartment, at half past ten.'

'Oh, is that all?' I could tell she was disappointed by the tone of her voice.

'It's not all, actually,' I said, 'the odd thing is that she looks exactly like me; well not exactly but very nearly!'

'Yes, I agree that is a bit odd, so tell me. You've got ages, it's not even nine!'

'We're an hour ahead,' I explained again, 'but, briefly; I think we might be related through my father's side of the family.'

'What, you mean your dad's been putting it about! Whoever would have thought it?'

I cringed, 'No, you idiot, through an uncle, before the war, or something. Look, I've really got to get ready!'

'But I haven't even told you about the Tarot revelations, and my decision to go back to teaching.'

'Right, but be quick, give me the info on the Tarot if you think it will put my mind at rest. We can leave the teaching discussion till we've got more time!'

'It's that Major Arcana, I looked him up on line when I was at work, there was nothing interesting on twitter, and I've practically given up on Facebook…'

'I'm in a hurry, Annabel…!'

'Oh yes, sorry. Well, there are seventy-eight cards in a Tarot pack and twenty-two of them are of major significance, and, wait for it, they are called the Major Arcana, so not a person after all! I've still got more to do though, nothing yet on Grim,' she giggled, 'yes, and before you say anything, I know he's the Grim Reaper, I was only joking, I'm not completely stupid you know. Call me when you found out more about your doppelganger.'

And she was gone. I was in the kitchen attempting to light the gas when the phone rang again.

'Is that Katherine Elliot?'

Oh no…! Debs this time, from the agency!

'Look we're really desperate, absolutely no one for St Yob's, I mean St Job's; we'll pay double!'

'Sorry, Debs, as I told Barb, I'm on holiday so you'll have to find someone else.'

'Can't you come back?' wheedled Debs, 'just name your price, anything!'

'I'm in Venice!' I practically shouted, 'so no, I'm not coming back. Leave me alone!' I put the phone on silent and went back to the mystifying dilemma of how to light the gas; it was definitely coming out because the kitchen reeked of it. How much do I have to breathe in before it kills me, I wondered; and was this my destiny, lured back to Venice to die in the Villa Alatri of gas poisoning?

I gave up on the tea idea and stuck my head out of the bedroom window to take in half a dozen deep breaths of fresh air, just in case; then I showered and got dressed. It was still only just after ten, so I flopped down on the bed and studied the room. A huge ornate mirror decorated with leaves and musical notes almost filled the opposite wall reflecting the tapestry behind the bed and an icon of the Madonna and Child beautifully etched in gold on wood; a huge chest of drawers that was far too big for the size of the room dominated the remaining wall. In the top left-hand corner, a black spider was dangling from a web in the elaborate coving and I wondered if I should move it outside but I decided not to bother; after all, I'd only be there for a week and if I got really lonely it would be something to talk to. I stood up and went back to the window; the glass was thin, and I could hear people chatting and laughing as they strolled along the narrow canal path that wound its way towards a tiny bridge to the far right of my view.

My doppelganger, that's what Annabel had called Sofia; someone who looks exactly the same as another person, a twin-stranger, often the harbinger of bad luck according to tradition. Well I certainly didn't need any bad luck! And what if Sofia wasn't a stranger, aside from the fact that I didn't know her, that is; she could simply be a long lost relative. Maybe that's why I was here, to reconnect with lost family; it didn't seem likely though, still... It was half past ten and I realised I'd been putting off our meeting, but I felt slightly reassured so I went downstairs and banged on her door.

It was extraordinary, like looking in a mirror! For a start, we were both the same height and we both had long, nearly black hair, but it was the similarity in our features that startled me most; the vaguely questioning, arched eyebrows, the full lower lip and slightly almond shaped brown eyes. Her nose was straight, and it even had the same slight bump on the bridge that I'd always hated. Actually, I don't look too bad I thought. Then she laughed, and I noticed that her teeth were a lot straighter than mine, huh, one genetic flaw I could have done without, must have come from my mother's side of the family. Or perhaps she just had a better dentist?

She waved me in, and I noticed the table was set for breakfast. 'Welcome Katherine,' she cried, 'come in and make yourself at home. The coffee is on and I've bought some fresh rolls, and there's cheese, and some Danish pastries; are you hungry?'

I was ravenous; all I'd had was a dry sausage roll the day before and somehow, in all the excitement, I'd forgotten about food.

'Go ahead, eat,' she instructed, in brilliant English with only the slightest accent.

I took a large bite out of a roll, 'Thank you so much...' I murmured, 'sorry, I don't usually speak with my mouth full, it's just that I suddenly realised how famished I was!'

'Famished... oh, you poor thing!'

'Yes, hungry, starving in fact,' and I covered my mouth to prevent crumbs escaping, 'Your English is amazing, Sofia!'

'Thank you, my grandmother sent me to boarding school in Switzerland. I can speak English, French and German, and Italian, of course; I'm a translator.'

Huh... my doppelganger, except she was multi-lingual, and had straight teeth into the bargain. I was starting to feel like the poor relation, the sad little church mouse.

'We're ignoring the elephant in the room,' said Sofia.

Wow, metaphors too, her English was better than a lot of the people who lived there.

'Yes, we should talk about that,' I agreed, 'but I've already discovered that my father had an uncle who was Italian, so I assume we are distantly related. Apparently, our genes are so random that anything can pop up, at any time, and it's probably just a coincidence that we've met!'

'I'm very pleased to meet you long, lost cousin,' said Sofia and we shook hands.

'Me too,' I said, and we both started to laugh, and even that sounded similar.

'I have to go into Verona to collect some work this afternoon, and tomorrow I'm taking my grandmother, Nonna, to the station; she's going to visit an old friend in Alatri. I'll be back on Tuesday, we could go out; I can show you around Venice. It's a shame Nonna will be away all week, she would have enjoyed meeting you and she might know something of our family links to England. She would probably laugh too; she's got a great sense of humour even though she's ninety-two!

'But this is the Villa Alatri, is there a connection?' I asked.

'Yes, this used to be a palace; of course, practically every house in Venice was a palace at one time. Serenissima, as Venice was known for ten centuries, was very prosperous and everyone was rich, well maybe 'everyone' is a slight exaggeration. Anyway, my family were from Alatri, a very ancient town in the south.'

I watched her closely as she spoke; it felt odd as if I'd suddenly developed a sexy Italian accent and straight teeth.

'You don't mind being here overnight, on your own, do you?' she asked suddenly. 'The old woman, Sibella, is just across the courtyard and she's always looking for company. She's even older than Nonna! But if you go, don't let her scare you with stories; she can be very amusing if you take it all with a pinch of salt.'

Another metaphor, I was impressed. I stood up to go, 'Yes, maybe she can throw some light on why we're so, you know, similar… if she's been around that long. And thanks for lunch; I suppose I should go shopping.'

47

'Take this, I won't need it,' said Sofia.

She went into the kitchen and I could hear her opening cupboards and drawers. Finally, she returned and handed me about a week's supply of food in a large carrier bag. 'Here, this will keep you going. I'll see you when I get back.'

I forgot to ask how old she is, I thought, as I climbed the stairs back to my apartment. I was tired. It wasn't even midday, but I felt exhausted, too much was happening and what I needed most was a lie down but I had to unpack the food first, Sofia had given me heaps and it all had to be fitted into the miniature fridge. I tried to light the gas, a cup of tea would liven me up. Tom would have been able to light it; he was good at stuff like that. Still, I persisted, after all, I'd done it the night before, then I noticed the microwave sitting on a shelf behind the door. Problem solved, who needs an oven if you've got a microwave, especially if you've got a toaster and a kettle. I felt quite upset about the lack of kettle.

I sat at the table in the hall-diner clutching my cup of tea and feeling quite proud of myself. I'd got here against all the odds, and despite Mum's and Annabel's negativity. I'd made a useful contact in Auntie Flo, and I liked her too, so I wasn't being selfish and only thinking about myself and a convenient place to stay before any future trips overseas. And next time her car might start, and I'd be sure to check that I was at the right gate when I got to the airport. Plus, I'd found a new cousin who was really nice, and accomplished, not to mention

48

good looking... haha... And she lived in Venice; I might even get 'mates' rates' next time. I was SO lucky! Everyone, including me, had made a big fuss over nothing at all. I sipped my tea and smiled to myself then something in my head said, 'Hang on, what about the scary dreams?' I tried to ignore it but the memory hovered over my head, oppressive as a black cloud. 'Go away...!' I said aloud but it persisted, 'Can't...' it whispered, 'I exist, whether you like it or not; just look around you, isn't it obvious?' And it was obvious, for there was no denying that the Villa Alatri, with its shallow stone steps and ancient wooden door, that in my dream I was trying so desperately to reach, was, without a doubt, the very same house.

Then I remembered Sibella, the aged crone who lived across the courtyard! Yes, she might know. She would certainly be able to shed some light on the past; after all, she'd been around for almost a hundred years, according to Sofia. I left my tea and ran down the stairs and across the courtyard.

She looked surprised when she opened her door.

'Ah, Sofia, come stai,' she murmured, 'c'è un problema?'

OOPS...! She thought I was Sofia, and I knew just enough Italian to understand that she was asking, 'how I was? And if there was a problem?' GAWD...! Difficult, or what...?

'I'm not Sofia,' I explained slowly, enunciating every syllable.

Sibella looked puzzled; then she waved her arms to the heavens and rattled off a stream of invective in Italian of which I understood not a jot. It was simply too fast and too complicated. To be honest, I could just about ask for a cheese sandwich and a cappuccino. It obviously hadn't occurred to Sofia that I couldn't speak Italian, or she would never have suggested I call on Sibella.

'I'm sorry, um… I don't suppose there's any chance that you speak English?' I asked but she just looked even more puzzled and threw her hands in the air again and crossed herself; and then she slammed the door.

'That went well,' I muttered, 'I wonder if there are any more old ladies I can scare out of their wits?'

It would have to wait until Sofia returned from Verona. I made up my mind to tell her about the dream, she would think I was mad, but most people seemed to, so one more wouldn't make any difference. I did feel bad about Sibella though because she must have thought I was some sort of demon, or Sofia's evil twin.

She was incredibly old; I just hoped she didn't die before Sofia got back to set the record straight! It looked as if it was going to rain, but that didn't bother me too much, being a typical English rose, um… or was I? I grabbed an umbrella that was propped up in the hall, along with my bag, and a map, and went out determined to find my way around without resorting to my phone for directions; no more Googling for me I decided as I

50

headed for the tourist hub. Actually, I needn't have worried as on almost every corner was a sign that said 'Rialto', or 'St Marks' so it was impossible to get lost, in daylight at least. I soon came to a tiny square that looked slightly dilapidated in the dismal November light, but I could see how it had once been majestic with its grand porticos and friezes. A quartet was playing something I vaguely recognised, Puccini, I think, and people were sitting at tables outside a small restaurant hoping that the rain would hold off. I sat down and ordered a glass of Prosecco, and I know it was early and the sun wasn't yet over the yard-arm but I was on holiday for goodness sake. I closed my eyes to listen to the music; it was very soothing, even to my troubled soul. I opened them when it stopped just in time to see the young cellist give a little bow. He smiled at me and I smiled back, he was very good looking. Annabel would be really jealous. I'd persuade her to come back with me next time, she would love it!

'OO, ooo….! Helloooo….!'

What me? I turned around; Shirl was just coming out of the little restaurant, and she was heading my way.

'It's me, Shirl, remember? I was hoping I'd see you; just me left now, my friends have gone home and it's nice to have some company.'

She plonked herself down in the seat next to me.

'Oh, Prosecco… lovely, what a good idea; do you want another one? Er… Kate, isn't it?'

'That's right, Kate,' I was surprised she'd remembered, 'I won't have another one, not just yet, I'm tempted but no thanks Shirl; maybe later though.'

The waiter came over and she ordered a drink and said how wonderful everything was, all in perfect Italian and they started having a long chat and he smiled, and she giggled. I couldn't believe it, Shirl, who looked like the typical English woman abroad, with her flashy jewellery and raucous voice, was fluent in Italian. I just sat there feeling embarrassed and unable to join in, a bit like a parrot with a cover over its cage.

'Wow, I am so impressed!' I gasped when he walked away. 'Where did you learn to speak Italian like that?'

'My family came to live in Rome when I was eight; we stayed for five years then we went back to Manchester. I suppose it's one of the reasons why I'm always here, everyone is so relaxed, and they enjoy life. I'd like to buy a house over here, not Venice, obviously, but maybe somewhere a bit more remote. I saw a great place down south, an old town house, in Alatri, have you heard of it?'

I nearly fell off my chair, talk about coincidence. 'You'll never believe this Shirl...' I could hardly get the words out, 'I'm staying at the Villa Alatri, and that's not all, apparently the family who own it have all sorts of connections with Alatri.'

'Well, isn't life strange?' said Shirl.

'Yes, very strange,' I agreed.

The waiter brought her drink and a few complimentary slices of pizza. 'Prego, Signorina, prego,' he murmured, and he blew her a kiss when she thanked him.

'See it pays off, and it's worth it just to be addressed as Signorina, haha... Anyway, I'd like to hear about this place where you're staying. And why do I get the feeling that there's more to it than you're saying? I'm very intuitive; in fact, my friends say I'm a bit psychic.'

What, Shirl, this slightly overweight woman with bright pink lipstick, and bracelets that jangled every time she lifted her drink to her lips, could she be psychic? But then I thought, why not, no one would look at Julia and say to themselves, 'Oh yes; weird Tarot woman, it might be best to avoid her!'?

'You can tell me you know,' she added, 'it might make you feel better and I wouldn't tell a soul.'

'It started with a dream...'

'It often does, luv... go on, I'm all ears, and I can give you my unbiased opinion, for what it's worth.'

'In my dream I'm here, at the Villa Alatri, or I think it's me, I'm not sure, but it's sometime in the past... so how can it be me?' It took me some time to relate everything, the dream and the Tarot reading, and about how I lived opposite the cemetery, and even then I missed bits out. I finished by telling her all about Sofia and how closely we resembled each other, and about my unfortunate encounter with Sibella.

We were there for an hour or more and the wine was flowing. I'd given up any idea of restraint; my brain seemed to work better when it was lubricated.

Shirl sat for a long while in silence. I looked at her face, she appeared to be in some kind of a trance and I wondered if I should shake her, or splash her face with water, or wine, but eventually she spoke.

'That is the strangest story I've ever heard, very strange indeed. As I see it, there is an unresolved issue somewhere in the past, but it can't be your past no matter what the Tarot reader told you, you're too young. I'm guessing you didn't mention this dream, which was probably for the best or you might have been even more frightened by what she said. Now what would be unresolved? Assuming that it was a murder, as we suspect, what would be the motive, and of course, 'who done it?' as they say. And if it was so long ago why does it matter anyway?'

'Unless it means,' I hesitated, it all seemed so ridiculous, 'unless it means that someone is in danger in some way and I'm here to find out who that person is, and how I can prevent it, whatever 'it' is, from happening!'

'Let's hope it's not you,' said Shirl, 'it would be like some grim replay of the past.'

I shuddered, 'Oh yes, Grim, he popped up in my Tarot reading, or rather he popped out, on his own; it was my first card as well.'

'Looks to me as if death is on the cards then,' murmured Shirl, 'so to speak; another Prosecco, luv?'

'Better not.' I looked up at the sky, 'it's going to pour any minute.'

'If you take me back to your Villa Alatri, I might pick up some vibes, you never know. Actually, I've got a better idea, we should have thought of it before, I can explain to Sibella that you're not Sofia, and we can ask her all the questions you like.'

'If you're sure you don't mind; it is your last day here!'

'Hell, no… it's absolutely fascinating! Come on, quick; let's hurry before we get soaked!'

CHAPTER 5

Sibella didn't seem at all keen to open her door to Sofia's evil twin, but she relented in the end and looked me up and down suspiciously; then she turned to Shirl and did the same.

I smiled apologetically, 'I'm really sorry for what happened earlier, Sibella, and we've brought you these,' and I handed her a box of fondants that we'd bought on the way back from the square.

Shirl translated for me, 'Mi dispiace per quello che è successo primo…'

Then she went on to explain that I wasn't Sofia, I was a relative and would she mind us asking her a few questions about the villa. Sibella gave a toothless grin and chuckled, then she threw open her door and waved us in to a vast living room. I shivered, it was freezing! There was a huge empty fireplace at one end and a table that could have easily seated twenty diners, but it was set with a heart-wrenching single plate and cutlery.

'Did she have a big family?' I asked Shirl, I could see this was going to take some time.

The old woman looked sad when she answered.

'She had eight children,' said Shirl, 'five sons and three daughters, three of them are dead and two of her sons emigrated, to Australia. The other three have moved away to Rome and Milan and she hardly ever sees them. She says that Sofia is more like a daughter to her, that's why you gave her such a shock when you arrived on her doorstep, she just couldn't understand what was going on.'

'That is so depressing! Can you ask her about the villa, please, and Sofia's grandmother?'

'I'm going to ask her if she knows anything about a murder' said Shirl, 'that's why you're here so what's the point in beating about the bush. She might even know why it happened, not sure what you're supposed to do about it though.'

She turned to Sibella, and spoke to her in a soft gentle voice, 'Sibella, do you know anything about the history of the Villa Alatri? Was there ever a murder nearby?' Shirl talked for a long time and I got the impression that she was explaining about my dream because she kept glancing at me with frightened eyes and crossing herself. She listened carefully and then she picked up the corner of her skirt to wipe tears from her eyes before rattling away in fast Italian.

'She has a very strong regional accent,' said Shirl and she took out a tissue and dabbed her eyes too, 'she says it makes her unhappy remembering the past because it's all gone now!'

I went to stand up, 'Perhaps we should go.'

'No, she wants to tell someone, she never has company and she misses having her family around her. She's been a widow for more than forty years. Her mother told her about the murder, it was a young girl, she must have been about seventeen, and you were right, she was strangled. It was the end of the nineteenth century; her grandmother was very young when it happened, but she remembered it well because it made such an impression on her. She said she was afraid to go in the street after dark; it was very dark in Venice even when Sibella was small. She was born between the wars.'

'Ask her why she was strangled, if it's not upsetting her too much. And does she know the name of the young girl?'

'Caterina,' said Shirl, 'her name was Caterina.'

Caterina, Katherine, Kate, I shivered but it wasn't because of the cold, not this time.

'She came from a rich family in the south, from Alatri,' Shirl glanced at me and I thought her eyes were going to pop right out of her head. 'She says it was because of a necklace. Someone had left it to her, her grandfather I think.'

'She was murdered for her necklace? Surely, she wasn't wearing a valuable necklace in Venice, in a dark alleyway?'

'No, maybe not wearing it, but they could have been trying to find out where it was kept. Sibella says it was a wonderful thing, studded with all the jewels of the Orient, diamonds and sapphires from India, and rubies from Ceylon. She thinks it might even have been brought back by Marco Polo, and for some reason people were convinced it was hidden here, in the Villa Alatri.'

'Did they catch her murderer?' I asked.

'She doesn't know, says her memory is failing and she wants to die.'

'That's so sad!' I was really depressed now.

'And she says that she's glad Sofia has you because she has no one else and her Nonna, her grandmother, is very old.'

We said goodbye and I promised to call in again. I wouldn't be able to speak to her though because Shirl would be off home in the morning, but I could smile, and bring her some more fondants. Then we went upstairs to my little apartment and I made tea for us both in the microwave.

Shirl sipped her tea thoughtfully. 'You know what you should do, Kate...' I shook my head, 'you should go to one of them hypnotists, one that deals in past lives; you know, reincarnation and all that. They believe in it in India and lots of other parts of the world...'

I looked around me; true, it did seem familiar, but reincarnation, was that even possible?

'... or it could somehow be inherited memory, something in your DNA, that's if you're looking for a more scientific explanation. Look, I leave early tomorrow so I need to pack by nine, at the latest, but let's go out; I bet you haven't been anywhere yet. You're going to be fine; Sofia will be back soon, and I'll show you around a bit tonight so you won't be completely at a loose end. There's a great restaurant just around the corner but we'll head for the town centre first. Come on; get your glad rags on.'

'Haha... I hope that's a joke,' I said.

I found out where the crowds were when we got to St Mark's Square. It swarmed with people of every nationality, filling the cafes and restaurants and all no doubt paying extortionate prices for the privilege.

We were walking back over the Rialto Bridge when the rain started. It fell in sheets and everyone ran for cover, but I put up my umbrella and did a little twirl, 'I'm singing in the rain...' I sang.

'Come back with the brolly,' squealed Shirl, 'you're daft, and I'm getting soaked.'

We were only a few streets from the restaurant but by the time we got there the rain had already seeped into my cheap leather boots and Shirl was complaining that her hair had gone straight.

'Looks like the floods have arrived,' she said, 'you should have brought your wellies.'

I laughed, 'I know a song about wellies, as well. Do you want to hear it?'

She grinned, 'No, you're alright, luv!' Yes, I was definitely going to miss Shirl.

We ate spaghetti bolognaise and downed a couple of glasses of red wine and laughed, a lot, and she told me about her girls! She was only in her early forties, but she had two grown up daughters, Sarah, the eldest, who was at Leeds University studying psychology, and Naomi, who was two years younger and a hairdresser. She lived in Wakefield with her boyfriend Liam who was 'a lazy bugger but a good laugh'.

'He's a barista, which is nothing to do with the law,' explained Shirl, 'no; it just means he's fantastic at making coffee; a much-underrated skill, apparently!' and, she added, 'Sarah's the brainy one, got it from my old man, I reckon!'

I wasn't so sure because it turned out that Shirl was a translator like Sofia; she said the best thing her mother could have done for her education was taking her to live in Rome for five years as it meant she was fluent in two languages and people were always looking for translators. The rain had stopped when we left the restaurant and we walked back slowly, gossiping all the way. Then we hugged and promised to keep in touch, and she wandered off into the night while I gazed up at the wooden door with the iron grill, gripped by a strong sense of foreboding.

I'd just let myself in when my phone rang, 'Singing in the Rain'; Shirl must have changed my ringtone when I went to the ladies!

It was Annabel.

'How's it going, Kate, me old mate?' she asked, then without waiting for a reply, 'I just had to tell you about the awful day I've had! I can't tell Lucy, she's never here. I don't know why I ever agreed to flat share with her in the first place. Oh, yes, I do actually, it was because you and Tom moved in together or I could have shared with you.' She paused but before I could even open my mouth she was off again. 'Anyway, I know she wants James to move in, he's here most nights; I can hear him snoring in my room. Well not in MY room exactly, I mean I can hear it from my room.'

I was beginning to think I preferred Shirl; at least I could get the odd word in with Shirl!

'Are you still there, Kate…?'

'Hi, Annabel, yes I'm here,' I sighed, 'so what's happened that you can't tell Lucy?'

'I might tell her if she was even here! I'd still rather tell you though, she's so sensible, even more sensible than you are; er… usually; I think it's a form of OCD because she's SO sensible, and she thinks I'm incompetent, which is rubbish!'

I spluttered with laughter but managed to turn it into a cough, 'Oh, I wouldn't say you're incompetent, Abel!'

'I've been SACKED! Can you imagine? Me… sacked! And all because I was reading up on the Tarot; if I'd had my reading instead of you, Julia would probably have spotted it in advance and then I could have got in first and handed in my notice! Oh, the ignominy of it all… sacked…!'

She was beginning to sound like Lady Macbeth, I'm sure she could have got a part at the National.

'And EVERYONE does it, Snap-chat, Facebook, Instagram, Tweets, everything… not just me, so why have I been singled out? It's accepted behaviour; imagine how BORED we'd be otherwise!'

'Well yes, that does sound um… unfair…' I murmured in the most sympathetic voice I could muster; after all, if she'd been sacked, she had no one else to blame, 'So, did you find out anything new,' I asked, 'you know, anything relevant?'

'It's fascinating, Kate, this whole Tarot thing, some people swear by it and have to consult it before they do anything, and it can change their lives, that's a bit extreme though. Others say that it's a psychological tool to tap into the subconscious because really you know all the answers already, deep down.'

Julia said that, she told me that my memories might be beyond my reach in the normal way, they could be just buried in my subconscious. I thought about my dream and the hair on the nape of my neck quivered.

Annabel was still babbling on, 'And some people think the subconscious can be linked to a past life; or they could be memories from a person who has lived before whose genes you may have inherited. I'll let you know more as I progress with my research, I'll have loads of time as I haven't got a job, I might even go to the library! Looks like I'll have to give up this flat anyway...'

She paused for breath and I was just about to reply when she gathered strength and started again.

'The thing is, Kate, as you know, I'm going to give the teaching thing another go...'

Another go? To my knowledge she'd only ever done a few stints of obligatory teaching practice.

'...and that will be next September with the new intake of littlies... bless... and we'll make pirate maps and... stuff... and it will be brilliant but I thought I'd begin with a bit of supply teaching, like you, Kate, just to get back into it… and I wondered if I could share your flat… please?'

I actually dropped my phone at this point and had to scramble round on the floor to retrieve it before I could answer. I could hear a tinny voice saying 'Kate, Kate, hello…oo… are you there?'

I put it on the bed and turned on the loudspeaker, 'Yeah, I'm here, Abel; I dropped my phone.'

'Well can I, you know, share?'

'But you hate my flat,' I gasped, 'you said it was creepy, and morbid!'

'It's different if it's you and me,' she said, 'we'd have a good laugh. And we could buy some of those nice blinds, the ones that let the light in but keep the view out. We'd probably forget that the creepy old cemetery was there at all.'

I somehow doubted that, but I had to admit it would save the trouble and expense of moving. And it was a nice area, very green; and Mum and Dad were just up the road on the other side of the park. I relented, 'Okay, we can sort it out next week when I get back. You can have the box room, I'll move my stuff. If you want you can move in now, Mum's got a spare key.'

'Oh, thank you, Kate, I love you! And I think the box room is really sweet, but next week will be fine, when you're here, I'd hate it on my own, and I'll have to check with Lucy that James can move in and take over my rent, though I'm sure they can't wait to see the back of me, and he earns loads in the city! Oops, gotta go! They're coming in and I'm on the land line, and it's strictly verboten!'

And she slammed the phone down just as I was just opening my mouth to reply. Well if she moved in with me at least I wouldn't be getting huge telephone bills because I didn't have a land line! I find it's always best to look on the bright side.

I gazed out of the window; raindrops were racing down the glass panes blurring the lights on the bridge. A solitary figure rushed past under an umbrella; then all was still except for the sound of the rain lashing the rooftops. I was alone, again, and it felt worse somehow after being with bubbly Shirl for most of the day. It crossed my mind to ring Mum, but it would only confirm her suspicions that I should never have come here on my own. I poured a glass of wine from the bottle that Sofia had given me and vowed I'd cut back tomorrow.

I was certain I wouldn't sleep; what if I had the dream? Where would I go? This wasn't London where I could always be guaranteed to find company of some sort. This was a strange city, a dark, watery, and unfamiliar city, and I didn't even speak the language. I considered knocking on Sibella's door but she'd be asleep; and Sibella was quite scary anyway, looking like she did, all wrinkled and bent, and shrunken, as if she already had one foot in the grave. I shuddered, then I told myself to calm down, after all, there was no point in worrying; I was here, full stop, and I had to make the best of it, so I finished unpacking and got ready for bed and put on one of the films that I'd downloaded onto my laptop before I left England.

CHAPTER 6

I woke sometime later; it was cool, even though the sun was streaming through the windows casting bright rays on the tapestry above my bed. The room seemed to have grown, there was a red velvet armchair and a finely carved table topped with a mirror, and the walls had painted murals of lions, and cherubs, and cornucopias overflowing with ripe fruit and flowers. The familiar oversized chest of drawers was now some distance away under a large window on the other side of the room, and an ivory topped washstand with a blue patterned basin stood at the far end. Italian voices were echoing up from the streets and I could smell roses, and patchouli, and oranges, and I felt incredibly happy. Almost immediately it started to blur and fade, tears filled my eyes and when I woke for the second time I was crying, and the room was filled with the grey light of an early November morning. What was happening to me? I sat up and reached for a tissue and blew my nose, I could still remember the room clearly, just as it had been in my dream, before it had been divided into apartments with black spiders living in the corners. I was sure now that, somehow, I had known the room before. A sceptic would say that it was a memory etched deep within my genes, a recollection passed down through the generations and hooray, I was the lucky recipient! But I knew what Shirl would say because she was already convinced that I was a reincarnation of Caterina.

It was still raining, and I could hear voices and a strange rattling noise, so I climbed out of bed and looked down on the pathway that ran along the canal. It was a gaggle of girls, most likely a 'hen party' as one was still wearing a soggy bridal veil, and they were pulling suitcases and slipping and sliding over the wet uneven path.

I tried to remember the Tarot cards I'd chosen. I wished I'd written them down, maybe then I'd have some idea of what I'd got myself into. There was 'Death', the Grim Reaper with his scythe; and 'The Hanged Man', indicating a state of limbo, where I was at this very moment, hanging between the present and the past; and 'The Moon'. Julia said that in my spread it represented deception. I couldn't help wondering when destruction would strike; the three dreaded Ds, death, deception and destruction.

I got into bed and tried to go back to sleep but it was no use, I was wide awake now. Sofia would be back on Tuesday, and maybe later today I'd text Louise and we could arrange lunch as she'd suggested. After a while I got up and went into the kitchen to find some breakfast and my thoughts strayed to Tom. The simple truth was that I wasn't accustomed to being on my own. I'd lived with Tom for the last five years and we'd fallen into a day-to-day routine assuming that things would always be the same, but 'she' was plodding along behind us both, like a tortoise in a marathon, slow and steady, and determined to win. He said that she made him feel young again, well fair enough; all I needed now was someone to make me feel young again! And, anyway, I didn't mind that much, because I knew I was right, he was horribly boring, even though my mother referred to him as 'a good catch'! 'She' was doing me a favour, Tom had become nothing more than a tedious and slightly irritating habit, one that it was time to conquer, once and for all!

I suddenly felt happier, it was getting light at last, so I dressed and went outside. The statue of the lion stood guard over the courtyard in his bed of faded geraniums; he looked lonely too. Sibella's shutters were closed when I passed her front door, and I wondered for a moment if she was still alive, then shaking off my morbid thoughts, I headed down the stone steps to the alley and walked to the fish market. 'Not a soul about, anywhere,' I muttered to myself; then I laughed because the market was closed and I wouldn't be seeing a sole either, or a cod. Oh gawd, I really was going mad! I'd quite forgotten it was Sunday but some of the stalls were starting to open in the Rialto market, so I bought a couple of postcards and wandered over to St Mark's. The rain had stopped but there were large puddles in the square, and a fine mist lay over the Grand Canal, making everything soft and somehow ethereal. A few people were emerging from their hotels in search of coffee, or souvenirs, or pulling suitcases towards the crowded vaporetto stop. I hurried on, unsure of where I was going but anxious to put some distance between myself and the Villa Alatri; I seemed to be always running away.

It was nearly eleven when I returned to the villa and I'd just closed the wooden door behind me when Sibella came out of her apartment.

'Bongiorno, bella Caterina,' she cried merrily and then she grabbed me by the hand and pulled me back into the alley, urging me to follow her. I followed out of politeness, but I was curious too; where was she taking me? We wound our way through a multitude of tiny streets and all the while she jabbered away at me encouragingly. Somewhere in the not too far distance I could hear a bell; oh no, was she taking me to mass? We rounded a corner into a tiny square and it became apparent that she was! 'San Giacomo dell Orio', she announced happily as she took my arm and led me towards the entrance.

She crossed herself and did a little curtsy as we went in, then she smiled up at me and pointed to a wooden pew. I sat down and looked around; it was beautiful, with an altarpiece depicting the Madonna and Child and an ornate wooden roof that I found out later was made from a ship's keel. Did she think I needed saving?

I put my arm around her bony shoulders and gave her a squeeze, I could feel her thin flesh beneath my hand; she was as fragile as a tiny bird.

'I'm really sorry, Sibella, I can't stay,' I murmured, 'you see I'm not a Roman Catholic.' I could have mentioned that I hadn't been in a church for years, apart from on the odd tourist visit, but she couldn't understand me anyway.

'Mi dispiace, Sibella, I'm really sorry.' I stood up to go and she looked at me sadly as I pushed my way out. Maybe I should have stayed; it would have made an old lady happy, and I thought of her children far away, and the huge dining table set for one, and it made me sad to think that now she was all alone. I turned around and tried to get back in, but it was no use, the place was bursting at the seams, so I sat on a bench and chewed my nails until they started to come out again.

I waited for ages; she was one of the last and I thought I'd missed her, but she finally emerged. 'Sibella,' I yelled, 'I'm over here!' I didn't know what to say, she couldn't understand me anyway, so I suppose it didn't matter. I ran across to meet her and she looked really happy to see me, so I was glad that I'd decided to wait. She tutted at me and wagged her finger, yes, I was right the first time, she did think I was in need of saving.

The shop where we'd bought the fondants was open, so this time I grabbed her hand and pulled her inside and pointed up at the shelves, 'Fondants, Sibella?' I enquired.

'No, cioccolato,' she replied and grinned a toothless grin. Oh, chocolate, of course, I had to agree, I definitely preferred chocolate too so I bought two large bars and we set off home.

'Il mio Leone,' said Sibella when we were back in the courtyard. Then she shook her head and muttered in her strange dialect and I felt annoyed with myself because I couldn't understand what she wanted to tell me.

'See you later,' I said anyway, 'Si, alla prossima,' replied Sibella and she threw her arms to the heavens in disgust at my stupidity and disappeared indoors.

I was tired, it had been a long morning one way and another, and it was too late to text Louise to arrange a lunch date for today. I made tea in the microwave and went to sit in the tiny sitting room. It felt even more familiar than the bedroom, with its pale terracotta walls and long curved window. I checked my phone for messages, but there were none and I debated whether or not to call Annabel, or Mum, but decided to let sleeping dogs lie and went to the bookcase instead. There was very little in English, apart from a few novels that previous visitors had left, and there was nothing I fancied until I found a book on the history of Venice and I settled down to read until I dozed off. It was gone four when I woke up and the light was already fading. November wasn't a good time to be alone with no one to distract or entertain. I decided to text Louise.

'Hi Louise,' I wrote, 'I hope you remember who I am. We met on the vaporetto and you said I could get in touch if I found myself at a loose end….'

No, that sounded much too needy, I deleted it and tried again, 'Hi Louise, Kate here, from the vaporetto, was just wondering if you're free for lunch tomorrow?'

I was surprised when Adam called me straight away.

'Kate... it's Adam, how are you? Louise is having a siesta. We were hoping you'd get in touch; Louise says she feels outnumbered! Are you enjoying Venice?'

'I love it,' I replied breezily, I was trying to sound genuine and enthusiastic. Well, I did love Venice; it was just that everything had become so strange, so it wasn't quite that simple.

'We can do tomorrow. There'll be four of us; my cousin Gio, and his mate Antonio, and Lou, of course. Is that okay with you? They're a laugh, and Gio is always asking me when I'm going to introduce him to a nice English girl.'

'Oh great, I hope he's not expecting too much!'

'I'm sure he won't be disappointed; actually, I'm looking forward to seeing you again. Shall we say midday, on the Rialto Bridge?'

'Um... think I can make that,' I giggled, 'yep, sure I can, in fact; so, see you tomorrow, Adam.'

'Looking forward to it, Kate...!'

He was looking forward to seeing me again, but what about Louise? And why did I keep laughing in that silly, girly way? Oops, I really was looking forward to seeing him! Still, at least Gio would be there, and Antonio, so things were looking up. I turned on all the lights and went into the kitchen to make scrambled eggs in the microwave; I'd watch a film or two and have an early night and, hopefully, I wouldn't be disturbed by visions of the past, or ghosts of the departed!

CHAPTER 7

Adam was all by himself at the top of the Rialto Bridge; I noticed him as soon as I started up the steps, he was leaning against the parapet watching the water traffic. He saw me straight away and I ran up to join him.

'Kate,' he shouted above the noise of the crowds, 'good to see you!' and he kissed me on both cheeks, 'Look at that, it's nearly as bad as the M25.'

It was true; water buses vied with gondolas and speed boats for space on the water, whizzing in and out and barely missing each other.

'All part of the fun, I guess,' he added, and he laughed, and I noticed that his eyes were the colour of the water, which was a bright aqua now that the sun had come out.

'The others are shopping for tat; well Lou is mainly, and the lads have gone to make sure she doesn't get ripped off; though actually, I reckon they're more likely to get ripped off than she is! Anyway, how's it going? You must be quite a seasoned traveller, coming away on your own? I'm not sure I could cope with it; I'd be worried about getting lost or feeling lonely with no one to talk to... pathetic really.'

I laughed because he looked anything but pathetic; I couldn't imagine him ever getting lost, and he was far too good looking to ever be lonely for long.

'I don't usually travel about on my own,' I explained, 'it's just that I needed to get away and everyone else was busy. I've been doing a spot of teaching, you know, for teachers who are away having nervous breakdowns!'

'I should imagine that would be hard, I nearly did the same myself.'

'What? You mean you're a teacher as well?'

'God, no...! Nearly was though, I did a career swerve and finished up in journalism, freelance travel writing to be precise. It's great actually. Whereabouts in London are you based?'

I grimaced, 'Highgate, right opposite the cemetery, the bottom end.'

'Oh right, yes, Highgate Cemetery, 'the soaked Carrara-covered earth for Londoners to fill."

'Wow, yes, John Betjeman!' I was really impressed.

'Grim poem though, isn't it? Apparently, some of our family are residents, a long time back though.'

'Where do you live, Adam?'

'Well, funnily enough, I'm in Kentish Town, just down the road from you, small world isn't it?'

'Kate!' Louise was running up the steps two at a time.

'It's great to see you! I've been stuck with these three since we arrived. 'This is our cousin, Gio Barletta. And Gio's friend, Antonio D'Este, he says he doesn't speak much English, but he gets by.'

'I'm sure it's better than my Italian,' I said; I was beginning to feel inadequate again. 'I speak a bit of French though,' I added, and they smiled encouragingly, or perhaps patronisingly. Anyway, it made me feel slightly better, but I reminded myself not to tell Sofia about my language skills in case she decided to switch to French, just for fun!

'Let's have pizza, and lots of wine,' suggested Gio, 'but not here, follow me, I know a small restaurant, very good... no tourists, only locals.'

We followed him back over the bridge. It was all starting to look very familiar. 'My apartment isn't far from here,' I told him, 'I'm staying at the Villa Alatri.'

'The Villa Alatri!' he looked shocked but he soon recovered and smiled at me.

'Have you heard of it?' I asked.

'Yes, actually I have,' and he added quickly, 'but I don't know why, just something somewhere... I'm not really sure...' and he looked away as if he was trying to find a reason to change the subject.

'Ah, over there!' he said at last.

It was enchanting; tiny but elegant, and painted in a bright sunshine yellow, with an ironwork balcony and ivy that trailed over the windows onto the striped shutters below.

The patron came out immediately when he saw Gio. They began a long conversation in Italian and I noticed them glancing at me several times as if I were being discussed.

'What's going on, Antonio?' asked Adam. 'We can't keep up, they're talking too fast.'

'It's Luca, he's a friend of Gio; he says he knows Kate. He says he's seen her before; that she lives here, and she speaks Italian.'

They all stared at me, 'It's complicated but I can explain,' I murmured, 'shall we go in first?'

Gio came over and took my arm, 'I will sit next to the beautiful Caterina and she will tell me her story.'

We sat near the window; Louise sat on my right and Gio on my left, Adam and Antonio were across the table and all four were staring at me intently. I wasn't sure where to begin; no way could I tell them the whole story, they probably wouldn't believe me anyway, either that or they would be terrified. I thought for a moment while they waited, I could sense impatience.

'Don't worry, Kate,' said Louise; and she smiled reassuringly, 'we know you're English and that you don't speak Italian. We're not blaming you for anything, we're just curious, that's all.'

'I do know her though,' I paused, '…that woman he was talking about, the one who looks like me.' I wondered if it would have been simpler just to deny it, but it was too late now, instead I told them about how I had turned up at the Villa Alatri only to be confronted with someone who looked exactly like me, apart from the fact that Sofia's teeth were straighter than mine. I wished afterwards that I'd left that bit out; and that Sofia was Italian, and she spoke fluent English, German and French.

Then I went on to tell them that she was probably a distant cousin, and how we had lost touch with half of the family many years back. No one said a word until I had finished, although I noticed that Gio jumped very slightly when I mentioned the Villa Alatri.

'It's very curious,' said Louise, 'I wonder if there's someone out there who looks exactly like me?'

Adam grinned, 'I hope not, one of you is bad enough. I'm only joking,' he added when she glared at him. 'Actually, it's quite possible for it to happen to any of us; it's just that normally we'd never meet so it's a huge coincidence that you showed up on her doorstep, Kate. That is so strange, what are the chances?'

I sighed, 'Yes, I suppose it is strange... Oh well, that's enough about me.'

I left it at that, I wasn't sure I wanted them to know the real reason I was here; that I had felt compelled to come to Venice, in November, on my own; which was something I'd never normally do given the choice. I looked round expectantly waiting for someone else to speak and they seemed to accept that I'd said my piece and preferred not to pursue it further.

Gio said that he and Antonio shared a flat on the island of Murano, just across the lagoon, though Antonio added that Murano was really a group of islands joined by small bridges. He was a glass blower and he often did demonstrations for the tourists. 'You must come to Murano, Kate,' he said, 'the glass is very beautiful! Murano has been renowned for glass blowing since the thirteenth century when we were banned from making glass in Venice for fear of fire.'

'I think you speak very good English, Antonio,' I said.

'Oh, it's for the tourists,' he replied, 'they want to know everything.'

Adam laughed, 'Huh, more like if he's nice to all the ladies they buy more glass and he gets more commission.'

'Have you got a boyfriend?' asked Gio, and he shuffled his chair closer to mine.

'Gio, behave!' scolded Louise, 'You'll frighten Kate if you sit so close, you've only just met.' She smiled at me, 'Don't take any notice, he's just trying it on, he thinks anyone is fair game, especially if they're English!'

'How did you and Adam meet,' I asked her.

'Me and Adam,' she practically exploded with laughter, 'about thirty years ago, give or take a minute. We're twins, Kate. He's my brother!'

Well I'd certainly got it wrong! I'd thought Adam and Louise were an item, and to begin with I'd suspected that Gio and Antonio might be too; instead it turned out that Gio was some sort of Casanova, and Adam and Louise were siblings, twins, in fact, though they looked nothing like each other. As for Antonio, he gave away nothing, only that he was a glass blower.

'I live in Wiltshire not far from our parents, I've got a job in Trowbridge; I'm a solicitor,' she added.

79

'Lou's the one making all the money,' said Adam.

I'd call Annabel when I got back and tell her that Adam and Louise were twins, it would give her a good laugh. I had a horrible feeling she might like Gio though, he was very good looking with dark passionate eyes, and he was tall and handsome, and a stranger. Could he be the King of Wands that Julia mentioned? Or maybe the other one, what did she call him, 'a tricky fellow'? Yes, I was certain that Gio was a tricky fellow, it was written all over him, but Annabel always seemed to be drawn to trouble makers.

'I'll walk you back, if you like,' offered Gio when the meal was over, 'you might get lost otherwise.'

'No, she won't,' said Adam, 'because we'll all come with you, Kate, though you probably know your way around already.'

It was late afternoon when we arrived back at the Villa Alatri. It looked sinister in the gloom but maybe that was my imagination. All the lights were off; Sibella must have been worrying about Sofia's electricity bill again. I asked everyone in, it would be good to have some company even though the night before had been fine, and I'd slept till late.

'Sofia is away but you can come in, I've got some instant coffee, I can heat it up in the microwave.' There was no response; they just stared at me as if I'd suggested taking poison!

When did people get so elitist over coffee, for goodness sake?

'Or I can do tea,' I added, 'I've got some tea bags?'

'Oh, I could murder a cuppa,' said Louise, 'lead on, Kate.'

Sibella looked out of her window and waved as we went past; I expect she wondered who everyone was.

'Who is that old woman?' asked Gio, 'she looks about a hundred years old!'

'Sibella,' I said sadly, 'and apparently she's well over ninety; and all by herself now that her children have left, and they're probably at least sixty years old. And she's got a huge table for a huge family and she just sits up one end on her own.'

Louise sniffed, 'OMG, with no one to talk to, and probably just dry bread to eat!' she wiped her eyes.

'Oh, come on Lou, give over,' said Adam, 'it's not 'Les Miserables' you know, and I expect this Sofia keeps an eye out for her, when she's here. Anyway, it must be ages since her children left home, surely she's used to it by now!'

They followed me up the stairs and I unlocked the door, and suddenly the whole place came to life as I fussed around heating up cups of water to make tea, while everyone else took over the tiny sitting room.

'I like it,' announced Louise, 'it's sweet, and odd that it's so small when the house is so vast. I know there's Sibella across the courtyard but even so! Sofia's apartment must be huge. Oh, I can hear a phone buzzing somewhere, is it yours, Kate?'

'Yes, over here... no problem, I'll get it,' said Gio. 'Ciao, ciao, who is speaking?'

It was Annabel; and he'd switched on the speaker, so I could hear the surprise in her voice from the other side of the room.

'Hello, I'm Annabel, is Kate there?'

'Yes, but why do you want to talk to her when I'm here? And why didn't you come to Venice with your friend?'

'She didn't ask me actually,' said Annabel, 'and who are you anyway?'

'Give me my phone, Gio,' I leaned across the sofa and tried to take it back, but he laughed and backed away.

'Here you go, Kate,' cried Adam and he snatched it from Gio and threw it across to me.

'Who was that?' asked Annabel, 'he sounds really nice.'

I switched the speaker off, 'It's just Gio...'

'Gio...! Gio who, and where did you meet him? Are you having a party, without me?'

'No, it's not a party but I'll ring you later when everyone's gone.'

'Oh, okay, bye.'

'Ciao, bella,' shouted Gio as I rang off.

They went soon after, to catch the waterbus back to Murano and their laughter and chatter was replaced by silence.

'Come out with us on Wednesday,' said Louise before they left. 'We'll take you around the lagoon; Antonio has a boat. And you must bring Sofia, it will be interesting to meet her and compare; I'll tell you if you really look alike.' They trooped noisily down the stairs and across the courtyard and I stood at the top of the stone steps and waved until they were out of sight.

'Hi Abel,' I said, 'sorry I couldn't talk earlier I was busy making tea and everyone was here.' Then I told her all about Adam and Louise and how they were twins, and that when I'd met them on the vaporetto I thought they were a couple. After that I told her about the restaurant and being mistaken for Sofia; and about Shirl, and Sibella; I'd only been in Venice since Friday evening, but it felt much longer! Annabel hardly said a word which was unusual for her and I wondered if she'd just put the phone down, but when I'd finished she told me that she thought it was all intriguing.

'Maybe you should see a hypnotist, like Shirl suggested,' she said thoughtfully. 'It's all very well getting warnings from Tarot readers, but really you need to know why this is happening and how you can stop it. There must be a reason, what's the point otherwise?'

'How's everything your end?' I asked, I felt mean hogging the conversation although she did it all the time.

'Same as ever, except Lucy says she's okay with it if I go. Actually, I thought she looked really pleased, though she was trying to hide it. I thought I'd go to Mum's for a few days. I haven't seen them, or my brothers, for ages. I was going back at Christmas anyway, but since I've been virtually evicted from my flat...'

'You haven't been evicted Annabel; you said you were leaving, and James could move in.'

'Yeah, well it feels like I've been evicted, they were very peculiar the other night, asked how long it would take for me to pack, and could they help! I should have come with you and met Gio and the others but instead I'm stuck here!'

I was starting to wonder if I was making a big mistake by allowing her to move in with me, 'Okay, gotta go, I have to plug my phone in,' I said at last.

Sofia would be back tomorrow so just one more night to get through on my own. I pulled the curtain across to shut out the darkness; it would be fine, what was that old adage about there being nothing to fear but fear itself?

CHAPTER 8

I opened my eyes and looked up into a firmament that was frosty and bright with stars. The stone lion was standing directly in front of me, and I was shivering, and reaching out blindly with my arms, as if seeking something that wasn't there. I heard Sibella's door open, and I saw her startled face peering at me through the pale light as she padded over to me. Then, clasping my hand tightly in her bony fingers, she led me across the courtyard and into her apartment. It was bone chillingly cold, even colder than outside, and I could hear my teeth chattering as she wrapped me in a thick blanket and sat me down in an overstuffed armchair.

'Riposi, Caterina, riposi...' she murmured soothingly, as she tucked the blanket around my bare feet and legs, 'riposi, dormi, dormi...'

'Thank you, Sibella,' I whispered, 'I've never walked in my sleep before, not until now.'

'Si... si, eri sonnambulo... riposi...' and she patted my head gently as if I were a small child, and stroked my hair until I fell asleep.

When I awoke the next morning, I could hear her as she bustled about. She made a surprising amount of noise for someone so small and diminished. She was sweeping the floor around me, and she sang quietly as she filled a saucepan with water and put it on the stove. I didn't want to open my eyes, I felt safe, as if Sibella were taking care of me, saving me from harm. She smiled down at me and gave me a cup of watery coffee, and a lump of slightly stale bread, and some of the chocolate I'd given her.

I had to leave eventually, although I could happily have stayed there until it was time for my plane to whisk me away. She waved from her doorway, 'Sofia,' she said, and I nodded; yes, Sofia would be back, maybe she would let me stay with her, since it was obvious I was so useless on my own. I staggered up the stairs to my little apartment heading straight for the shower, and once I'd washed my hair and made some tea I felt a bit better. I thought about ringing Shirl and telling her about how Sibella had rescued me from the garden, but I really didn't feel like talking to anyone; most of all, I needed to think.

There was a knock on the door, it was Sofia.

'Poor Kate,' she said when I opened it, 'I've just seen Sibella and she told me you'd been sleepwalking.'

'Yeah, she found me outside, in the flower bed, with the lion!' I felt like laughing, it seemed so ridiculous. 'She took me in and looked after me; she was so kind.' I paused, 'Did she tell you about my friend Shirley as well?'

'Yes, and she said you were asking about the murder that happened here over a hundred years ago. How did you hear about that? It's practically ancient history; of course, Sibella loves to talk about it, it puts her in mind of her mother and her grandmother.'

'It was Shirl that translated for me! I forgot to tell you that I don't speak Italian.'

'You must get dressed and come downstairs with me; we'll have lunch and you can tell me everything that's happened while I've been gone.'

I looked down at my ancient cotton dressing gown with the fraying hem, and I sighed, 'Sorry, Sofia, what must you think? Just give me ten minutes, you go on, I'll come down and find you.'

Sofia's apartment was warm and smelled of fresh coffee.

'Sit down and relax,' she said, 'tell me everything that has happened so far. I'll pour you some coffee, would you like milk?'

'Yes, lots of milk, please... er... I don't really know where to begin.'

'Tell me first how you found out about the murder, no one around here would know anything about it, apart from a few very old people like Sibella, and not many of them are left.'

So, I told her about my dream, and how I'd recognised the Villa Alatri as soon as I arrived. I described my terror when he placed his hands around my neck, and how I'd felt his foul breath on my cheek as his fingers closed around my throat... I stopped, recoiling at the memory and unable to speak for a moment.

'But... why would that happen to you?' she asked. 'What possible reason could there be? After all, both the victim, and the man who killed her, are long dead.'

'The Tarot reader told me that something was unresolved, something in my past, though actually she didn't know about my dreams because I didn't tell her about them!'

'A Tarot reader, well, how bizarre! If it wasn't for the fact that you know about the murder, I'd be convinced you were suffering from some kind of a breakdown.'

I nodded, 'Yes, that would be easier to understand, but it's all true, the dream and the Tarot reading!' Then I told her about Annabel, and how she had won the Tarot reading in a competition, and that it was supposed to be her reading and not mine.

'But I'm sure she knew I wasn't Annabel,' I murmured, 'because she seemed to know everything about me, how I'd just split up with Tom, and...'

'You mustn't worry, these fortune tellers are clever, very intuitive, you give them clues without realising; but you say that you recognised this place as soon as you arrived? That's the most curious thing of all. The murder, well that could have been something you'd read about somewhere and forgotten, though I don't know where; or possibly just coincidence, the mind plays tricks. Are you sure it was the Villa Alatri?' She shook her head, 'What am I saying? It must be, because we resemble each other so closely, and we obviously share the same genes, the same DNA, and my family has lived in this villa for hundreds of years.'

We sat quietly for a while, each of us lost in our own thoughts.

'I had another dream,' I said quietly, 'just the other night, it was... different. Actually, I'd almost forgotten about it because of everything else that's happened.'

'Go on,' she said, 'tell me...'

'I thought I was awake. Have you ever had one of those dreams where you're certain you're awake and yet you're not?'

'Yes, I know what you mean, it usually happens to me when I have to be somewhere and I'm late or stressed.'

'Well, I woke in the night, or I thought I did, and the room had changed. It was much bigger, and the walls were decorated with lions and cherubs, and there was a red velvet chair, and a wash-stand with a blue and white jug. I was sad when I woke up, and when I realised it was only a dream I cried.'

It made me feel sad just remembering.

The colour drained from Sofia's face; she looked deathly pale and I was worried she was going to faint. 'It's the way it used to be,' she gasped, 'when my parents were alive; not the wall paintings of course, they were long gone, though there were traces here and there, but the room was bigger. They decided to divide the house into apartments, they'd only just started when they had the accident; they died instantly.'

'I'm so sorry, Sofia, I had no idea!' I was mortified. Here was I going on about my problems when she was an orphan.

'It was a long time ago, twenty-four years to be precise; I was only six at the time. They often went away leaving me with Nonna and Grandpa, I didn't mind because I loved them so much and they used to spoil me. My parents had a speed boat and it crashed onto the rocks, they didn't know anything about it, or at least, that's what I was told. No one really knew what had happened. Grandpa died soon after, Nonna says the shock at losing my father, Roberto, was more than his heart could stand. She brought me up; we'd just moved to our house in Verona so that this place could be turned into holiday apartments, we both stayed there, and life went on. My Mother was pregnant at the time so I would have had a brother, or sister.' She shook her head as if trying to dispel unhappy memories, 'I told Nonna about you and she says you must come again when she's here. She has an old box with photos and a family tree that she wants to show you.'

'I'd like that,' I said, 'and it's amazing that we're related but it still doesn't explain why I'd see this house as it used to be; or why I'd remember Caterina's murder as if it were happening to me. My friend Shirley thinks I may be a reincarnation of Caterina.'

Sofia laughed, 'Well, it's one explanation, I suppose, though some people believe that memories can be inherited, especially if something traumatic has happened to someone in a previous life.'

'Don't you believe that the soul can exist apart from the body,' I asked, and I wondered where the question had come from because it didn't sound like me at all.

'Only if there's no other explanation,' said Sofia. 'Look let's forget all this and go and eat. I know a nice little restaurant; it's very near here and not at all touristy, in November at least!'

'I might already know it! Is it bright yellow, with an iron balcony, and trailing ivy?' And I told her about Gio's friend who thought he'd recognised me.

'What? I don't believe it! Well, perhaps we'll go somewhere else; and how odd that he remembered me!'

Sibella was dead-heading the geraniums in the flower bed when we left. She patted the stone lion and gave a gummy smile.

'Ciao, Sofia… ciao, Caterina,' she murmured.

'Ciao, Sibella!' we chorused.

'She thinks you're my long-lost twin,' whispered Sofia, 'and she's very happy because we've found each other at last!' and she laughed and took my arm.

Sofia was good company and we created quite a stir in the restaurant as everyone was convinced we were twins. We didn't try to explain, it was easier not to, but they must have wondered why only one of us could speak Italian, and luckily, we didn't see anyone who knew Sofia. The red wine probably helped too because I was more relaxed when we got back, but I also felt slightly guilty as I'd gone on a bit about Tom and Lorna and probably bored her half to death.

She agreed that I should stay with her for the three remaining nights and we went upstairs straight away to pack up my belongings.

Sofia's rooms were large and airy with high ceilings and intricate coving that went all the way around, rather than just halfway as they did upstairs, and it was evident that the Villa Alatri had once been a grand residence in spite of the peeling paintwork and worn rugs. She showed me to a large room with a double bed and pale blue curtains trimmed with heavy lace, 'This will be much better for you,' she declared breezily as if she was trying to lighten the mood, and she added, 'there's no hurry tomorrow, I haven't got to work so we can have a lazy day.'

I was exhausted after my bizarre sleepwalking episode the night before, and when I sank down into the feather-soft bed I'd completely forgotten that tomorrow was Wednesday, and that I'd arranged to meet Adam and Louise for our trip around the lagoon on Antonio's boat. My mobile rang at precisely eight thirty the next morning, well not rang exactly, just a tuneful rendition of 'I'm singing in the rain' that made me laugh because it reminded me of Shirl. I yawned and stretched, 'Hello...' I mumbled sleepily.

'Hi Kate, sorry, did I wake you up? It's Adam, remember? We'll be with you in about half an hour, hope that's okay?'

'Yes, great, lovely...' I stifled a yawn.

'Are you still up for coming out? You sound worn out; not been knocking back too much of the vino, have you? Look, we'll get as close as we can, and I'll come and get you when we're moored. And don't forget to bring the mysterious Sofia.'

I rang off and leapt out of bed, 'Sofia, are you up?'

'Yes, I am, and I was just about to call you. I remembered you said we were going on a boat trip at some point today, around the lagoon?'

'Yes, Adam just called; they're on their way now. Thanks so much for letting me stay, Sofia. That bed might be an antique but it's really comfortable!'

Sofia laughed, 'It's the frame that's antique, Kate, not the mattress. Shall I make a picnic; we've still got most of the food I gave you when I left for Verona.'

'Great idea, I haven't eaten much, I've had loads of wine though! I'll have to lay off it for a bit when I get home.'

'It's easy to drink too much here, the wine is so good. Come on, get dressed, your friends will be here soon, I can't wait to find out if they can tell us apart.'

Adam was alone; he was standing in the courtyard staring at the lion and he glanced around when he heard us. 'Hey, I've seen another lion like this somewhere else…' then he stopped and his jaw dropped in disbelief.

'Well, I've seen everything now…!' he seemed lost for words, 'the likeness is extraordinary! How…? Why…?'

'I know, it's impossible to explain,' murmured Sofia, 'we're obviously related, descended from the same family, though one that divided many, many years before we were born. Maybe if we all waited long enough it could happen in any family.'

'It's odd you should say that,' said Adam, 'my sister Lou is the image of our great, great aunt; same hair, eyes, everything. The difference is they were born more than a hundred years apart; only one Louise though, thank goodness.'

I was silent; it felt strange to be discussed in that way, like some freak of nature, no more than a replica, though Sofia was too, as if we all just popped up from time to time over the centuries, different people, different times, but basically the same.

Antonio was moored in the canal behind the villa, the one that I could see from my bedroom in the upstairs apartment. He was at the controls and anxious to be on his way. Louise was sitting with Gio; she looked like a glamorous Russian countess in her fake fur hat. We piled on board, and we were off, speeding towards the wider canals and out into the open lagoon. The wind whisked my hair around my face and I pulled on my black beanie to hold it down; Sofia had a headscarf tied around her head, like some old fifties film star, but she still managed to look elegant. I could look exactly like that, I thought, I just need a silk headscarf; I glanced at Louise, or a Russian hat, why hadn't I thought of that?

Adam grinned at me, 'You look very sensible in your woolly hat,' he said as if he could read my mind, and he winked and added in a fake Yorkshire accent, 'Aye, you can't beat wool for warmth!'

'There are a hundred and twenty islands in the lagoon,' announced Antonio, 'most of them are very small. It's the Lido that protects the lagoon and all its islands from the open sea.'

'What's the Lido, Antonio?' I asked.

'It's a narrow strip of land with beaches and hotels, lots of people stay there when they want to visit Venice, and Murano where we make the glass; and Burano, that's the island of the lace makers. And over there is the cemetery island, San Michele; see, with the high walls and cypress trees. It's made up of two islands, and lots of famous people are buried there; for instance, have you heard of Igor Stravinsky, or Sergei Diaghilev of the Russian ballet?'

'So, why did they build the cemetery on an island?' asked Louise.

'There's no room in Venice,' said Gio, 'and the graves have to be above ground, not below, because the water table is high, and they were worried that the dead might spread the plague, which is probably why they shipped them out here to begin with.'

It seemed obvious put like that.

'You can't stay there now though,' he added, 'they move you after ten years, so they don't run out of space.'

That shut us all up for a bit, although I had a few questions to ask, like where did they go next? Mum would say it was my morbid streak again.

'We'll go to Murano first, and I will show you my glass blowing skills.'

'Watch out! Antonio wants you to buy something,' warned Gio, 'he thinks we're tourists!'

'You mean I'm not,' I asked.

'Yeah, you are, but best if you don't remind him,' whispered Adam.

'This is home for me,' declared Antonio proudly as we turned into a narrow canal. 'The Rio dei Vetrai, my family has lived here for over a hundred years. Come, come, I will show you the treasures of Murano.'

We followed Antonio into a cavern-like store, twinkling like an Aladdin's cave, with glass ornaments of every variety and in every colour imaginable. It was hot inside, particularly after the wind chill of the boat ride; my cheeks were tingling, and my mouth felt almost numb with cold and I wasn't sure if I could speak properly. At the end of the room two glass blowers were holding lumps of coloured glass over a flaming cauldron till they melted and stretched like molten lava; then they blew into rods creating bubbles of pliable glass which were prodded and tweaked until fragile shapes appeared; a horse with spiky legs and a curling mane, and a curved, blue, translucent dolphin, leaping from some imagined ocean. They held them up to show the crowd who watched from a cordoned-off area, cheering and applauding.

Antonio stood at my side, 'Look at the chandeliers, see how beautiful they are, we call them 'ciocca', which, in English, is a 'bouquet of flowers'. Some of them are very old, and very valuable, and every piece of glass is individually made to form leaves and garlands in all the colours of the rainbow. It's my turn now and you will see how talented I am.

Antonio went around the barrier to talk to Paolo and shortly afterwards the door slammed as Paolo left. I could see him through the plate glass window, strolling along next to the canal; he seemed so happy, and he was laughing and greeting people as he went. His life was so different to mine; I was pondering on this when I turned back and looked up at the chandelier as it swayed slightly in the draught from the door. My eyes felt dry, and my vision started to blur, making the colours blend into one, and suddenly, I was swaying too as the room spun around me. A small girl was dancing on tiptoe close by and I could hear music. 'Dance, Caterina, dance...' she implored in Italian, and somehow I understood her, and she smiled at me with big, brown eyes that were fringed with long, black lashes, 'Dance, Caterina, come on…please…' 'Elisabetta,' I cried, 'Elisabetta…I haven't got time to dance…' and I laughed at her enthusiasm and reached out my hands to take hers. 'Oh, very well, little one, but not for long…' the light from the chandelier seemed to vibrate as we spun around the room to the music, and I could still hear Elisabetta's laughter as, too soon, everything faded into darkness.

When I came to, Louise, Adam and Gio were looking down at me curiously from what seemed like a great height, while a woman I didn't know was gripping my ankles. The beautiful 'ciocca' still swayed above me, mesmerizing me, drawing me back into its sparkling depths; it was hard to resist its pull. Somewhere in the distance, I could hear Antonio, instructing the growing crowd of spectators to leave; then Adam took off his coat, and lifted my head gently so that he could place it underneath. Oh, that was much better.
Sofia was on the floor next to me, and she was stroking my hair and making soothing noises; I looked up at her and it was as if I was looking in a mirror, at a different version of myself, a more confident, accomplished self.

'Katherine, can you hear me?' she asked, 'Who is Elisabetta, Katherine?'

'I… don't know…' I murmured, 'I don't know anyone called Elisabetta…'
Adam bent down and took my hands, 'Come on, Kate… it's not important! Hold onto me, can you get up? Lou, fetch a chair, will you?'

I turned my head and saw Louise out of the corner of my eye as she went off to find a chair. I was starting to feel silly, like I'd just tripped flat on my face in the street. The woman who was holding my legs lowered them slowly to the floor, 'Do you feel better now, dear?' she queried, 'Or would you like us to call an ambulance?'

I struggled to get up, but I felt strangely weak. An ambulance, eek... no! Anyway, how would they get an ambulance here? I'd have to get in a helicopter. I'd be a poppy show, whatever that was; I just had a vague recollection of my Gran saying it when I'd dyed my hair pink, light years ago.

'No, er... thank you for helping me... I'll be fine now; you've been very... um... helpful...'

'We'll take you home, Kate,' said Sofia, 'lean on me, it's not far to the boat.'

Adam put his arm around my waist, and he and Sofia helped me back to where Antonio's boat was moored. He'd raced ahead, and the engine was already ticking over ready to go. He didn't seem very pleased.

'It's okay,' said Gio, 'he'll get over it, there's lots of time, and he can show off some other day.'

Antonio glared at him, 'but I was going to take you to Burano. Burano is unique; the houses there are painted in many different colours; and then to Torcello, the island in the swamp where Ernest Hemingway lived.'

'His aunt makes lace on Burano,' whispered Adam, 'and she was probably hoping to sell us something. He never stops, he must dream up anecdotes to amuse the tourists all day and every day, just never knows when to shut up.'

'How are you feeling now, Kate?' asked Sofia when we were out on the lagoon and Murano was fading into the distance.

'I'm fine,' I said, 'and I'm really sorry I've spoilt everyone's day. Antonio knows so much about the area, and he had all sorts of plans that I've ruined. And he's let us come out on his boat which is really nice of him.'

'Yes, but there'll be other days,' said Sofia softly, 'and I think he likes Louise. He's trying to impress her, look, he's letting her steer;' she giggled, 'and Gio's trying to get a look in too.'

I glanced up at Adam's face; he looked worried, 'If it's anything like her driving I'm not so sure it's a good idea; she's written off two cars in the past three years! Where are the life jackets?'

I was pleased when we got back to the villa, I couldn't wait to get inside and hide away. I was so embarrassed by everything that had happened; I was nothing more than a liability, and they probably wished they'd never met me! We said goodbye on the steps and Adam promised to call me when he got back to London, and they said they hoped I'd feel better in the morning. Even Antonio said he would look forward to seeing me at some time in the future, though I found that hard to believe, but it seemed I'd got it wrong and they liked me, in spite of everything.

'What happened to you on Murano?' asked Sofia. 'I've seen people faint before, I used to work with a girl who was always passing out, but it was different somehow. You were talking to someone; her name was Elisabetta. Do you know anyone called Elisabetta? You were reaching out as if you were trying to hold her hands, and you were talking to her in Italian! How is that possible?'

'I don't know, perhaps it was because of the ciocca, the chandelier; it was almost as if it sparked a memory, and there was a child, a little girl, and I didn't want to leave her. We were so happy, me and Elisabetta.'

Sofia shook her head, 'Yet you don't know anyone by that name? The odd thing is...' she paused and stared at me as if she was worried that she might upset me further, 'the odd thing is, I do recognise the chandelier, or one that is very similar. It used to hang in this room; it was one of the things Nonna moved to our house in Verona. My mother loved it; it's still there; you'll see it some time, when you come back.'

I gazed around the room with its high ceilings and the long windows that were beginning to feel more familiar with each passing day. I sighed, 'I'm not sure if I should come back at all, Sofia, I'm causing too much of a disruption; surely, you won't want me back?'

'Of course, I do! We'll sort this out, I promise. My home is your home, and you are always welcome,' she chuckled, 'even if you are a disruption. Make yourself at home here! Now would you like coffee, or a nice cup of builders brew?'

Wow…! Her English was brilliant! 'Yes, please, a cup of tea would be wonderful!'

She grinned, 'Just what the doctor ordered?'

CHAPTER 9

I slept well again. The sun was shining when I woke up and I felt much happier. Sofia wasn't up so I decided to call Mum to let her know I was still alive. The phone rang and rang, and I was just about to ring off when she picked it up. I could hear the panic in her voice straight away.

'Katherine, is that you, what's wrong, you haven't had an accident, have you?'

Oops! I'd forgotten we were an hour ahead and it wasn't even seven o'clock in England!

'No Mum, I'm fine, there's nothing wrong, really. I just forgot about the time difference.'

'Oh, that's a relief, only twenty to seven here, we were still in bed. Dad's got a late shift.'

Oh gawd! Even twenty to eight would have been too early for Dad. 'Sorry, Mum, I only called to give you an update, I'm coming back tomorrow. The week has gone really fast!'

'Well I knew you were fine because I spoke to Annabel the other day and she said you'd made friends; she said you were having a party when she called, you always did make friends easily, I hope they're nice.'

'Yeah, really nice, and actually one of them, Adam...' I couldn't help smiling when I said his name, which was rather worrying, 'well, he lives just down the road in Kentish Town. Anyway, I'll call tomorrow when I get home; I'm getting a plane by the way, not a ship so you don't have to worry.'

'Oh, Kentish Town, how funny, it's a small world, isn't it?' said Mum, 'Speak soon then, safe journey!'

The house was silent but Sibella was up and about. I could hear her broom swishing back and forth as she swept the last of the autumn leaves into a pile. I decided to explore, after all, Sofia had told me to make myself at home and so far I hadn't ventured further than the ground floor.

The staircase rose from a hallway on the other side of the house, where a door opened onto the canal path. It was next to the corridor leading to the old kitchen; yes, there was definitely an old kitchen; somehow, I knew that for certain. I was tempted to go in there first, but I was curious to see what was on the other side of the wall from my tiny bedroom on the next floor up. The stairway curved in a gradual spiral of wide dusty treads, framed, on either side, by banisters that looked almost oriental, with elegant curlicues, and long graceful leaves carved into the wood. It was obvious that no one used this part of the house, and why would they? It was too vast for one person and I could see why Sofia's parents had wanted to divide it up into holiday rentals. It was a house that needed a large extended family, with aunts and uncles, and grandparents, and children running up and down the stairs, laughing and shouting, and music, and the smell of cooking, just like it was in my dream and before Venice became little more than a museum.

I wandered from room to room, incongruous, an outsider with echoing footsteps, and strange garb. Greying dust sheets covered the heavy furniture, and dead house-flies decorated the window sills, and then I found it, the other room, or the rest of my tiny bedroom. It seemed disproportionate, as if part of it were missing, which, of course, it was. The window looked down over the courtyard where Sibella was still brushing furiously, I tapped on the glass and waved, and she didn't hear me at first, but she glanced up eventually and I saw the shock on her face, until she realised it was me. I looked back at the room; an ancient armchair, draped in red velvet brocade, nestled in the far corner next to an elegant, marble washstand topped with a blue patterned jug and a matching china basin. I closed my eyes for a moment and the rich fragrance of rose oil, patchouli and oranges washed over me in a soothing wave of sweetness

'What are you doing up here, Kate?' called Sofia, and I felt suddenly guilty, as if I'd taken advantage of her hospitality.

'I'm sorry, Sofia,' I murmured, 'it was rude of me, I should have asked.'

'No, it's fine; I should have given you a guided tour. It's just that sometimes I'd prefer to believe that this part of the house doesn't exist. Mad, I know, but it makes me wonder how my life would have been, you know, if I'd had brothers and sisters, a proper family.'

I didn't know what to say, nothing really felt right.

'Perhaps I could share your family, Kate?' she said at last.

I laughed, 'What my horrible brother, well I'd happily have given him away when we were small; he was a pest, though actually I miss him now.'

Her face fell, 'Oh, no…! Did something happen to him?'

'What, Greg? Oh no, well, yes… he went to university in Newcastle and he never came back. He's getting married.'

She smiled and looked relieved and I felt sorry for her. How awful always to assume the worst, but it was hardly surprising considering what had happened in her past.

'It's your last day in Venice, we should go for a walk; you could buy some souvenirs, something for your mother and father, and your brother maybe? And this afternoon Sibella has invited us to tea, she wants to tell you the story of the lion, it's pretty gruesome though, I'm warning you!'

Souvenirs…? And I hadn't even got around to writing Auntie Flo's postcard, I'd forgotten completely! Who writes postcards anyway these days? I wondered if she had an email address.

'It's a lovely house, Sofia,' I said as we went down the stairs, 'and it seems a pity that no one is living here. Maybe you could turn it into restaurant with tables in the courtyard; or a wedding venue, you'd make a fortune. Perhaps Greg could book it, there's lots of room for the immediate family to stay.'

She laughed, 'I'll give it some thought. It's really cold today so don't forget your gloves and you can borrow my boots if you like? I bet our feet are the same size!'

Our feet were the same size, which was just as well because I only had my trainers, and the cheap boots I was wearing when Shirl and I got caught in the rain, and they were still damp.

It felt almost as if we were falling into a routine when we left Sibella in the courtyard. She waved as we passed, 'Ciao bella, Sofia, Ciao bella, Caterina,' and we called back, 'Ciao, Sibella.' I was beginning to wish I could stay with my new-found family, I'd learn Italian and we'd start a restaurant; I wondered if it was possible.

La Serenissima, it certainly looked serene in the hazy, autumn sunshine that glinted on the water and threw deep, mysterious shadows under the bridges. We wandered through the beautiful, Gothic fish market, where prawns and lobsters wriggled in deep layers of crushed ice beside slabs of multicoloured fish and calamari, and watched the swooping seagulls as they screamed and swooped over the fishmongers in their long aprons.

'Let's go to Burano,' said Sofia suddenly, 'you missed it yesterday and we can get a vaporetto from San Zaccaria near St Mark's.'

'Due biglietti per i gemelli,' chortled the woman selling tickets at the quay.

'Someone else who thinks we're twins,' whispered Sofia.

The vaporetto was crowded with tourists and soon we were out on the water again heading north for Burano and leaving the cemetery of San Michele and Antonio's island of glass far behind us.

'You'll see the lace shops on the quay,' said Sofia, 'some of the old women still like to sit outside in the sunshine, working away, dressed all in black. Nonna told me that when she was small hardly anyone came to visit Burano but now everyone comes to see the coloured houses. The old women are continuing the tradition, but not many young people make lace now, it's quicker and cheaper to buy it from China.'

Burano was as picturesque as the guide books said. The canals were like narrow streets linked by tiny bridges and flanked on both sides by rows of coloured houses, all strung about with freshly-washed bedding that flapped noisily in the breeze.

'Why are the houses so many colours?' I asked Sofia.

'It was because of the fishermen,' she replied, 'or so the story goes; they would come home drunk and forget which house was theirs, so their wives came up with the idea of painting them so that they would be easy to find. I'm not sure how true it is; now I think they paint them because lots of tourists want to visit to take photographs, and buy things they'd never dream of buying if they weren't on holiday!'

We found a secluded spot on the quay and perched on the steps to dip our toes in the water. Sofia unpacked some bread and cheese and a bottle of red wine, and we ate and drank until we felt relaxed and slightly giggly.

'It's time to go back,' she said, after a while, 'Sibella is expecting us.'

I took my phone out, 'Come on, let's take a selfie before we go... I can send it to Annabel, and Adam.'

Sibella had set her huge table for three and she'd made a very English looking apple pie and a chocolate cake. She only had coffee so Sofia went to get her tea bags because I said it wasn't a proper tea otherwise. Her coffee looked thick and black, and it was probably bitter too because she wrinkled her face every time she took a gulp. I was sure she would have preferred a nice cup of tea, but it was much too late to convert her, and she wouldn't even try it, not even a sip!

'Didn't Sibella want to tell me the story of the lion?' I asked.

Sofia giggled, I don't think the effects of the wine had completely worn off; 'No, not the lion, please...!' but Sibella had already heard and recognised the word as soon as I mentioned it.

'Ah... leone,' she murmured, and she smiled at me, and then at Sofia, slightly disapprovingly I thought, as if she guessed we'd been at the bottle. 'Si, il leone...' she began, and Sofia translated.

'Long ago, the Villa Alatri was a palace, one of the first in San Stae, and the owner was Marco Roberto di Lazio. He was named Marco after the great Venetian explorer, Marco Polo. He was a very powerful man with a great many servants.'

'It sounds like a tale from The Arabian Nights,' I whispered.

'Shhhh… you'll upset her,' hushed Sofia and Sibella paused to frown at me.

'One day he heard about two beautiful stone lions that ancient people had left behind on the Island of Poveglia out in the lagoon.' Sofia turned to me and added, 'Poveglia is a very mysterious island, it's supposed to be haunted.'

'Si, fantasmi…' muttered Sibella and she crossed herself before continuing…

'He wanted the lions to stand on either side of the gate. In those days it was a magnificent gate at the bottom of the stone steps; there was more space then, and they grew figs and olive trees because the garden was larger than it is now. He went across to the island to see the lions and they were as magnificent as he had hoped so he asked his servants to make a giant raft to bring them back to the Villa Alatri.'

'Si magnifico…' muttered Sibella and she turned and pointed through her window to the stone lion in the bed of geraniums.

'Yes, that is the very lion that Marco brought back from Poveglia,' said Sofia, 'he's been alone for hundreds of years because the other lion never made it.'

I glanced at Sibella, she was very animated when she talked about the past, even a past that was well before her time. She was talking again in rapid Italian, crossing herself and chuckling in turn; then suddenly she clapped her hands together and exploded into a peal of laughter and I noticed she had no teeth, none at all!

'Why is she laughing?' I asked Sofia.

'I'm not really sure; I've never found it that amusing. I'll tell you the rest of the story shall I, and then you can decide for yourself if it's funny.'

Sibella was still jabbering away, and slapping her hands together and laughing like a maniac.

'She says she's laughing because the story is so macabre and now that she's lived for so long she realises that all of life is macabre and so the only thing you can do is laugh at its absurdity.'

'Wow, that's deep,' I said, 'not to mention depressing. Anyway, what happened next?'

'She says Marco was very pleased with his new acquisition and he couldn't wait to get the other lion so that he had the pair, so they got the raft out again and headed across the lagoon and back to Poveglia. Then Marco went ashore and they tried to lift the lion onto rollers to take it back to the raft. The problem was that it had sunk into the waterlogged soil and so they threw a rope around it and heaved and pushed and pulled, and Marco was getting angry and impatient, but then they heard the voices of the dead rising from the earth.'

'No...why? What dead?'

'The victims of plague, of course, it was where they sent anyone suffering from the plague, or actually, anyone who had something that might contaminate or wipe out the entire population of Venice. I expect they made mistakes sometimes; you wouldn't want to end up there just because you had a bit of a chill! And there was a lunatic asylum there until the nineteen sixties; it's a horrible place, some people say that fifty percent of the soil is composed of human remains.'

I was speechless, I gazed open-mouthed at Sibella and she looked back at me with wide rheumy eyes. Then she nodded solemnly at Sofia and indicated for her to go on.

'She wants me to tell you the rest of her story.'

'I can't wait!' I said. God... would I ever sleep soundly again?

'The servants ran away, and who could blame them?'

'Well, not me...!'

'Marco wouldn't give up, he just kept pulling on the rope, and then...'

SLAP...! Went Sibella's hands and I nearly dived for cover.

'I expect you've guessed what happened?' said Sofia.

'No, you don't mean...'

'Yep, squashed as flat as a pancake, it just suddenly shot out of the ground and...'

SLAP went Sibella's hands, and she cackled again, laughing gummily until tears ran down her face.

'...anyway, that's why there's only one lion. Your tea is getting cold.'

'And did they get him back, Marco, I mean? Did his servants go back for him?'

'No, the lion was on top of him, and anyway the ground is so soft on Poveglia that he'd gone in nearly a metre...'

By the time we left Sibella and crossed the courtyard to Sofia's, I felt as if I'd fallen into another world; one of ghosts and strange dreams where murder and a gruesome death lurked, waiting for me around every corner.

'Sibella will miss you when you leave,' said Sofia, 'and so will I, will you come back? Come for Christmas, you can meet Nonna, and check out the family tree.'

I was about to say, 'Oh, yes please, absolutely, can't wait!' when I thought of Mum and Dad at home. Wouldn't it be dreadful if Mum finished up like Sibella, who had all those children and not one of them even bothering to visit? 'I'll come if Greg goes home for Christmas,' I said in the end, 'I'll have to let you know, but I'd really love it! Can I bring Annabel, please, she can meet Gio.'

Adam might come too, I thought, and Louise, it would be amazing. I went off to my room to pack and I was just doing up the zip when I realised it had been ages since I'd thought of Tom, just shows you, I decided, he was really boring!

Sofia came with me to the airport, but before we left the Villa Alatri I knocked on Sibella's door and we hugged, and she walked me to the gate to wave, 'Ciao, Caterina,' she called until I turned the corner.

A heavy mist covered the grey water of the canal; it deadened the sound of the vaporetto as we navigated our way out of Venice and into the lagoon; the atmosphere felt heavy and sombre and I could feel a headache starting over my left eye.

'Too much red wine,' said Sofia, which was probably right.

I nodded, and the pain shot round the back of my head, 'Ow…' I moaned.

'You could be dehydrated,' she added, 'but you won't drink so much when you get home.'

What, I thought, with Annabel moving in, she'll probably drive me to triple vodkas!

CHAPTER 10

The flight was on time and uneventful, and I went through passport control and security without incident. It helped just having hand baggage so I didn't even have to wait around at the carousel, and I chose the 'nothing to declare' route and swept out into the arrivals hall, where taxi drivers stood waiting for incoming business men, and friends and relatives stood in groups waiting anxiously for planes to land, or laughing and hugging each other and...

'Oo ooo.... Kate! Over here...! I decided to come and meet you, I've moved out!'

It was Annabel!

I hurried around the barrier; I was really pleased to see her, even if she was making 'a poppy show' of herself because no way could I have missed her, done up as she was in a sunshine yellow puffer jacket, and bright red lipstick, and she'd had long blond hair extensions added to her bobbed hair.

She lurched towards me on retro platform boots and grabbed my wheelie and my arm and marched me towards the station talking all the time.

'Lucy and James helped me to pack, and then James shoved all my stuff into his Range Rover and drove it straight round to your pad... It was like they couldn't wait to get rid of me!'

'Pad?' I enquired, I looked up at her; we were normally the same height.

'Yeah, your pad, opposite the cemetery, der...'

'Oh, that pad...'

'All my stuff is there now so that's it; you've got me now, instead of boring old Tom.'

'Did you pick up the key from Mum then, she didn't mention it?'

'No, I haven't had time; I've just been too busy with my Tarot research, and I've signed up with your agency.'

'Wow, you're serious about this teaching thing then?'

'Of course; I'm going to be brilliant...'

'Hang on, Abel, where's all your stuff if you haven't got a key to my... er... pad?'

'Oh yes, it's in the front garden so we'd better hurry; looks like it's about to rain, or snow, or something; I don't want it going all soggy!'

We hurried down onto the station platform. I was wondering what Sofia would make of this mad woman if she ever did get to meet her.

'I've got loads to tell you, Annabel,' I said when we were on the train and I'd managed to get a word in.'

She kept looking anxiously at the time on her phone, no doubt concerned about the possible sogginess of her belongings in my front garden. It didn't seem to have occurred to her that they might not be there when we got back. Even if they hadn't been stolen, the dustmen might have been and at this very moment all her worldly possessions

116

might be languishing on top of a pile of discarded egg boxes, and potato peelings, and worse, much, much, worse!

'Go ahead, lovely, I'll shut up for a bit, wish this train would speed up. Oh no... We've stopped...! I hate it when we stop in these tunnels; I think I might be a little bit claustrophobic!'

She eyed herself in the glass and her reflection stared back from the darkness.

'Your hair has grown, hasn't it?' I peered over her shoulder at the glass to where a second Annabel, perish the thought, was peering back, 'And I've only been away for a week!'

'Haha, very funny, I think it looks really natural actually,' she replied, and she ran her fingers through her long fringe, 'and I think it matches my own colour perfectly. Look, you can't see where it's joined on at all!'

'And what's with the boots?'

'Yeah, great, aren't they? I bought them down Portobello market; they're originals from the early eighties. I like yours though, stylish, Italian; expensive?'

'Sofia gave them to me; mine fell apart when they got wet.'

I had the feeling she wasn't really listening to me because she kept nibbling her nails and checking her phone for the time.

'You've got a strange man living downstairs, you know,' she said at last.

'What, oh yes, old Mr. O'Connor, he owns the house; he and his wife live downstairs.'

'He's Irish.'

'Yes, I know.'

'He's got a really red face; I think he drinks too much.'

'Annabel, how come you met Mr. O'Connor?'

'I tried the front door; thought it might be unlocked so I could bring my stuff in. Anyway, he threw open the door and asked what I was doing. I said, 'I'm moving in', and he said, 'well you can't, there's no vacancy; we're full up already!' Then he swore at me, in Irish, yeah, I'm pretty sure it was Irish!'

'Really, why, what did he say for goodness sake?' Perhaps she was right, and he had been at the whisky.

'I dunno, pog mo… something… I looked it up; it means 'kiss my arse! Of course, I didn't know that at the time...'

I was speechless.

'And I think he said slapper…and tart… not sure, he's got a very strong accent; and feck. Yes, I'm sure he said feck,' she paused, 'I thought you were going to tell me about your trip.'

'Oh, later, over a glass of Prosecco,' I stopped myself, 'better make that cocoa.'

The stations whizzed by and soon we were in the middle of London. I was dreading going down into the tube. If Annabel had suddenly become claustrophobic she wasn't going to be happy miles under the ground. Luckily, she seemed to have forgotten about it by the time we were going down the steep escalator, and along the windy tunnels, echoing with buskers plink- plonking away on guitars.

'Sexy hair,' shouted one as we went past, and Annabel tossed her long blond locks and smiled back at him.

'Could have meant me,' I said, and he winked at me and I winked back and threw him a quid. I was back on home ground, and it felt comfortable and familiar; the London Underground, sunny Goodge Street, Mornington Crescent, Camden Town, Kentish Town, Tufnell Park and, finally, Archway, where Dick Whittington and his cat Tiddles heard the Bow Bells urging him to return to a City that was paved with gold.

We came out of the station and turned up the hill, cutting through the newly gentrified back streets. A fairly substantial van was parked by the cemetery and two men were filling it from what looked like a pile of rubbish lying next to the road.

Annabel abandoned my suitcase and took off, looking like an ungainly giraffe in her newly acquired footwear. 'Stop...!' she screamed as she stomped along, 'It's all mine, it's my stuff!' I caught up with her; she was bent over gasping for air and trying to persuade them to unload.

'Can't do that, love; it's for charity, the bloke that lives here called, he said to come and take it.'

I looked at the van; it had Charity Donations badly painted in red letters on the side, but I had my doubts.

'Unload it, now!' I ordered, 'or I'm calling the police!'

'Load of rubbish anyway,' muttered his friend and they began throwing Annabel's worldly possessions back onto the road, 'doing you a favour taking it away, I was.'

It took ages getting her rubbish to my flat at the very top, and by the time we'd finished I was wishing we'd arrived a few minutes later when it had all gone off to its uncertain fate in the 'Charity Donations' van. Mr. O'Connor stuck his head around the door at one point to see what was occurring, but he soon popped it in again when he saw Annabel, and then it took at least three hours to unpack it all! We had to empty the box room first and I finished up with my computer and a tangle of wires heaped on the floor in the corner of my bedroom. Still, I felt calmer now that I wasn't on my own, the upheaval was worth it, and Annabel could out-scare any ghost who fancied crossing the road from Betjeman's 'Carrara-covered earth'. I couldn't wait to get those black-out blinds and then, just maybe, I could persuade myself it wasn't there at all. It was evening when we sat down in front of the television like an old married couple. I still hadn't told her about my trip and she seemed to be so caught up in some reality show that I didn't like to interrupt, and when I finally staggered off to bed she still hadn't asked me what it was I wanted to tell her.

I yawned, 'I'm going to bed, I'm completely knackered.'

'Oh, sweet dreams,' she said, 'and flying machines! See you in the morning.'

Sweet dreams! Well first thing tomorrow I'd enlighten her; I just hoped I wouldn't wake up screaming before I'd had the chance to warn her.

. I was exhausted and fell quickly into a dream; Adam was there, and Sofia, and dear old Sibella, and Louise, and Shirl, in fact it was populated by a whole host of people I hadn't even met less than a week earlier. Thankfully Caterina didn't show up, or Elisabetta, but I had a feeling they would very soon.

CHAPTER 11

We spent the weekend sorting out the flat. Annabel managed to fit all her belongings into the box room, just about, apart from the pile of sheets and some bedding from her old flat that we managed to cram into the airing cupboard at the top of the stairs. She still didn't have a proper bed, but there was a narrow camp-bed along one wall and she stuffed at least three black plastic sacks of expensive clothing underneath it. She said it was okay because it gave the bed stability and she had already ordered another proper bed on line, and it had drawers underneath!

When I got up on Monday there was a note from Annabel on the table,

'Your friend Barb called, from the agency, I've got a job to go to! Hooray!!! It's at St Yob's, haha… I mean St Job's, of course. It's GOT to be better than that putrid office and the money is FANTASTIC. See you later! Hope you had a good sleep, sans nightmares… smiley emojis… Abel xx'

Annabel, at St Job's…? They wouldn't know what hit them; no, more likely it would be the other way round; she had clearly forgotten the trauma of teaching practice; well her memory was going to be jogged very soon. Still, it was nice having the flat to myself after everything that had happened, and fine as long as it was light. I bustled about tidying up and made a few futile attempts to reconnect my computer, but the sun was out and it looked like it was going to be a warm day, well warm for November anyway.

Mr. O'Connor opened his door and popped his head out as I was clattering down the stairs in Sofia's boots. 'Mornin' Mr. O'Connor...' I called, and I raced along the grimy hallway and slammed the front door behind me before he had time to question me about the crazy person who had moved in. I crossed the road; the steep hill through the cemetery climbed almost directly in front of me, a temptingly short cut to the park en-route to Mum's, and I hovered by the gates. It didn't look too bad for a cemetery, better than the cemetery islands of Venice anyway, but it still gave me the shivers. Soon I was climbing the steep hill up to Highgate Village, and five minutes later turned right into the park where the willow trees trailed their branches over soaking grass and grey squirrels ran around my feet nibbling at acorns. I could hear the ducks quacking and splashing and squabbling in the waterweed even though they were still some distance away and when I reached the lakes, they rushed up the bank towards me begging for bread. 'Sorry ducks,' I murmured, 'no bread today because I've been away, but I'll bring some next time.' Then I walked up to the café in Lauderdale House and sat outside. I looked down at my boots, they were wet, and mud-stained, and I felt guilty because I was sure that Sofia would never have walked across a muddy park in such chic boots. Everyone else was inside the cafe staring out through steamy windows, all except for an old man in a wheelchair who was parked in the shade. I smiled at him and he raised one hand and gave a feeble wave and I noticed that he was shivering so I went over and asked if he would like to be pushed into the sun.

He nodded, 'Oh, yes, thank you, very kind of you! My daughter left me here and went to get a pot of tea; she didn't do it on purpose; it's clouded over since we arrived.' He smiled and nodded again, and he seemed to want to talk so I took a chair over and sat beside him.

'I've lived here all my life,' he said, 'up here, on the hill. My mother used to take me onto Archway Bridge when I was just a nipper; we'd look down on the whole of London from up there. She used to say, look, little Georgie, there's St Paul's Cathedral and Holloway Prison and don't they look small? Did you know you could see the Blitz from up here? Those planes came out of nowhere that night, and the bombs, well; they rained down like giant black marbles. The noise was terrifying and when they left all we could see was orange and yellow flames, leaping up, high into the sky, like the whole of London was on fire. I'll never forget it, never...' His eyes seemed to lose focus as he gazed up into the clouds that had come out of nowhere just like the planes that had bombed London all those years ago. I didn't know what to say so I patted his hand and looked around anxiously for his daughter. She came out a few moments later, a woman of about

124

sixty who was carrying a tray with cups and a teapot and a plate of toast.

'Has George been regaling you with stories of the war? Have you Dad?' she smiled at him.

'Yes, but I don't mind. Actually, I find it really interesting.'

'Not many people left to remember it now,' she said, 'and soon they'll be no one at all.'

I waved goodbye and wandered off down the bosky paths until I found a secluded bench; it occurred to me then that I had been so distracted that I'd forgotten to buy a drink; my life was becoming very strange. It seemed as if I couldn't even take a walk without the past being rammed down my throat and I wondered if one day, perhaps a hundred years from now, some descendent of George would suddenly have terrifying dreams and re-live the night of the Blitz, the dreadful noise, and the flames, and maybe he would feel compelled to walk up the long hill to Highgate and stare out at London through the iron railings of the bridge recalling the night that it was almost obliterated by Hitler's bombs, just as George had.

I was feeling thoroughly depressed when I stood up and continued on my way. Our house was just the same as it always was, but the whole street now looked more spruced up and cared for, and there was a row of trees along the pavement that weren't there, when I was 'a nipper', to quote George. Even though I'd only been away for a week I felt as if I was looking at it through new eyes. I'd sent a text to Mum so I knew she was in, but I glanced up at the open window that I climbed through if she was out when I got home from school, and I was tempted to climb in and surprise her, but I rang the bell instead.

'What have you done with your key,' she demanded when she opened the door, 'have you lost it, again?'

'Er... might have,' I mumbled.

When she'd finished telling me how 'they could be murdered in their beds' because 'anyone might find your key and just walk in', she wanted to know all about my trip to Venice.

I was tempted first of all to point out that anyone could climb through the permanently open windows and 'murder them in their beds', but I refrained and instead told her all about Sofia and Adam, and ancient Sibella and the Villa Alatri.

'I asked your Dad again, you know, about the Italian side of his family; anyway, he says he knows nothing, which doesn't surprise me. He has trouble remembering his name sometimes,' she grinned mischievously, 'he's getting on a bit y'know.' I didn't like to remind her that she was nearly as old as he was.

'Anyway, he said to ask his Auntie Flo, Grandad's sister. Apparently, she's very good on that sort of thing, she remembers all the old stories, so she would probably have some idea about why you look like this woman.'

'Sofia, her name is Sofia,' I said, 'and she's not just like me, we're almost twins; in fact, lots of people thought we were twins!'

'Yes, of course, Sofia; but it's funny how things like that happen. Flo might even have some photos hidden away somewhere, I wouldn't be at all surprised.'

I didn't mention my dreams though; or the Tarot reading, but as I was leaving a couple of hours later, she called me back.

'I meant to say, you should stay clear of these fortune tellers. Annabel told me you had your Tarot read by some gypsy, really Katherine you should have more sense, they're nothing but a load of diddycoys; they're just after your money!'

'And did she tell you that I only did it because she wouldn't, even though she won it in a competition?'

She laughed, 'No, but that sounds about right, I know what Annabel's like, she doesn't change, does she?'

Annabel was home already when I got back. She was lying flat on the carpet with a cushion over her face and for a moment I wondered if she was dead, it wouldn't surprise me the way things were going. 'Please god, don't let me have to resuscitate her!' I mumbled silently.

'Annabel, are you alright?' I cried, and I snatched the cushion off her face and threw it across the room.

'No, I'm not,' she moaned, 'I had to leave early; I couldn't stand it a moment longer… They're all bigger than me, even in my new boots…'

I gasped, 'You didn't wear those surely, not to St Yob's? What were you thinking?'

'I did, and it was a good thing, or they wouldn't have noticed I was there. But I might as well not have been there because they didn't take any notice of me, none at all.'

'I don't think you're meant to leave before the end of the day, Abel; how would they cope?'

'Oh, they didn't mind at all! The headmaster said I was wonderful, and would I go back tomorrow.'

'What did you say?'

'I didn't answer, I was already hotfooting it towards the nearest exit. I just waved and ran. Make me some tea Kate; on second thoughts, have we got any gin, or vodka?'

She was still babbling and moaning when I came back ten minutes later with two mugs of tea and some cheese sandwiches.

'So, does this mean your teaching aspirations are over,' I asked, 'and you'll go back to work in an office?'

'What…?' she sat up, 'No, no… definitely not, I couldn't bear it; perhaps I could be a gardener; or I might train as a pastry chef?'

'But you hate worms, and you don't even like cooking.'

She stood up and came to sit next to me on the sofa.

'Kate, there is something though, something someone told me in the staffroom at lunchtime, before I ran away.'

'What's up?' I asked; she looked really worried.

'I got talking to this teacher, another supply teacher like me,' she wrinkled her nose at the thought, 'he said he went to Wood Down School last week.'

'Oh, where Tom teaches, and...' I had trouble saying her name, 'and Lorna?'

'Yes, and it's really awful, Kate; I hate to be the one to break it to you.'

I stared at her stricken face, was someone ill... or... something...?

'She's pregnant; Lorna is, about five months, due early April; a girl apparently, called Genevieve. He said when he was there, they were all toasting the happy couple with champagne, in the staff room, but Lorna would only have a sip because, well you know...'

'But we only split up in October, are you telling me that he was seeing Lorna all that time?' Well maybe Tom wasn't so boring after all, he must have had hidden depths, Lorna certainly did.

I was stunned into silence but suddenly I saw the funny side. Lorna had got what she wanted so all those years of persistence had paid off. As for Tom, I just hoped he wouldn't regret it. Fair enough, he wanted to move on from me, but did he really want to find himself in a situation that he couldn't get out of? Mousy Lorna, how did

Annabel describe her? Oh yes, she had a face like a Viking, or was it a horse?'

'She's not nearly as beautiful as you, Kate,' said Annabel, as if she was reading my thoughts, 'but then you can do much, much better than Tom. I always wondered how it was you got stuck with him. She's done you a favour.'

We were both shattered after that, Annabel by her less than fulfilling return to the classroom, and me by the revelation that my boring partner had been carrying on with an adoring work colleague who had fallen out of the ugly tree and, according to Annabel, bounced off every branch on the way down, so we slumped in front of the TV again and I broke my pledge of at least a week without alcohol, and opened a bottle of Italian red.

I still hadn't told her about my dreams, and I'd meant to tell her about George, the old man in the park, but there just hadn't been time; events had conspired against me, again.

I was getting ready for bed when I got a call from Shirl who wanted to know all about the rest of my week in Venice. We talked for a long time and I told her what had happened in the Murano Glass Factory and about the little girl who wanted me to dance with her, and when I told her about the connection with the chandelier in Nonna's house she got very excited.

'You must see someone, Kate! You need to find out what this is all about. I think this is happening for a reason. We know Caterina was murdered for the necklace, what if someone is still searching for

130

it? If Sibella thinks she knows where it is her life might be in danger.'

'But Shirl,' I said, 'whoever murdered Caterina for the necklace is long dead, so who would even know about it, apart from us?'

'Hasn't it occurred to you that someone else might have some strange connection with the past, in the same way that you have?' I'm afraid for you Kate, the dreams will only increase unless you find out why, go to a hypnotherapist, someone with knowledge of past life regression, please... do it for me'

I laughed, 'If you want to hear something really amusing, how about this...' and I told her about Tom and Lorna and their baby.

She was horrified, 'You're not having a brilliant time at the moment, are you?' she said at last, and then we said goodnight and I went to bed.

Perhaps I'd tell Annabel about the dreams when we were more um... chilled. Yes, I'd tell her tomorrow.

CHAPTER 12

I was back in my room in my Venice apartment, only this time it was large and airy, and there was another window looking over the courtyard. A group of women sat gossiping and sewing in the corner and a younger woman was standing next to the marble washstand; and there was a little girl with her, she looked about eight years old. My mother, Lucia, and my sister Elisabetta, I was certain of it, and my mother was washing Elisabetta's hands and scolding her gently and she was laughing, a little giggly laugh like water in a stream. I sat down for a moment to watch her, happy little Elisabetta who always made me laugh; then I stood up and walked to the window and looked down into the courtyard. A man was there, he looked back at me and there was something about him that made me feel uneasy, something familiar, but I couldn't quite place him; he looked friendly enough, but then I remembered where I'd seen his face before and I screamed. Suddenly I was aware of people turning to stare, and my mother and my sister were running towards me as I fell to the floor. I screamed again, a scream that echoed around inside my head, reverberating and shrill, and a voice calling me by a name I didn't recognise...

'Kate, Kate, what's going on? Are you alright?'

It was Annabel.

My eyelids fluttered open, I was back in my bed in Highgate, and it had been a dream, just a dream; I was Kate, and this was where I belonged, or was it? I was beginning to wonder. Tom would say I was losing my grip on reality. Tom! Why the hell did I care what he thought...?

'It's five am,' complained Annabel, 'huh; I'll never get back to sleep now. I'll put the kettle on, get up, we'll talk. This thing with Tom must be affecting you more than you realise.'

I stumbled out of bed and waited for a moment or two trying to gather my thoughts; then I went and sat down in an armchair clutching my forehead, while Annabel muttered in my ear about it being five o'clock and why the feck was I screaming like that?

'It's a long story,' I began, 'and nothing at all to do with Tom!'

'What? You mean I've really got to sit here and listen to you rambling on for hours when I could be asleep? And I was so warm and cosy in my tiny box room.'

I glared at her, but I could tell she didn't mind really.

'It started when I had this dream that I was being strangled,' I explained, 'and it was before the Tarot reading so it wasn't anything to do with that.'

'Strangled...? You're having me on...' She whispered it close to my ear, as if she was afraid that someone or something was hiding in the darkness outside, ready to leap through the window and pounce.

So I told her, how in my dream I was being pursued by a man who wanted something from me, just as Julia had said, someone who was prepared to stab me in the back because he coveted something I owned; the beautiful necklace that Sibella poetically described as 'embellished with all the jewels of the orient'. Not stabbed though, just strangled, and I described it to Annabel, making sure to include all the gory details; his foul breath on my cheek as his fingers tightened around my throat, and how I struggled to breathe, and then my shock when I discovered that the Villa Alatri was, without doubt, the place where I had lived and died. I told her about my Mother, and my little sister Elisabetta, and Annabel had tears in her eyes when I told her how she'd begged me to dance, before I collapsed on the floor at the Murano Glass Factory.

'I don't understand any of it,' she murmured, 'why would it be happening after so many years when they're all... dead?'

'Shirl thinks it might be because someone still wants the necklace, and I think Sibella knows where it is; or perhaps she just thinks she does, but either way, it's still there somewhere and someone is determined to have it.'

'No, I still don't understand!'

'God, Annabel, what makes you think I do. I didn't even know that we had family in Italy until last week!'

'Why were you screaming in your sleep? Were you being strangled again?'

134

I struggled to remember; the dream that had seemed so real when I woke up was already beginning to fade; 'I saw the face of the murderer, I think; why would I have screamed otherwise? I remember looking out of the window and recognising him, he was in the courtyard; it was odd because it was someone I knew.'

'Well, who was it...' demanded Annabel, 'whose face did you recognise?'

I rubbed my eyes till I saw white blobs behind my eyelids, 'That's the trouble, I can't remember; no matter how hard I try I just can't remember his face! Shirl says I need past life regression; there are people that do it, hypnotists. She believes in all that stuff, you know, reincarnation. I'm more inclined towards some weird sort of inherited memory; or an earlier version of me maybe, but I suppose that would be reincarnation, wouldn't it? Oh, I don't know, I'm really confused!'

Annabel was staring at me like I'd gone completely mad.

'Lorna must seem very boring after you;' she chuckled, 'I expect Tom was always wondering what you'd do next. Still, best to look on the bright side, he's cleared off for good, and you've got Italian rellies so lots of free hols!'

It was nearly eight by the time we'd chewed it all over and then Annabel's phone rang.

'How much...?' she was saying, 'Well I might consider it if you 'up it' a bit more.'

'Don't tell me,' I said when she put the phone down; 'St Yob's want you back?'

'I'm going! They're paying me top dollar, I'll just leave early again when I've had enough, like yesterday; I can do this!'

I heard the door slam ten minutes later, I was already back in bed, it was okay when it was light, during the day; it was just the night I feared when my life turned into one of the scarier scenes from a Gothic horror movie.

She was home by lunchtime. 'It's no good,' she ranted, 'I wouldn't go back there if they paid me!'

'They do pay you,' I said, 'loads! Look, calm down and tell me what happened?'

'One of them had the audacity to ask me out!'

'You didn't have to say yes, did you? It's flattering to be asked out by a younger man.'

'He's thirteen, actually!'

'Okay, not good, you should have reported him.'

'Huh… they only did it for a laugh; they were all pointing at me. Then they started throwing chairs around the room, and when I went to get some paper from the cupboard, they…'

'Gawd, Abel, what… look, don't cry… you don't have to go back. What happened when you went in the cupboard?' I could hardly bare to ask.

'They locked me in, and I didn't get out until break time. Luckily someone wanted some pens and they found me, or I'd still be there.'

I laughed, 'Yeah, you'd be in the cupboard getting paid! It sounds perfect to me.'

'I suppose so, except I really wanted a wee, but you're right, I got paid for being locked in the cupboard. I'm not going back though; my next class was just as bad.'

I was surprised she'd stayed for the next class and I couldn't wait to find out what evil they'd perpetrated.

'They were nice enough, to start with. It was when I went for coffee; that teacher, the one I mentioned before who gave me the news about Tom and...' she paused, 'er... well, he gave me the note that some kid had pinned on my back.'

'I don't mind you mentioning Tom and... her,' I said, 'come on, what did the note say?'

'It said 'posh totty'! Well, actually it said 'POSH TOTY', in capitals, with only one T.'

I looked at her offended face for just a few seconds before bursting into giggles, I just couldn't help myself. She looked slightly more offended for a bit longer, but I could tell she was just pretending, then she joined in and we were soon both clutching our sides and laughing hysterically.

'You are a bit though,' I said when we'd managed to stop laughing, 'you know, posh totty.'

It was true, my dad always described Annabel as 'County', one of the horsey set, with all the right connections, and I knew that even without a job Annabel wouldn't starve because they had 'family money'.

She must have been reading my mind because her next words were, 'Why don't we just settle in, have a laugh and relax for a few weeks, at least until after Christmas? It's only a few weeks away. You've got your savings, and Mummy says she'll help me out, you know, pay my rent, and cover food and so on. It will give us time to think and work out what we should do next, you know, what we really want to do with our lives.'

Three days later we still hadn't decided on the direction our lives should take, but we'd had a great time mulling it over, and getting up late, and watching daytime TV till lunchtime. Jeremy Kyle was our favourite because he made us realise that nothing we could possibly do would drive us to the depths that some people seem to plumb on a daily basis. Sometimes we went out for rambles, Annabel's description not mine. They were actually more like sedate walks, in the park, or down to Parliament Hill Fields to watch the kites soaring high in the cold blue sky. I hadn't had any more of my haunting dreams and I'd come to the conclusion that living a stress-free existence was the way forward, well, until the cash ran out, that was.

Barb and the 'girls' rang every morning without fail, pleading with us to return to work and offering us huge financial incentives, but we refused to be swayed by their lamentations and in the end, we simply blocked their calls.

Annabel's bed arrived on Wednesday. Mr. O'Connor opened the door to be confronted by two enormous ape-like guys who probably worked night shifts as bouncers in some dodgy club.

'Bed for A bel Leggup,' said the larger of the two. Annabel charged down the stairs, 'That's me!' she shrieked, 'Though Leggat, actually, not um... Oh joy! My bed has arrived!'

Mr. O'Connor looked startled, he hadn't seen her since she arrived, and I think he was hoping he'd imagined it.

'I tort I seen it all,' he whimpered as they tramped through the hallway with a large box. 'Can you bring it up, please?' cried A bel Leggup brightly, 'I'll lead the way!'

I peered down over the top banister as they heaved it, puffing and grunting, while Mr. O'Connor watched from the bottom muttering something under his breath, probably some ancient Celtic curse.

'Oh, well done!' cried Annabel encouragingly, 'Jolly good, mind the wallpaper! Oh dear, never mind Mr. O'Connor, I've got some glue... Don't forget the mattress... And the chest of drawers...'

Chest of drawers...?

'No one said we had to carry this lot up all these stairs,' complained the first ape to the second, 'narra' ain't it, Pete, look lift your end a fraction, I'm catching me neck between the box and the wall every time we go rand a corner.'

At last the box, containing bed head, slats and under-bed drawers, plus a flat-pack chest of drawers and a double mattress, were spread out across the living room floor. I looked out of the window as the delivery men staggered back to their van, one was clutching his back and grimacing and the other was limping.

'I'm glad they didn't leave it on the doorstep,' I said, 'we would never have got it up here on our own.'

'Yeah, not easy,' she replied, 'still, I gave them ten quid.'

'Blimey, Annabel, you got more than that for being locked in a cupboard!'

'Oh, but that was much worse, at least they weren't abused, and we didn't pin any notes onto their clothes. Come on, got to unpack. I can't stand another night on that rickety old camp bed! Got a screw driver?'

'The door doesn't open properly,' I said, several hours later.

'Honestly Kate, it's not a problem, I can get through easily, watch me; see it's simple, I just have to turn sideways, and the bed is fabulous!'

'It takes up the whole room. You can just about open the underneath bit, and you have to climb across it to reach the chest of drawers at the other end!'

'Well, it's what it says it is, isn't it? A bedroom, and it's here now and I can't wait to try it! I could even have a visitor.'

'It would have to be a small visitor, one that could squeeze through the gap in the door.'

'I have good news,' she announced suddenly, and I cringed, 'it's okay, Kate, you don't have to worry. I have ordered blinds, I did it on line and they're fitting them on Friday! It's so exciting, don't worry, I'll pay. Aren't you glad I came?'

I had to admit, black-out blinds would be the icing on the cake; maybe then I'd be able to pretend that the cemetery wasn't there at all.

CHAPTER 13

Mum turned up the following day. It was only ten thirty, so we'd just surfaced, dragging ourselves from beds to sofa, and only stopping mid route to switch on the TV and the kettle, that we'd placed handily on the coffee table so that we could make tea without standing up.

She was horrified and ordered us to 'get showered and dressed straight away! Clear up this mess, make your beds, do the washing up… blah… blah… blah…'

I don't think anyone had ever addressed Annabel in such a way before, but it reminded me of when I was in my teens and living at home. I almost expected her to say, 'and no more pocket money until this flat has been cleaned and tidied.'

Still, we were spurred into action because it was turning into a bit of a slum, and a spot on the Jeremy Kyle show was becoming a real possibility.

She was even more horrified when she realised that she had to hold her breath and her stomach in, just to see around the door into Annabel's room and started muttering about the fire risk. Anyway, we did as she said and then presented ourselves and the flat for inspection. Mum, meanwhile, had been passing the day chatting to Mrs. O'Connor outside on the landing. She seemed to be reassuring her along the lines of 'No, there are only two girls living up here, the lad has left now, they're very respectable, no, definitely no parties, absolutely no drink, or drugs.'

We were ear-wigging at the kitchen door. 'Respectable, 'of course I'm respectable,' gasped Annabel, 'I come from one of the oldest families in the country!'

Right, yeah, and we all know what they were like!

Still, when she came back in we were done and dusted and raring to go because she'd promised us a pub lunch.

'Mrs. O'Connor thought you and Tom were married so she's very suspicious of Ms. Leggup.'

'It's Leggat, if you don't mind,' yelled Annabel indignantly, 'not difficult at all so why does everyone have such a problem with it?'

'I know that,' said Mum, 'but you've got a letter here and it quite clearly says Leggup.' I could see that she thought it was really funny. Annabel didn't though, 'Bloody cheek!' she exclaimed, 'it's that wretched agency; they're taking the piss because I wouldn't work for them anymore.'

'Language,' muttered Mum and she winked at me.

Annabel scowled as she ripped it open, then she grinned at us, 'Oh look, it's a pay slip; goody! Come on, lunch is on me!'

We were just leaving when I got a text from Adam.

'Hi Kate, hope you're feeling better. We met up with Sofia the other day and she wants us to come back here

for Christmas! I get home on Saturday so I'm around Sunday. Let me know if you're free. Love, Adam xx

'Why are you smiling like that?' asked Annabel, 'Who is that text from? Oh, its Adam isn't it; that guy you met in Venice? Hee hee... I hope he's respectable, especially if he's coming round here!'

I sent a quick reply,

'Great to hear from you, Adam! Call me on Sunday morning and we'll get together. Love, Kate xx

'We'll head up to the village,' said Mum, 'one of my favourite pubs. I hope they're still doing food, of course we can always have a bar snack if they've stopped.'

Luckily, they were still serving when we got there, and it was good to sit down after our route march up the hill. Mum had been training for some charity walk she was doing in the spring, so it was hard to keep up with her once she got going.

She stared out at the bird splattered wooden tables in the square. It was one of those November days when the air felt damp, and your hair looks flat and lifeless and flops over your face no matter what you do with it; and it had started to drizzle. We'd come into the warm; no one was outside, apart from a couple of teenage girls smoking furtively out of sight of their families who had taken up a whole table in the corner of the pub

'I used to come up here when I was very young; just like those girls,' said Mum wistfully. 'One day I sat opposite this gorgeous young man. I'm sure it was Donovan, must have been the late sixties, He had big soulful eyes, and long eyelashes and black curly hair. I wish I'd asked him, I've always wondered if it was him.'

'Who the hell is Donovan?' mouthed Annabel from behind her hand, but Mum droned on, 'Oh, yes, they had lots of well-known people performing up at the Gatehouse. Paul Simon came once, and I really wanted to go but none of my friends were interested.'

'What, the Paul Simon,' I gasped, 'he of Simon and Garfunkel?'

'Probably, maybe he wasn't as famous then, hadn't met Garfunkel, or something. Who knows, it was a lifetime ago!'

A lifetime ago, I found the words disturbing, was a lifetime ago so short a time?

'Yes, I'll have a shandy, please,' said Mum to Annabel who was anxious to get to the bar, 'and a cheddar ploughmans, I think. What about you Katherine?'

'Hello, anybody there? What do you want, Kate?' I shook myself and looked up at Annabel. She was combing her hair extensions with her fingers and it looked like a couple had already fallen out. 'Same for me; thanks,' I muttered.

'You can't still be tired, Kate,' said Mum disapprovingly, 'you didn't get up till nearly midday.'

The truth was I didn't feel entirely there; it sounds ridiculous I know, but even so. It was as if some other life was intruding on mine making me... despondent, yes that was it, not exactly depressed, just... despondent, as if something dark was lurking just behind my normally cheerful persona.

'Is Adam coming round soon?' asked Annabel when she came back from the bar, 'I can't wait to meet him! Is he good looking? He's sure to be more attractive than 'you know who', I always thought he was a bit pale and lethargic.'

I could tell Mum didn't agree just by her expression. 'He was a very reliable type,' she said, 'and you can't say fairer than that. You always knew where you were with Tom.'

'Ha...! Really..?' I felt suddenly angry about everything, Tom, Lorna, the forthcoming 'happy event', and all the weirdness that had overtaken me and made my life so strange. 'Actually, Mum,' I ranted, 'He got that... cow... up the duff while he was still going out with me! So... stuff that in your pipe and smoke it!'

Several people turned around to stare and the young barman smirked. Mum looked dumbfounded, 'Are you sure about that, Katherine? It doesn't sound at all like Tom to me.' She looked around at the staring faces, obviously worried that I was making a 'poppy show' of myself.

'Yeah, she's sure, definitely, and he was a rat, a slimy little toad,' added Annabel.

Yep, he was! A toad-rat, or a rat-toad, probably both; I pictured a toad with Tom's face and a long ratty tail and it made me laugh.

'She's hysterical, someone slap her!' cried Mum.

'No, I'm not, Mum,' I murmured quietly, 'just stop going on about Tom as if he's some kind of paragon of virtue when really he's an absolute bastard!'

'Really, Kate, there's no need for that, and keep your voice down, you're drawing attention to yourself!'

I shut up after that, but it did put a damper on our outing. Annabel tried to jolly us along with her constant rabbit about nothing in particular and it seemed to work in the end.

'Look over there, Kate;' she said just as we were leaving, 'see that poster? We should check it out, it looks interesting.'

Mum laughed, 'It's psychedelic, all those pinks and yellows. Reminds me of one of those old posters for 'Hair', and the record sleeve; I never saw it though, I was too young, unfortunately.'

Well, she was right there, it was psychedelic, and at the bottom in big letters it said, *'PAST LIFE REGRESSION THERAPY'* and Annabel was taking a photo of it on her phone.

'Oh, I don't like the sound of that,' said Mum, 'no, not at all!'

She turned left into the park towards home and we waved until she was out of sight.

'You were a bit hard on her,' said Annabel, 'after all, she didn't know about Lorna, and the baby.'

She glanced at me quickly wondering if she'd said too much, 'Don't worry, I'm fine now,' I replied, 'I just needed to get it off my chest. Right, now what was that poster all about?'

'Randolphus Lebedev Popov, um… slightly pretentious, isn't it?' I remarked when Annabel showed me the photo of the poster on her phone.

'Foreign,' she said, 'I think, I'll check him out on line.'

I read on, 'Do you suffer with unexplained fears and phobias? Have you considered that your irrational fears may be founded in something that happened to you in a previous existence?'

Unexplained fears and phobias…? Well, not exactly, in fact, until quite recently I'd considered myself well balanced and no-nonsense, and there was no mention of weird dreams, or doppelgangers, but maybe he didn't include those.

'You have to do it,' said Annabel, 'you have no choice and this Popov person sounds like he might have the answers you've been looking for. It wouldn't hurt, and at least you'd be doing something!'

I couldn't believe what I was hearing, 'Oh, and what makes you so sure it won't hurt, what if it sends me completely doolally,'

'You are already, admit it, doolally and absolutely bonkers. It could only improve things! Ring him now!'

He answered the phone after two rings, 'Randolphus Lebedev Popov, how can I be of assistance?' He had a strong accent, Russian, I think.

'He's there,' I whispered, 'what shall I say?'

'You want an appointment! Kate, for goodness sake; why else would you be calling him? Just get on with it!'

'I have ze feeling that you have some issues,' came a voice from the ether, 'and maybe I can help you? My vates are very reasonable. Is it about past-life regression, my dear? I sense a certain vibration in your voice.'

He reminded me of Julia and her Tarot cards, but I wasn't sure why, all a bit alternative I suppose, and equally scary.

Annabel nudged me in the ribs, 'just get on with it!' she hissed.

'Yes, yes…' I stammered, 'maybe you can help me. When would you be free to see me?'

'Any time today, or tomorrow, I've had a couple of last-minute cancellations,' said Randolphus, 'I like to keep my veekends free for yoga and meditation.'

I turned to Annabel, 'he says today, or tomorrow. No way can I do today; I'll have to prepare myself. And tomorrow the blinds man is coming…'

Annabel grabbed the phone out of my hand, 'She can come tomorrow afternoon. Yep, definitely, her name is Katherine Elliot, yes, three pm, see you then.'

She pressed the red button on my phone before I had the chance to argue. 'He's says he 'vill be happy to see you, and please do not drink any of ze alcohol'. Well, I think that's what he said, he's not wery easy to understand.'

CHAPTER 14

Friday morning, I woke up to the sound of loud banging and Annabel screaming, 'Coming…!' at the top of her voice, which had me wondering for a bit in my somnambulant state, but then the doorbell started ringing as if someone very impatient was leaning on the bell. 'I said I'm coming,' shrieked Annabel again and I heard her thundering down the stairs.

I jumped out of bed and ran to the window; a van was parked in the road and a man was standing by the gate looking up at me. I saw him smile as Annabel opened the door and then ran out to hold the gate open so that he could get through with his um… large parcel. I jumped out of bed and made a rush for the bathroom before they got to the top, up four flights of stairs to be precise, so I had time to grab my makeup and clothes, and a fresh pair of knickers, and still get there first and be able to emerge looking totally respectable in no time at all; unlike Annabel who appeared to be attired in a frilly nightie, her blonde hair extensions swinging seductively in the breeze. I was surprised that Mr O'Connor wasn't out there as well muttering his usual curses in Gaelic! What was it he said to Annabel? 'Pog ma… something'? Not pleasant, not pleasant at all! I expected to see him pursuing them up the stairs.

I listened as she issued instructions.

'There are three front windows,' I heard her say, 'we're trying to block out the view over the cemetery.'

'I don't blame y' for that,' he replied, 'awful, can't see why anyone would want to look out over that! Cor... creepy innit, all those dead people.'

'Absolutely, Mr. er...?'

'You can call me Merv, luv... hehehe heh...'

I waltzed out of the bathroom to rescue her even though I still hadn't done my makeup.

She beamed at me, 'Merv is just fitting the blinds; can he start with your room?'

Merv collected up his belongings and trotted obediently into my room eyeing us up and down as he went. I could almost hear him salivating.

'Where did you find him?' I asked her, 'He's possibly even creepier than the cemetery.'

'I told you! On-line of course, but he's got wonderful blinds, and he's really cheap!'

'And where are the O'Connors?'

'They went; I saw them leave about an hour ago with a couple of suitcases; they got in a taxi, probably off to see the family in Dublin.'

'How do you know they've got family in Dublin?'

'Mrs. O'Connor told me, the day I moved in.'

I had to hand it to her; Annabel was great at finding out things, taking people into her confidence and inveigling all their little secrets. I didn't even know she'd spoken to Mrs. O'Connor. Anyway, I was glad they'd gone because we hadn't warned them that we were having blinds put up and they might have objected to screw holes in the woodwork.

'There y'go... Great, aren't they?' announced Merv, 'they look white but y'can't see through them at all; modern technology, clever innit?' He turned to Annabel and winked suggestively, 'Took y' curtains down luv, they need binning. You going t' see me out then?'

I went for a lie down. It was quite true, with the new blinds I could almost forget the cemetery was there, watchful and... expectant. I shivered. Annabel opened the door and came in and sat on the bed, she sighed dreamily, 'He was nice, quite dishy actually.'

'He was at least fifty,' I said, 'and he was wearing a wedding ring. Why didn't you wake me up earlier?'

'You were sleeping, like a log; I didn't want to disturb you. You're seeing Randi whatsit this afternoon and...'

'Oops... I forgot all about that! I don't think I should go. I've only had one weird dream since I got back.' I stood up, 'I'm going to cancel it, now.'

'Oh no you're not,' she blocked the doorway and held her arms out, so I couldn't get by, 'it's not that simple, Kate! What about Venice, and Sofia, and the necklace, those dreams were only a message, just a small part of it. You've got to sort this out, once and for all! It won't go away!'

We left at half past two and walked down to where Mr. Randolphus Lebedev Popov, now rather dubiously re-christened Randi by Annabel, had his 'healing rooms', which was how he described his premises on the poster. We'd checked his credentials on-line the previous evening and all the 'posted comments' professed him to be a 'wonderful human being', and 'fully understanding of the problems we all face due to past life traumas' etc. etc. Most of his clients seemed to think they'd been Joan of Arc, or a servant in some royal court or another; I couldn't find any peasants, or foot soldiers, or housewives.

It was about a mile away and turned out to be a first floor flat over a barber's shop, and there was a sign that said 'healing rooms' and an arrow directing us up a dingy passageway to an even dingier doorway covered in graffiti.

'Don't do it...' hissed Annabel.

I sighed, 'But I'm here now, it might be alright inside. Do you want to go? I can do this on my own.'

'Are you joking? I'm not letting you go in there by yourself; you might never come out again! What if he's a pervert, a weirdo?'

I pushed the door, it opened straight away, and I must admit my voice was shaking when I said, 'Come on then, Abel, I'd rather you came with me, just in case...'

'Ah, Miss Elliot, velcome to my home and healing rooms.'

I looked up; a tall man, with wild red hair, was standing at the top of the stairs. I'm not sure why, but I'd expected him to be old and grey, a bit like Einstein, or Freud, and just for a moment I wondered if I should make Annabel do it instead of me, in the same way that she had made me take her place for the Tarot reading. I looked at her expectantly.

'Don't even think about it!' she said quickly, which I thought was a bit unreasonable given the circumstances.

Randi's 'healing rooms' looked like some sort of hippy paradise. Wind chimes hung from the ceiling and garlands of paper flowers and fairy lights edged the windows and overflowed onto a potted plant, like some giant mutant Christmas tree.

He gazed down at me from a great height, I reckoned he was in his forties or maybe more, perhaps his red hair was dyed, and he was sixty? Either way I was beginning to wish I hadn't agreed to come.

'Your friend can vait here, vould you like to follow me? May I call you Katherine?'

I could see 'my friend' making faces behind his back as he led me into a smaller room. She seemed to be indicating that we should scarper... at full speed... without a backward glance, but I knew it was too late for that.

'Would it be alright if she comes in with me to vatch, er... watch?' I asked.

'No, no, Katherine, ve can't have ze distractions, no distractions at all. She must vait here, read ze magazines.'

The room was a stark white and unadorned, in fact it was hard to imagine a greater contrast to the

155

first, and it was devoid òf furniture apart from two large leather armchairs. A small side table sat next to one of them and on the top was a notepad and a pen, evidently the tools of his trade, so no overheads and it suddenly occurred to me that I hadn't asked how much I was paying for this fiasco.

'Please sit, Katherine. Do not vorry; it is not painful, usually.'

What did he mean, 'usually'? I sat and he settled down opposite to me, our knees and noses were nearly touching.

'Zere is no need for pendulums or metronomes' he said quietly, 'just look into my eyes, Katherine, into my eyes, vat do you see there? I'm going to take you back, back, many years, before you arrived in your present existence, you are travelling back in time, many, many years…'

His eyes were startling; grey flecked with green and amber, and I gazed into them, deeper and deeper until the room no longer existed and there was nothing but pale light and then, very slowly, a different room emerged, gradually shaping itself into a solid form, and I saw a marble washstand and a small child with long black hair, and she was dancing and begging me to join her. Then I was in an alleyway and the moon was only visible in the thin strip of sky because the alley had widened. I ran towards a large villa with stone steps leading up to a gated courtyard, and I somehow knew it was the Villa Alatri. Frantic voices sounded all around me, and I heard a shrill scream that reverberated, on and on, inside my head, till I could bear it no longer; and after that... nothing, nothing at all. My eyelids snapped open; Randolphus Lebedev Popov was on the far side of the room, his back pressed flat against the wall reminiscent of a pinned butterfly, or a moth; yes, Popov was definitely a moth. He had terror in his eyes. Annabel was standing in the doorway and I presume she'd just arrived because her look was one of total confusion rather than fear.

'Very interesting, very interesting indeed,' mumbled Randi when he finally found his tongue, they stood in complete silence and stared at me for what seemed like an age. 'What did I say,' I demanded, 'tell me, please; what did I say? I need to know!'

'You were talking...' said Annabel at last, 'loads, I could hear you in there, 'you were yelling about the opera over and over, you were really excited about it, wasn't she Randi?'

He gazed at her for a few long moments and then at me, as if he was wondering how he could escape; or maybe he'd just never been called Randi before.

'Miss Elliot,' he murmured, 'I have never seen such proof of a previous existence in my forty years of psychiatry and past life regression therapy!'

'Psychiatry,' mouthed Annabel.

'Forty years,' I mouthed back. Well that was one question answered, he did dye his hair, though, of course, he could have been a child

157

genius psychiatrist at six; it seemed unlikely though.

'Did you know you can speak fluent Italian?' he asked me, 'I am fluent in Russian, and ze Baltic languages, but my knowledge of Italian is sketchy, and you had a very strong regional accent. I managed to record a little of it and I vonder if perhaps I might use it at a forthcoming conference on ze migration of souls. There vill be many experts in residence, perhaps they could throw some light on ze content. I don't know how to advise you for the moment. I hope you aren't in danger, ze other personality is a very vibrant presence and, I don't vant to vorry you, but zere is a remote chance that you and she are becoming one and ze same person. There's no charge, I can use our therapy session for one of my more er… interesting case studies; if you feel ze need please come back and see me again.'

'He's hoping you never darken his threshold again,' declared Annabel when we were back in the street, 'he's frightened half to death of you. And how come you've never mentioned to me that you're a fan of opera; and why were you speaking Italian?'

'I don't speak Italian,' I said, 'I can just about order a cappuccino for goodness sake, you know that. And I've never been to an opera in my life!'

'Oh, you should go, they're very romantic, especially the Italian ones like Boheme, all death and attics, and weeping, you'd love it!'

'Thanks, Abel, they sound like just what I need at the moment, and I'm not entirely ignorant, I do recognise the odd aria.'

We trekked back up the hill to Highgate, the street lights had started to come on and someone must have decided to stage a late firework display because rockets kept zooming overhead sending stars shooting into the heavens and down over north London. There would be empty cardboard tubes all over the street come the morning.

'It's what Julia said,' I murmured, 'she used the very same words, 'I don't want to worry you'.'

She giggled, 'Don't you mean, 'I don't vant to vorry you,'?'

'Ha... all very well for you to laugh!'

'Yes, well the gypsy warned you,' chortled Annabel.

We walked on in silence for a while then she said, 'I'm starving; what's for dinner?'

'I've got a shepherd's pie in the freezer, we can have that.'

'Did he mind?'

'Did who mind?' I asked.

'The shepherd, of course, did he mind?'

'No, he didn't mind, not at all!'

I should have been worried, but quite honestly, I wasn't, I felt calm, or maybe just resigned. I was certain that Caterina wasn't some kind of malevolent spirit; and, even though her death had been violent and premature, I was sure that she was kind and light hearted when she was alive. I was certain now that she was trying to tell me something of importance, and I wondered if it was to do with the jewelled necklace that Sibella had described. There had to be a reason for everything that had happened; the dreams that had somehow led me to Venice and the bizarre predictions of the Tarot reader; and, most of all, my strange connection to Sofia. But why was it happening to me and not her? After all, she still lived in the Villa Alatri, and she'd known Sibella all her life; could it be that the answer lay here in England? I knew that I was an essential part of an intricate puzzle and once all the pieces were assembled then perhaps the mystery of Caterina's murder would be solved but why was it so important after so many years had passed?

I dozed in front of the TV long after Annabel had gone off to her little box room, but eventually I staggered from sofa to bedroom and collapsed exhausted on my bed. It was as if I was afraid that the present might disappear completely if I didn't hold on to it and I could sink deeper into the past, perhaps never to return. I woke early feeling washed out, and when I looked in the mirror a ghostly white face stared back at me, it was mine, hollow cheeked with black circles under my eyes; like a nineteenth century poet in the last stages of tuberculosis.

'Oo… you look awful,' cried Annabel when she saw me, 'and Adam is coming tomorrow so you'd better perk up!'

Perk up? I went back to bed and slept soundly for four hours. She brought me a cup of tea around midday and suggested we headed to the nearest alternative health emporium, Sierra Madre Holy Organic, which always sounded to me more like an upmarket Spanish restaurant. I agreed, I was ready and willing to try anything!

SIM HO, as it was known to its avid fans, was less like a shop and more like a small market place; I presume that was why it was called an emporium. I could smell weed the minute a skinny, bearded guy opened the door, it kind of drifted out into the street with him. Inside, a girl with dreadlocks sat in a corner displaying a sign that advertised 'henna tattoos and braiding', and there was a stall devoted to all things 'nut and gluten free', and another selling hookah pipes; anyway, you get the picture? I headed straight for essential oils at Annabel's insistence because she said they'd be sure to have something to help me sleep. We emerged onto the street soon after feeling slightly high and giggling for no reason in particular. Everything seemed more vibrant, oppressively so, as if I was about to get a migraine, and I was clutching three tiny bottles each containing the essential oils of rose, and orange, and, wait for it, patchouli. The rose oil was horribly expensive because it came from Marrakesh and was difficult to extract, requiring literally thousands of fresh petals; which meant I was responsible for the demise of countless roses! Whether that was true or not, I was assured that a combination of the three would resolve all my problems.

It wasn't until we were halfway home that I realised the significance of the oils I had chosen, rose, and patchouli, and orange; still, it worked like a charm and I went to sleep that night enveloped in exotic fragrances that soothed and calmed my troubled spirit.

CHAPTER 15

Adam didn't ring till gone eleven. He was tired after the journey back from Venice; there had been a flight delay which meant they arrived late in the evening. Louise had already left for Wiltshire because she had work first thing on Monday morning.

'I'll come and find you early afternoon,' he said, 'I've got to unpack and shove some things in the washing machine.'

I couldn't wait for him to arrive, and Annabel was desperate to ask him all about Gio and whether he would be coming any time soon. I was feeling quite shy; after all, this was someone I'd only known very briefly, and actually met up with just three times. The blinds had been down ever since Merv fitted them, but we opened one in the lounge so that we could watch for him coming down the road.

'There he is!' I yelled at last.

'About time too,' moaned Annabel, 'Oo… he's very good looking, sort of angular; lovely cheekbones, and nice hair.' Then we raced each other down the stairs to open the door and stood gasping in the hallway while we waited for him to ring the bell.

'Kate, great to see you,' he said as we flung the door open, and he gave me a squeeze. Annabel stared up at him with fawning eyes, 'Hi Adam,' she murmured, 'I've heard so much about you!'

I felt happy just seeing him there, 'Hi Adam, it's great to see you too. This is my friend Annabel.'

'Oh, the one Gio keeps going on about. I'm pleased to meet you, Annabel.'

'Likewise...!' She grinned at me and gave him a little curtsey.

We clomped noisily back up the stairs. It was lucky the O'Connors were away as this was our second male visitor after Merv; and the fourth if you counted the bed men.

'You're certainly tucked away up here!' exclaimed Adam when he saw our tiny flat and Annabel had demonstrated how she could only just open her bedroom door, 'but that it was enough if you really wanted to get in there.'

'Not sure about your cemetery view though, it's a bit grim, especially at this time of the year, good thing you've got those blinds!'

'Oh, they were my idea,' she said, 'we only got them the other day; Merv fitted them!'

Adam and I exchanged glances, he looked amused.

'We went around to visit Sofia and she says she wants you to go back for Christmas, and she's invited me; and Louise as well; apparently Antonio's a bit obsessed with Lou!'

'And me, I want to come too; I can't wait to meet Gio! And Antonio, of course,' cried Annabel, and she gave us a quick burst of 'Oh, oh, Antonio, and his ice cream cart', and only stopped when I told her that it probably wasn't politically correct because the days when Italians pushed ice-cream

164

carts around London was long gone. I was starting to wonder if she'd been possessed by the ghost of some long-dead, music-hall artiste. After all, if it could happen to me...

'I'll open some Prosecco,' she said 'does anyone fancy pizza? We can order and get it delivered?'

I'm not sure how it happened, but soon we were telling Adam about my 'therapy session' with Randolphus Lebedev Popov.

'What an extraordinary name,' said Adam, 'Russian, I presume. It's an intriguing story, are you telling me that you felt you already knew the Villa Alatri? And possibly a past life that ended with someone strangling you? I don't understand any of it; all seems a bit far-fetched to me.'

I didn't know what to say, it seemed more insane every time I repeated it.

'I know, I don't either,' I murmured, 'but there must be a reason and I suppose I'll find out soon.'

'She thinks it's something to do with the necklace, and Sibella,' added Annabel. 'Kate, tell him about all the delicious smells, you know, the roses and oranges, and the mysterious room with the little girl, and don't forget the bit with the chandelier, on Murano, wasn't it? Oh, the pizza's here, I'll go down.'

Adam and I looked at each other in silence. He probably wondered what he'd got himself into.

'Was that why you fainted in the glass factory?' he asked me when I'd finished. He poured the remaining Prosecco into our glasses while Annabel got the plates and another bottle out of the cupboard.

'Red, this time,' she said, 'you have to have red with pizza.'

By the time Adam left he was well and truly clued up. He knew all about Tom, and Lorna and the baby, and my Tarot reading that should really have been Annabel's, and my day out with Shirl; every detail washed down with ample servings of pepperoni pizza and lashings of Italian red; and embellished by Annabel, as if any embellishment were needed.

Luckily, he only lived a mile or two down the road so he decided to walk to clear his head instead of catching a bus. He promised to be in touch and I hoped he would, even though my revelations were enough to put anyone off. I was wondering how I could spend Christmas in Venice with a clear conscience, wouldn't Mum and Dad be really disappointed? Perhaps Greg and Mary would be there, that might let me off the hook, though somehow, I doubted it.

I wandered over to see Mum a few days later. Annabel was meeting her mother in the West End; for lunch she said, but I suspected she was really on the same mission as me, to find out if we could both clear off and spend Christmas at the mysterious Villa Alatri with clear consciences. She said she couldn't wait to see it for herself, but I think she was probably equally keen to get to know Gio.

The weather was freezing. A biting wind swept across the park lifting the last of the leaves and blowing them into dusty piles, and everything looked dead, apart from a few evergreen trees and some holly with bright red berries. I didn't stop at the café this time; it was sure to be closed anyway with so few people about. Mum's kitchen was warm and inviting and, as usual, the central heating was set higher than was absolutely necessary, and she had the oven on as well. It was easy to forget the arctic conditions outside; inside it was more like the Costa Brava.

I sat in a large comfy armchair that had stood in the corner for as long as I could remember, while she ladled homemade veggie soup into bowls.

'I'm just wondering what's happening over Christmas, is Greg going to be here?' I asked tentatively.

'Yes, of course, and Mary; they went to her family last year so it's our turn. And, you'll never guess, old Auntie Flo is coming too, along with her new boyfriend.'

Whoa, I couldn't believe it! What happened? Flo was so shy about it when I saw her, and 'new boyfriend'! Like she'd had hundreds, but perhaps she had!

'What, Jim...?' I gasped, 'The house will be bursting at the seams! Where will you put them all?'

'Actually, Katherine, I wondered if Greg and Mary could stay with you, it's only down the road. I know you've got Annabel there, but if she's going

167

to her parents, well, you could have the box room and Greg and Mary could have your bed. I don't want Flo to be embarrassed and I think she might be with Greg here; you know she and Jim aren't married.'

She had it all worked out!

'Well if all goes to plan, my place could be empty,' I said.

She looked at me with a puzzled expression. 'Are you moving? I thought you were happy there now you're not on your own, and with those new blinds up it must be really cosy; and you can't even see the cemetery anymore.'

'No, of course I'm not moving; it's just, would you miss me if I went away at Christmas? Only I've got the chance to spend Christmas in Venice, and Annabel is coming too if she doesn't have to go home. Greg and Mary could have the flat while we're away.'

'Well, of course we'll miss you, Kate! Wouldn't you rather stay here with us; you haven't seen your brother for a while.'

'I'll go and see them when the weather improves; it's horrible up north at the moment, even colder than here,' it made me shiver just thinking about it, 'and I saw Flo just a few weeks back, though I'd like to see her again, and Jim. You'll like him, he's nice.'

She smiled, 'Of course you must go to Venice; it will be beautiful. I expect they have all sorts going on for the tourists, it will be busy, mind.'

I hugged her, 'That's brilliant, Mum... thank you! I'm not sure of the details yet, I'll have to speak to Adam.'

'Oh, I see, Adam is it?'

'We're friends, that's all, he's very nice but I've no intention of getting involved with anyone, not at the moment, I've had quite enough of that!' I laughed, 'I'm going to play the field, and don't look at me like that.'

'Well, not for too long, I hope. Your biological clock is ticking!'

Dad came in just after we'd eaten and said he would walk back with me as far as the park.

'She's going to Venice for Christmas, with Adam,' said Mum as we were leaving, and I saw her catch his eye and they exchanged worried glances.

'Do you mind if I'm not here for Christmas?' I asked him when we were walking up the hill. He laughed, 'You were only there a week or so back weren't you? Mum reckons you're keen just because this Adam is going too. That's not why you're going, is it?'

'No, of course not; you know me better than that, Dad. I just really like Venice, and Annabel is coming as well. We thought it would be a laugh, you know, something different, otherwise it's always the same old thing; not that I don't enjoy that too,' I added, in case he got offended.

'Mum is just a bit worried because of all this carry-on with Tom. He was around for quite a long while and we thought you might end up getting married,' he grinned at me, 'eventually.'

'She doesn't have to worry; I've got used to it and I'm much happier without him around, especially now Annabel has moved in, it was a bit creepy before.'

I wondered then how he would react if I told him about my strange dreams, but I decided not to risk it; if he told Mum she'd only worry more. 'Can you speak Italian?' I asked instead.

'Italian...?' he looked at me with a concerned frown on his face, 'No, of course I don't speak Italian; don't you think you'd know if I did? Why are you asking?'

'It's... just that I seem to have a natural affinity for the language, and Mum said we had family over there.'

'Family over there? Cor, that was donkey's years ago. I only found out myself because old Auntie Flo started delving into the family history. I never met any of them, and certainly no one who spoke Italian, or had any connection with any of that lot. We're all a mixture, Kate; Flo has found all kinds of 'so called' relatives all over the world. We've probably got some distant cousin in Timbuktu as well, for all I know.'

'So, has Flo made a family tree?' I asked.

'Yeah, it took her ages; she's been visiting graveyards and old churches for years. Mind you, she's always been morbid; Mum says that's where you get it from. She's even sent off for some DNA testing kit. Risky, I'd say; you just never know what you're going to find out, could be something nasty.'

I took a deep breath, 'Um... actually Dad, the reason I'm interested is because I found someone who's related to us, in Venice, and we're going back to stay with her.'

We'd almost reached the park gates, but it was obvious I'd left too many questions hanging in the air. I could almost see them popping out of the top of his balding head in the shape of brightly coloured question marks. 'Pub...?' he said, 'Good idea!' I replied, and we crossed back over the road and found a quiet corner in the Queen's Head, him with a pint of best, and me sipping a large gin and tonic.

'Right,' he said, 'start from the beginning; what's this all about, Kate?'

I sat quietly for a moment or two, trying to decide how much I could tell him without him reporting back to Mum that I was, in his words, 'a sandwich short of a picnic'.

'I suppose you could say I feel an affinity with Italy, and, like I said, with the language; and with Venice in particular...' then I stopped because he was looking at me with such a curious expression and I wasn't sure what to say next.

'Go on... don't stop there,' he said at last.

'The thing is...' I hesitated, 'the thing is, this person who is related to me, well, she looks exactly like me; and she told me that some of her family moved to England, though that was probably more than a hundred years ago.'

171

He stared at me disbelievingly, 'Is that what this is about, Kate, someone who looks like you? Total strangers look like each other sometimes, probably more often than we realise. Are you sure you're not getting carried away with all of this? The mind can play funny tricks you know; sometimes it fills in the gaps, especially if we're looking for something. Maybe you should move, come back home for a while, we've been thinking of getting a dog, you always wanted one.'

I smiled, I'd always wanted a dog, but it was a bit late now, I was old enough to get my own dog. Still, it would be company for Mum; maybe Sibella could get a dog and then, perhaps, she wouldn't feel quite so depressed by all those empty chairs around her huge table.

'No, really, Dad, I'm fine. I won't see Flo over Christmas, but can you tell her that I'm very interested in her research. And, I know you don't believe me, but I'm absolutely certain that Sofia and I are related. Great about the dog though, I think it's a brilliant idea, we could take it on long walks.'

We finished our drinks and said goodbye and I ran into the park, feeling light-hearted and slightly giddy because of the gin. Hooray, I was off to Venice, with my new friend Adam. He'd make sure I got on the right plane! I skipped along the path, and down the road, no longer noticing the bitter chill of the wind and the gathering dusk, and giving an invisible finger to my biological clock, and the treacherous Lorna!

Annabel was back before me and she had a big grin on her face. 'They're all off to Cornwall to stay with friends, so I'm off the hook; I'm free to go to Venice, assuming that you are; though I'd say by your happy demeanor that you are!'

Happy demeanor...? Well, I guess she was right; my demeanor was happy!

CHAPTER 16

Shirl sent me a text the following day,

'Hi Kate, are you about on Friday? I'm coming down to see some friends so thought I might call in for a goss and catch-up; that's if you're free? Luv, Shirl xx'

I sent a text back straight away,

'Fantastic Shirl - I can't wait to see you! We're heading back to Venice for Christmas, will tell all when you get here! Xx'

'We... who's we?'

'Haha... tell you on Friday, I'll meet you at the station. Text me when you're a couple of stops away.'

'Oh, very mysterious... Right, well I suppose I'll have to wait then. Ta... ra... xx'

Annabel was asleep when I went to meet Shirl. She was recovering from the night before when she'd got in after midnight, and I was just about to nod off when the front door slammed and she clumped up the stairs in her horrible retro platform boots, and burst into my bedroom.

'Sorry, meant to phone, hope you weren't worried...' she rattled on before I had the chance to reply, '...only I was having such an amazing time with Joe, he's the guy I met at the library when I was doing my Tarot research?'

'Tell me in the morning Abel,' I moaned, 'I'm really tired.'

'Oh, yes, 'pologies, didn't mean to disturb you,' she backed out of the door and a few moments later I heard water running in the bathroom, then her door banged shut and the house was silent again.

Shirl seemed frazzled when she stepped off the escalator. She was wearing a grey padded coat over her ample figure that made her look a bit like a beached whale, and the wind in the tunnels had lifted her frizzy perm so that it stood up on the top of her head like some sort of Mohican. And, worst of all, her lippie had come off.

'Kate...!' she shrieked as soon as she saw me and she rushed over to press me to her padded bosom. 'Oh, I must look terrible, 'ere hold this,' she handed me her purse while she fished around in her handbag for a hand mirror and a bright pink lipstick, 'had to catch the train before six to get here and it's been all go ever since. Hang on a mo, I can't go anywhere without my lippie!' She applied a thick layer of orchid pink, and then took out a lip pencil and drew a cupid's bow that went slightly over the edges all the way round; then she smacked her lips together and grinned a vibrant grin and I noticed that some of the orchid pink had come off on her front teeth. 'Here, have you still got that ring tone I put on your phone when you were in the lav? You know, 'Singing in the Rain'?'

'Of course...!' I switched it on and we did a little dance in the tube station which caused quite a stir. I think some people thought we were part of a flash mob and they were waiting for the rest of us to appear.

'Is it far?' she asked me as we left the station, 'only I need to spend a penny, and I'd sell my body for a cuppa!'

'About ten minutes, but five if we hurry!'

'Right, I think I can hold on for about five minutes and you can tell me about Venice while we're walking; just don't mention any canals, or lagoons, or anything involving water! Coo, shame it's not the Sahara!'

'You are so lucky...' she said when I told her about Adam and how Sofia had invited us both back for Christmas, '...and this Adam, what's he like, is he sexy?'

I laughed, 'Sexy...? He's a friend, that's all! And I thought you told me you'd be happy never to go back to Venice.'

'Well, I can change my mind, can't I?' She put her arm through mine and we picked up pace. 'Wow...!' she cried when she saw the cemetery stretching away into the distance on the other side of the road, 'I'm not surprised you're having weird dreams. That's enough to give anyone the heeby-jeebies!'

I unlocked the door and let us in; there was still no sign of the O'Connors, I'd have to ask Annabel if they'd gone away for Christmas, she'd be sure to know.

Shirl dashed off to the loo then sat down on the sofa sighing with relief and took off her boots to rub her feet.

'Mmm... I can smell roses, and oranges, and what's that other smell?' she asked, 'No, and it's not my feet... don't tell me, its patchouli, isn't it? Flower power, great combination...heady...!'

'It's to help Kate sleep,' explained Annabel, 'it reminds her of the room in her peculiar dreams and for some reason that relaxes her. I don't know why, I think it would freak me out completely! Tell her about the weird hypnotist, Kate.'

'You mean you took my advice and went to see a past life therapist...' Shirl looked surprised, 'and what did you find out? Are you Caterina?'

'Nothing, nothing at all,' I murmured, 'actually I can't tell you because I don't remember anything. I was completely out of it!'

'She was shouting,' said Annabel, 'and it was really loud. I was in the next room, but I could hear her yelling, 'Opera, opera, opera', and it was all in Italian. Oh, and Otto, she definitely mentioned an Otto, whoever he is; or it could have been otter? And lion; yes, leone,' she smiled, 'Leo, it's almost the same as lion, so I recognised that at least. He recorded some of it but he asked if he could keep it for the Hypnotist Convention, lucky really because we didn't have to pay and as neither of us is working at the moment...'

'What a shame you didn't keep a copy; I might have made some sense of it!'

It was true, I'd completely forgotten that Shirl could speak fluent Italian, 'Are you sure it was 'opera', Annabel?' asked Shirl, 'And I wonder who Otto is, could he be the murderer? Unless it was otter, but why would it be otter? I'm not even sure they have otters in Italy. It's all a bit odd isn't it?'

I looked at them, 'Odd...! Odd doesn't quite cover it if you don't mind my saying!' I was feeling quite miffed, especially when they ignored me and went on talking as if I wasn't there.

'Maybe she was an opera singer in a previous life,' suggested Annabel, 'anything is possible, isn't it?' she shuddered, 'Gawd, you should have heard her! I rushed in then and she was throwing her arms around and clutching at her throat like she was being strangled.'

'The mind is strange and unpredictable,' declared Shirl. She seemed to have taken on a more serious persona, a world away from orchid pink lippie and 'Singing in the Rain'. 'Are you sure it was opera? I mean, could it have been sopra?'

Annabel bit her lip, I could see that she was trying hard to remember, 'Sopra, sopra, well I suppose it could have been. Why, what's a sopra?'

'It means 'above',' said Shirl mysteriously.

'Why would she be shouting 'above'; above what...? It makes even less sense than yelling about some opera; and what about the otter?'

Shirl suddenly seemed to remember I was there because she turned to me and looked deep into my eyes and I had the uncomfortable feeling that she was trying to hypnotise me as well, then she said,

'It's that necklace, isn't it? Caterina is trying to tell you where it is; maybe she wants you to find it! You have to call this Randi and ask him for a copy of the recording, do it now before he goes off on his convention. I only hope it's not too late.'

'But... I didn't keep his number,' I stammered, 'and anyway, I'm sure he won't be there.'

'I've got it on my phone,' said Annabel, 'I'll call him... it's ringing...' and she thrust her mobile into my hand and I held it reluctantly to my ear. I had no wish to converse with Mr. Randolphus Lebedev Popov, and I didn't think for a moment that he'd have any desire to speak to me, terrified as he was by my revelations. 'Put it on speaker,' she urged, 'then we can all hear!'

'Answer-phone,' I whispered, and Annabel and Shirl gazed back at me wide-eyed as his strange mesmerising voice echoed around the room.

'My healing rooms are unavailable until January so all ze bookings for past life regression therapy will take place after zat date. You have taken the first step towards solving your problems in your present existence merely by calling me. Therefore, I urge you to call back, please, call back when I am available. Many of our fears are ze result of trauma and loss in previous existences, of which zere may be many. Much of this can be resolved through sessions of hypnosis in my healing rooms in London. Do not be afraid, you are part of ze great circle of life...'

'Goes on a bit, doesn't he?' muttered Shirl as she pressed the 'off' button, 'Anyway sounds like he's gone so we're already too late.'

I heaved a sigh of relief, 'Sorry, Shirl, stupid of me not to ask for the recording; I wanted to get out of there, and we just ran, it was all too... weird, wasn't it?' I turned to Annabel who was staring straight at me with a vacant expression.

'Gawd, Kate, he's only gone and put her under,' gasped Shirl. 'Look her eyes are all glazed over. Shall I click my fingers?'

'Don't know, Shirl; are you sure it's safe to do that?'

'No, choice, we can't leave her like this!'

'Circle of life,' murmured Annabel, 'it's the circle of life...'

I couldn't help giggling, probably hysteria, 'Ha-ha... she's gone all Lion King on us, quick before she starts singing.'

Shirl clicked her fingers right under Annabel's nose and she jumped and turned her head to look at her. 'Why did you do that?' she asked angrily.

'You'd been hypnotised,' said Shirl, 'by Randi whatsit... on the phone.'

'Don't be ridiculous,' snapped Annabel, 'I was just having a snooze; I've had a few late nights... Huh, like I'd be hypnotised as easily as that...!'

'Oh well, looks like he's cleared off, so we'll never know if it was opera or sopra,' said Shirl, 'and that voice; I don't think he sounds Russian, could be anything, but it's enough to put the fear of God in you. I know, let's have another cup of tea and then you can give me a cemetery tour.'

'Whoa, not me,' murmured Annabel, 'I'm keeping the blinds down, I've had enough hocus-pocus for one day. I might ask Joe round, we could do some research together...'

'Nudge, nudge...' muttered Shirl.

'Isn't he at work, down at the library?' I asked.

'Oh, I never thought of that; boring... still not coming though, you and Shirl go; I've got to decide on my wardrobe for Venice.'

We left her slumped in front of the TV and crossed the road to the cemetery.

A pale sun shone from a watery blue sky as we gazed up at the giant head of Karl Marx, and he stared back at us through empty, unseeing eyes.

'WORKERS OF ALL LANDS UNITE...!' read Shirl, 'Oh, he's a lot bigger than I expected, look at those staring eyeballs. Yuri Gagarin, you know, the first man in space, he came here just to see him; I've been reading about it. There are so many famous people in here; it's a sort of 'who's who' for dead people, George Michael, Malcolm McLaren, Bert Jansch, Charles Dickens; one hundred and seventy thousand in all! And there's a tunnel that goes from the mausoleum at the top gate; it runs under the road to the old cemetery. Perhaps I could come back when I've got more time and we could do a proper tour?'

Shirl was in her element! The tiny paths beckoned and we wandered off between the trees, where the weeds seemed to have run amok, and ivy scrambled over the weather-beaten stones. It had clouded over, and I felt suddenly closed in, enveloped in a strange, unnatural stillness. Shirl was marching ahead, chattering non-stop about body snatchers, and the Highgate vampire, when she suddenly came to a halt beside the marble figure of a tall angel, with feathered, out-stretched wings, and we almost collided.

'Well, she doesn't look at all happy,' she murmured.

'Yes...' I whispered for fear of disturbing the still air, 'but she looks... reproachful rather than unhappy.' I walked over and pulled the grass away so that we could read her name. 'Lucia Caterina di Lazio,' read Shirl, and I froze.

'No, surely not... it can't be...' I reached for Shirl for support, I was trembling. 'Lucia Caterina di Lazio',' I read it again, just to make sure, while Shirl eyed me with a look of concern, 'the mother of Caterina and Elisabetta, she's here, beneath our feet.' I stared down at the sodden earth and shivers ran up and down my spine.

She put a reassuring arm around my shoulders, 'No, Kate, I'm sure it's not her, it's just a coincidence, nothing more!'

'How can you say that after all that's happened? You were the one that made me believe that nothing was a coincidence, that all of this was happening for a reason.'

I looked up at the sad face of the angel and she looked back at me, and I felt as if, somehow, she recognised me.

'We should leave,' said Shirl, and she took my arm and marched me back down the path. 'I've got to get down to South London this afternoon, they're expecting me.'

'I'm so sorry,' I said softly, 'I've frightened you. You don't have to go, please stay.'

'Oh, of course you haven't frightened me,' protested Shirl, 'it takes a lot more than that to scare me! Come on, I can't be late, you've got to help me to find the tube station, or I'll have to resort to my Google again.'

We walked back in silence, which was very unusual for Shirl. I could tell she was worried, but didn't know quite what to say to reassure me.

'Try not to fret, luv, it'll sort itself out, sometimes you have to trust to fate,' she murmured, and then she hugged me and waved before disappearing down the escalator. I looked around, everything was normal and unthreatening; people came and went. None of them were being haunted by strange dreams and voices from the past, or if they were there was no indication of it, but then I looked quite normal, so no one would guess that any of it was happening to me either. My pace slowed; I was beginning to dread my return to Venice.

Adam was waiting for me by the gate.

'Are you feeling okay?' he asked when I got nearer, 'you look... pale, and sort of, tense.'

He kissed me on both cheeks and led me up the path to the front door, 'Key,' he said and held out his hand. I gave him the key and he unlocked the door, I still hadn't spoken. 'Annabel...' he called up the stairs, 'quick, open the door; and put the kettle on, Kate's not feeling well.'

She flung open the door and peered down at me. 'I'm fine,' I said, 'don't fuss.'

I sat on the sofa and stared at the blinds, it was no good; I knew exactly what they were hiding; tombstones, and crosses, and a strange marble angel who clasped a single lily in her left hand, while the other pointed across the path in an accusing fashion. Annabel brought me a cup of tea and Adam made me a sandwich, and when I'd eaten, I felt slightly better.

'What's going on, Kate?' he asked, 'we're all off to Venice, for Christmas, it's going to be great!'

'I'm not sure...' I murmured, 'not sure...'

'What do you mean, you're not sure?' demanded Annabel, 'I've practically packed. Did something happen in the cemetery?'

'Lucia Caterina di Lazio... Caterina's mother, she fled to England after Caterina was murdered. I think she's buried here; her name is on a tombstone, there's an angel, she looks... reproachful, and she's pointing, do you think she's pointing at me?' Maybe she wants me to do something to make everything right, but, honestly, Adam, I don't know what I'm supposed to do!'

Adam patted my hand; it was a slightly patronising pat, 'Of course she's not pointing at you...!' I saw him glance quickly at Annabel, 'We'll help you, Kate, you're not alone, we're here and together we'll find the solution. Did you say her name was Caterina?'

'Yes, and Lucia was her mother, and little Elisabetta was Caterina's sister. They lived at the Villa Alatri, until... she was strangled, and I'm certain she was murdered because of the necklace, the one that Sibella described.'

The next day I called Auntie Flo to ask her about her family tree and I was surprised when she said she could scan it and send it to me by email! Clever old Flo, it arrived almost straight away, page after page, crammed with names branching off in all directions over the last hundred years or more. Elisabetta was there, Elisabetta Lucia di Lazio who married Thomas Elliot in eighteen eighty-five, my great, great grandfather Thomas, and my great, great grandmother Elisabetta Lucia; her mother was Lucia Caterina, and her father Marco Giovanni di Lazio. My connection to the di Lazio family and Sofia was established. Now I just needed to speak to Sofia's Nonna, to see if she agreed with Flo.

Then I called Sofia to tell her, and to let her know that we would be arriving in the week before Christmas, me, and Adam, and Annabel.

I dreamed of Venice again that night, but this time it was peaceful, full of soothing voices and the sound of lapping water. No one followed me into a dark alleyway to throttle me, and there were no malevolent faces peering up at me from the garden.

I awoke to the sound of my phone vibrating on the bedside table, it was Adam.

'Kate,' he said, 'you'll never guess! I remember where I saw the other lion, you know, the same as the one at the Villa Alatri; well, it's on Poveglia, the plague island. I did an article about the place about five years ago, and the stone lion was there. It had toppled over and was lying in the mud.'

I could hardly believe it, 'You mean Sibella was right, her lion did come from Poveglia!'

Adam laughed, 'Yes, of course, Sibella knows everything!'

CHAPTER 17

Time passed quickly. Christmas trees appeared in the windows, and gardens glittered with fairy lights. We shopped for presents in Camden Market and decorated the flat with fallen branches, sprayed silver and gold and strung with shiny red and green balls. Every morning we found a pile of Christmas cards on the door mat, mainly for Mr. and Mrs. O'Connor who still hadn't returned. We pinned our cards to the new blinds as an extra barrier and it had the added advantage of us being unable to open them at all. One morning Annabel presented me with a card she'd picked up in the hall and opened by mistake; it was from Tom and Lorna and I felt so angry that I tore it into tiny pieces and threw it into the rubbish bin.

'The cheek of it,' she cried, 'how dare they upset you like that? So insensitive, mind you, I'm not surprised, I always thought he was a...' but I never found out what Annabel thought he was because she'd opened another card and was staring at the contents with a horrified expression.

'It's from Julia, you know, the Tarot reader, she wants to know how I am, and she's sent a twenty percent off voucher for my next reading; as if.'

'You didn't have a reading in the first place,' I reminded her, 'it was me, and it really wasn't helpful, not helpful at all. Anyway, why did it come here?'

'Oh, nothing mysterious about that, look, Lucy's forwarded it from my old address. I'll throw it away, shall I?'

'Probably best,' I said, I had no intention of visiting Julia again. Shirl would say my destiny was already written in the stars and, if anything, the cards had simply warned me to be careful. Julia had said much the same, that a reading only clarified existing situations so that we could see the way forward; still, one reading had been enough for me!

We got a card from the O'Connors the following day addressed to 'Katherine Elliot and A bel Leggup', obviously Eileen O'Connor had a sense of humour, but Annabel managed to control her indignation long enough to open it. Inside it read, 'From Eileen and Patrick O'Connor, with very best wishes for a peaceful Christmas' and a short letter was attached with a pin that said, 'Away longer than expected because we have a precious addition to the family, Lysette Eileen, born at the beginning of last week! Now you girls have a wonderful time, and if you can't be good, be careful! Best wishes, Eileen xx'

'Whatever does she mean?' asked Annabel, 'We're always good; well I am anyway, not so sure about you!'

Adam popped in all the time for cups of tea and accused us of being idle.

'What does he mean, 'idle'? Huh... it's simply not true,' said Annabel.

'Idleness, you know, lazy,' I explained, 'because we're not at work.'

'I know what it means, Kate, but really, what a sauce, we're just having a much-needed rest! The last thing I need is someone lecturing me about being idle!'

One day I met him in the park. We sat on a bench huddled together because it was so cold and I told him about my encounter with George and his tale of the Blitz, and how when he was just a nipper he watched the bombs raining down on London.

'His life is almost over now,' I murmured gloomily into my woolly scarf.

'God, cheer up, Kate,' said Adam, 'you've got your whole life ahead of you, and when you've sorted out this... situation that you've got yourself into, well, everything will get back to normal. You need a job, find a proper teaching job, that's what you're trained for, not as a stand-in for teachers in the worst schools who are probably away having nervous breakdowns.'

'I used to do that, Adam. For about four years I had my own class, you know, after I left uni, I wanted a change, it was all just too predictable, and I had other plans.'

'Really, like what?'

'I wanted to write, but somehow I've just never got round to it. For a start, I thought I'd have more time and be less stressed if I didn't have a permanent job, but, in fact, it's turned out to be quite the opposite. I've been more stressed because

I didn't know where I was going to be sent next, and some of the schools were horrible, and Barb and co at the agency were always on the phone, even when I told them I wasn't free. Then there was all this business with Tom, plus the scary dreams, and, honestly Adam, I do try to rise above it, but sometimes it gets too much. Actually, I suppose I miss having a proper class.'

'Well, change back again; you've got a lot to offer.'

'And,' I continued, 'why did you say I'd got myself into this situation? I didn't, it just happened; you're being passive aggressive!'

'No I'm not!' he said indignantly, 'anyway, it's cause and effect; everything is cause and effect, or action and reaction; you know, Isaac Newton? It's not fate; it's far more scientific than that; if you had a computer that recorded everything, since the beginning of time, then you'd be able to work out exactly what was going to happen next.'

I stared at him, 'What...? Remind me why I like you, Adam.'

'Obviously because I'm so intelligent, of course...' he replied, 'not to mention good looking, articulate, very fit...'

'Yep, I remember now, and conceited, and...' I racked my brains for insults but I couldn't think of anymore, perhaps I was too cold, and anyway I knew he was joking. Actually, he did seem to be quite knowledgeable about all sorts of things, poetry, and physics, and he was definitely more clued up about everything than... 'you know who'.

Mum and Dad came around for dinner a few days before we left for Venice and we exchanged presents. Dad had told her all about Sofia, and how I was convinced that we were related so I opened my laptop and showed them Flo's family tree; it seemed to encompass practically every English county.

Mum got out her reading glasses and pored over it, 'English, see, those are all typically English names; I can't see anyone foreign!'

'Except this one,' I said, 'look, Elisabetta Lucia di Lazio!'

Dad borrowed Mum's glasses and balanced them precariously on the tip of his generous roman nose. 'So, is Elisabetta on Sofia's tree as well?' he asked when he had studied it at length.

'Yes, I think so, in fact I'm sure, but Sofia's grandmother has the family tree so I can confirm it when we get there. And look at this,' I added, and I showed them the selfie I took of the two of us on our trip to Burano.

'You're right, you could be twins!' said Mum, 'The resemblance is extraordinary! Well, you just never know what's around the corner!'

After that we polished off a couple of bottles of Italian red and they went home in a cab because Mum said her legs felt all wobbly.

CHAPTER 18

Beautiful Serenissima; like an exotic ship on black water, reflecting and consuming her shimmering festive lights, and merging them into ribbons of colour, like oil in a puddle. Okay, poetic, I know, but well, it all looked so beautiful!

We were back in Venice, Adam and me, squashed together in the fuggy atmosphere of the vaporetto as it sped across the lagoon enveloped in a mist of flying spray. Annabel was there too, looking about ten pounds heavier than usual, and fanning her pink face frantically with a copy of the Lady magazine.

I nudged her, 'You look like you're having a hot flush, why don't you take your coat off?'

She glared at me, 'Well, I wouldn't be wearing so much if you hadn't made me bring that silly little suitcase, huh... budget airlines...!'

I glanced at Adam and he raised his eyebrows, 'Posh totty,' he whispered.'

'Hot totty,' I whispered back.

'I can hear you,' said Annabel, 'I'm not deaf you know, just a bit hot! Anyway, why did you tell him about that?'

'Oops, sorry, Abel, I just thought it was a funny story, and I didn't think you'd mind. Look give me your coat, you can put it on again when we get there, it's not far now.'

'Okay, s'pose so,' said Annabel. She rose slowly to her feet and had just taken one arm out of a sleeve when the vaporetto lurched violently and she shot forward and landed on top of a pile of suitcases.

She floundered for a long moment trying to stand up, while Adam and everyone else in the cabin struggled to suppress their giggles and I bit my lip hard to stop myself from joining in. Luckily, she saw the funny side and we helped her back onto the seat and were soon exchanging smiles and greetings with everyone, and the atmosphere of repressed excitement suddenly seemed to bubble over into jollity.

We got off at San Stae, along with about twenty other people, and this time it felt friendly and unthreatening and I knew exactly where I was going. I thought of Shirl and how she'd rescued me, and it made me smile. How could I have been so ridiculous? It would have been easy to give up. I could see Annabel was impressed because she was peering into the dark alleyways, and up at the tall buildings, and gasping and muttering 'WOW...!' and 'AMAZING...!' every few seconds. Then we turned down a familiar alleyway and there in front of us was the beautiful Villa Alatri all strung about with lights. Sofia was waiting for us and she ran to open the tall wooden gate with the metal grill, and there was the stone lion in the flower bed, and the olive tree next to Sibella's front door, and they were covered in fairy lights too; white ones that made the courtyard glow with a pure silvery light. I ran to hug Sofia, and then Sibella who was looking frailer than ever. She was arm in arm with another old lady who stepped forward and kissed me on both cheeks. 'So you're Caterina,' she murmured, 'the likeness is remarkable,' her English was excellent, but I had no reason to think it would be otherwise, 'I am Sofia's grandmother.'

'Come in out of the cold,' said Sofia, 'I'll show you to your rooms and then we'll eat. Sibella has made supper for us in her house; as you know, her table is large enough to seat everyone comfortably.'

'Mind if I share your room, Kate,' whispered Annabel in my ear, 'this place freaks me out and, basically, I blame you for telling me all those weird stories. I promise I won't snore.'

'Oh alright, I suppose so, but definitely no snoring, and no kicking, it's a double bed!'

'Great, we'll have a midnight feast; it will be just like when I was in the girl guides... thanks Kate, I don't think I could have slept on my own, much too creepy.'

'And no, you can't share as well,' I said to Adam who was taking it all in and looking hopeful.

He laughed, 'What...! I thought my luck had changed!'

Sofia grinned, 'No, Adam, you're upstairs; your room looks over the courtyard.'

Over the courtyard, I shuddered as my dream came back to me in a blinding flash, but I still couldn't recognise the face that stared up at me, even though I was certain I knew him.

Sibella's table was covered with a cloth of fine Burano lace, and she and Nonna had decorated it with sprigs of olive leaves and tall white candles. There were glasses of iced water, with slices of fresh lemon bobbing at the surface, and carafes of wine gleaming, ruby red in the warm, candle light. A large lump of parmesan sat on a wooden board, filling the room with its unmistakable aroma of old socks.

'OMG...!' What a huge table,' exclaimed Annabel, when she saw it, 'there's room for twenty people at least, and there's only six of us.'

'Come, come,' murmured Sibella in English, and she beckoned to us to sit down.

Sofia grinned, 'Sibella says she's going to learn English so that she can speak to my twin, though she may have left it rather late.'

'Maybe she's going to live to be one hundred and ten,' said Adam, 'and then it will all be worth it!' and he winked at me from across the table. I felt my cheeks flush in the light of the candles, so I stood up quickly and followed Sofia into the kitchen, where Sibella and Nonna were piling heaps of pasta carbonara onto plates. Sofia handed me a big bowl of salad, balancing a basket of garlic bread rather precariously on the top, and I tottered back to the table feeling more flushed than ever.

Afterwards, we went back to Sofia's, where the fire was crackling away and it was warm and cosy. I was feeling quite light-headed with the heat, not to mention the wine, when Nonna left the room and came back with a small wooden chest that she threw open with a flourish revealing a lining of faded, lavender velvet.

We crowded round as she took out a scroll of paper that was yellow with age and torn at the edges. I searched for Caterina and Elisabetta and there they were; the daughters of Marco Giovanni di Lazio and Lucia Caterina. A daughter, Caterina Maria born 1855, and ten years later a second daughter, Elisabetta Lucia born in 1865 and married in 1885 to Thomas George Elliot, my great, great grandfather.

There were photographs too, some of the earliest I'd ever seen. 'Look at this one, Kate;' murmured Sofia, 'do you think she looks like us?'

'Gawd, if she was alive now, you'd be triplets,' declared Annabel, 'she's exactly like the two of you! It's so WEIRD!'

She did, though rather solemn, and much younger. It was Caterina, she looked about sixteen, and she was perched sedately on a sofa next to a little girl with dark hair and an eager face, and I knew, without a shadow of a doubt, that she was Elisabetta, the little girl who loved to dance.

It was clear that I shared my ancestry with Sofia Lazio, but nothing explained my strange connection with Caterina, or why I slipped in and out of her life in such a terrifying way. I felt happy in the Villa Alatri, almost as if I'd come home, but I was afraid too.

I woke early the next morning. Annabel was still asleep on her side of the bed. Her face was calm and untroubled, nothing ruffled her peace of mind; there were no ghosts or insistent spirits pestering her for attention. I got up and went into the living room, Nonna was there already sitting in a big armchair with a shawl wrapped tightly around her knees.

'Come and sit beside me, Caterina,' she called softly, 'sleep sometimes escapes me, and Sofia's house is warmer than Sibella's, but I want to talk to you in any case. Sibella tells me that you are curious about the girl who lived here, many years ago. She was Caterina, just like you, but, as you know, she met a tragic end when she was very young, even younger than you are now.'

'Did Sibella tell you about my dreams as well?' I asked her.

'Yes, she did, but she's very religious and it frightens her. I'm rather cynical in my old age but her life has been... I'm not really sure how to explain, maybe more sheltered and restricted by circumstance; she's not as worldly as I am. She had eight children and they kept her very busy. I was envious of her, I only had Sofia's papa, his name was Roberto after my father, and I always hoped for more babies, but it wasn't to be. We were richer, we travelled, and I lived in Verona after Roberto married and they moved into this house. He was so lovely, he had big brown eyes and long lashes; when he was little, he was almost too pretty to be a boy, and he was enough for me really, I couldn't imagine loving anyone as much as I loved dear little Roberto. Then they had Sofia and she took after him, and so do you, Caterina.'

She took my hand but I didn't know what to say, both she and Sibella had lost so much.

'My grandmother told me about it; she was just seventeen when Caterina was murdered, and if she had lived, she would have been one of our great aunts. Sofia may already have told you that I married into the Di Lazio family, but we already knew each other well, our social circle was very small. Today you would probably say that I had an arranged marriage. But Caterina's mama came from a wealthy Venetian family too; it was her grandfather who left her the jewelled collar and it was very valuable, an antique that should have been in a museum and locked away, not bequeathed to a young girl. There was a rumour that it was hidden here in the Villa Alatri, and someone decided that Caterina had hidden it, or that she knew where it was kept. That was the motive for her murder; there was nothing random about it and, strangely, everyone seemed to know who was responsible! Her murder changed everyone's lives; it made the children afraid to go out to play, and our mothers and grandmothers made sure that we were aware of the dangers.'

'Can you tell me what happened after she died, please? I've seen her mother's grave; it's very near where I live.'

'Yes, she fled to England for safety with little Elisabetta, who was just seven when it happened.

They had family there and so she thought she would be safe, but he followed her. He wasn't about to give up, maybe he thought she'd taken the necklace with her; who knows? Her husband, Marco, died when Elisabetta was only a baby so his brother, Eduardo, decided to pursue and catch whoever had murdered Caterina. He was young and strong; he took two of his closest friends with him and they must have succeeded because, somehow, it ended there. They wanted revenge, revenge is very important to Italians, even now. Lucia and Elisabetta never returned to Venice, which is why you are here now, a descendant of Elisabetta and her husband Thomas Elliot, and I'm very glad of it because, when I die, Sofia will have you.'

'But how do you know what happened with such certainty?' I asked, 'It's more than a hundred years ago!'

'Oh, you forget how old I am, and I have a very good memory. My life is almost over, I am nearly one hundred years old and it has flown by, forty years, fifty years, gone in the blink of an eye, our time on earth is short.'

'Maybe we never really leave,' I said quietly, and I saw a look of panic in her eyes.

'Yes, perhaps you're right, but I am old, and you are young, and I prefer not to think too much about it,' she smiled, 'and perhaps I'll find out soon.'

She got up then and wrapped her shawl around her shoulders, 'I must go back to Sibella now, she likes it when I stay; we grew up together, two little girls, and now two old women.'

I watched her as she walked down the path, she seemed unsteady on her feet and I wondered if I should have taken her arm, but she turned and waved from Sibella's front door by the olive tree and I waved back and shut the door. I could hear Adam; he was just coming down the stairs by the kitchen corridor. I still hadn't been to the old kitchen, maybe it wasn't even a kitchen anymore, but I somehow knew that it once was.

'I like your jim-jams,' he called when he saw me.

I had tears in my eyes, but I wiped them away and did a twirl, 'Oh, these old things! And shhhh... be quiet, it's early and you'll wake Annabel and Sofia!'

'Er... too late, I'm awake already,' murmured Annabel sleepily, 'has anyone boiled the kettle yet. And Adam, I'm relying on you to call Gio, now I'm here. I haven't come all this way just to listen to stories about someone's ancient history, even though it's, er... really interesting.' She glanced at me sheepishly, 'Oops, 'pologies, Kate, couldn't help overhearing.'

'I thought you were keen on Joe, from the library,' I said, 'and anyway, you might be disappointed when you meet Gio; he came over as a bit of a sleaze. Sorry Adam, I know he's your cousin!'

'Couldn't agree more, and actually I've already called him, and he and Antonio will be here by ten.'

'No...! Adam, I'm not even dressed!' shrieked Annabel, 'and, basically, Joe is just a friend, so there!' and she rushed back into our bedroom slamming the door behind her.

'Did someone mention Antonio?' called Sofia from the kitchen, 'only I don't want to see him. He won't leave me alone since Louise went, and I'm not at all interested in him! And yes, I have boiled the kettle, and I really don't understand why English people are so obsessed with tea!'

'Nor me,' said Adam, 'I'm a coffee drinker; I don't understand the tea obsession either!'

We went into the kitchen and sat at the breakfast bar on tall designer stools, while Sofia poured not-quite-boiling water over the teabags, I'd have to tell her about that. It was all beautiful; Italian chic, with pale grey and white units running around the walls, and a tall window that would have looked over the canal if it hadn't been for the long charcoal linen blind. It was easy to forget that we were in one of the oldest cities in the world and not some modern docklands apartment.

'Was there another kitchen at one time?' I asked.

She looked up quickly from her pouring; she seemed surprised, 'Yes, of course, why do you ask?'

'This isn't the sort of kitchen you'd find in a house like this,' I said hurriedly, 'you know, it's very modern so I assumed...' I didn't know what else to say. Why was I even bothering to pretend that it was just a throwaway question?

'Drink your tea and then I'll show you,' she said, 'and don't worry, Kate, it's time I got used to your strange... incites.'

Adam winked at me, 'Yes, we all know about your strange incites, Kate.'

We walked down the corridor beyond the staircase; it felt cold and neglected, compared to the rest of the house. Sofia seemed uneasy and I wished I'd never mentioned it.

'It's just a storage room now,' she explained, 'so it's in a bit of a mess. I bought quite a lot of new furniture and I didn't want to sell the old stuff. I'm not sure why because some of it is probably very valuable; I'm just sentimental I suppose, and maybe it's a link with my parents.'

It was large and cold, and stuffed with heavy antique furniture. A tall bookcase, complete with dusty volumes, stood next to an old cooking range, and a vast sofa, draped in a cotton sheet that had fallen off at one end, revealing worn burgundy velvet. I closed my eyes and then wished I hadn't because my eyelids felt heavy, as if part of me wanted them to remain closed, and I could hear chattering voices, and laughter, and I wanted to join in. There was an overwhelming fragrance of basil and oregano, and the rich scent of just picked tomatoes, and someone was chopping something pungent; garlic, yes, it was garlic and it filled my nostrils, chasing away the scent of the herbs. I smiled, I felt warm... content, but someone was shaking my arm and I was trying hard to ignore it; and the insistent yelling in my ears that drowned out the laughter, and the chatter, and the bubbling pans on the range.

'Kate! Kate, wake up! Come on... look at me, where are you, Kate?' I turned my head slowly and opened my eyes. Adam was shaking me as Sofia watched, ashen faced, from the doorway, as if she were anxious to get away. I looked around and caught a flickering glimpse of a shadow and heard a small giggling laugh that faded slowly as my senses returned. I tried to smile but my mouth refused, 'I'm okay, Adam, really. Don't worry, Sofia; just one of my little turns!'

He was leading me out of the room and up the corridor, back to Sofia's domain with the pretty blinds and the modern kitchen where everything gleamed with a patina of newness. It seemed somehow strange, as if I didn't quite belong, but they sat me down in an armchair and fussed around asking questions, while Sofia wrapped a blanket around my shoulders and told Adam to fetch a glass of water.

'I'm fine, really,' I insisted, not very convincingly, 'I'm getting used to it and in a way... I quite like it,' it surprised me nearly as much as it surprised them.

'What do you mean, 'you're getting used to it?' asked Adam, 'and what exactly are you getting used to? Honestly Kate, you'd gone, vanished, and I was really worried that you weren't ever going to wake up! You were practically... catatonic!'

I threw off the blanket and stood up, 'Look, I'm okay! No harm done, you don't have to worry about me.'

'Really, what happened, Kate;' asked Sofia gently, 'please tell us.'

I looked at them; they were both staring at me like I'd grown another head.

'I can't explain...' I fumbled for words, 'it's as if I slip back in time, but I don't really mind because it's... welcoming, and somehow more alive in some ways than the here and now. I think I'm seeing everything through Caterina's eyes. I don't know if I'm her, you know... a reincarnation, like Shirl says... or if, maybe, I'm just picking up on her memories somehow, though I'm not sure how. As I said, I can't explain it, and I hate it when her life ends, obviously...' we looked at each other in silence not knowing what else to say and Sofia took a gulp from the glass of water that Adam had brought me. 'It's frightening,' she murmured at last, 'why would this be happening to you and not me?'

'Maybe you've had enough to cope with already, or perhaps Caterina wanted us to meet,' this sounded ridiculous to me even as I said it, but Sofia nodded pensively.

'Perhaps you're right,' she murmured softly.

CHAPTER 19

'What's going on in here?' asked Annabel, 'Do you like my coat; I got it last week in Fenwicks.'

'Which question should I answer first?' I asked.

'Um... do you like my coat?'

'Is it made of fake fur?' enquired Adam, 'And the hat, is that fake fur? You know sometimes they use real fur and say it's fake because real fur is cheaper.'

'Of course, it's fake fur, as if I'd go around in the fur of a real animal! And what sort of animal is this shade of peach in any case?'

I laughed, 'You're so funny, Abel! Yeah, it's great, a lovely shade of peach, and no wonder you couldn't get anything else in your suitcase! You should lose those awful platform boots though; they cheapen the whole ensemble.'

'Bloody cheek! Sofia, you've got yummy taste, what do you reckon?'

'I think you look gorgeous, Annabel, but your outfit is so classy whereas the boots are more... well, casual.'

'Adam... what do you think?'

'Oh no, I agree with the others, those boots don't go with the rest of the... ensemble; actually, they make you look like a demented giraffe!'

'What, you can't be serious, these are genuine vintage; they cost a fortune down Portobello Market!'

'Bit harsh, Adam,' I whispered as she clumped off, 'she loves those boots.'

'Well someone had to say something, and tact doesn't work with Abel, you have to be direct, to the point!' He'd certainly got the measure of Annabel!

'What about these, any better?' asked Annabel re-emerging from our bedroom, 'are they more tasteful, Adam, or do I still look like a... what did you call me?'

'A demented giraffe...?'

'They look much better with that coat,' I said tactfully, 'you look lovely and at least you won't be looking down on Gio.'

'Is he very short then?' she asked suspiciously.

'He's not tall,' said Adam, 'but not short; just average.'

'Average, not sure I like the sound of that,' said Annabel.

'It's just that those boots make you very tall,' and I added, 'giant... in fact, they make you miles taller than me, and we're the same height normally.'

'Um... what was my other question, Kate?'

'Oh, nothing important, we were just discussing the old kitchen.'

She looked around hopefully, 'What old kitchen? Where?' she asked, 'Can I see it?'

'No!' we chorused.

'Fine, there's no need to get excited, I haven't got time anyway, there's someone at the door, got to powder my nose, guys, so can you open it?'

Gio was alone; apparently Antonio had given up lusting after Louise, and Sofia, and was chasing after an American girl he'd met the day before at the glass works.

'Ah, Caterina,' he cried when he saw me, 'Welcome back to Venice! Did you bring your friend?'

'She's gone to powder her nose,' explained Adam, 'good to see you, mate!'

He looked puzzled, 'Why is she powdering her nose?' he asked.

'It's an English expression, Gio,' said Sofia, 'and she'll be back in a minute so have a seat.'

I was baffled, surely they hadn't set up some kind of blind date; no wonder Annabel was done up like a dog's dinner! Whatever was she thinking?

'Shall I see where she's got to?' I asked breezily.

She was just coming out of the bedroom as I opened the door so I pushed her back in. 'What are you up to, Annabel?' I hissed, 'Just because he's Adam's cousin well... it doesn't mean you're going to get on with each other, does it? Why don't we all go out together and if you like him there's always tomorrow!'

'Are you mad? It's just the same as internet dating, isn't it? Actually, it's better because you know him already, so no nasty surprises, you know, the usual thing, baggage; like wives and half a dozen kids!'

I couldn't believe what I was hearing, 'Blimey, Abel,' I gasped, 'what sort of life do you lead?'

'Um... well, I suppose it's interesting, and never boring. Do I look okay? You know, sexy, but not too keen, and attractive, but not over the top? All that stuff.'

I shrugged, 'S'pose so, good thing you took those boots off though.'

'He is short, isn't he? You didn't want to tell me, and I've gone to all this trouble.'

'I thought you were aiming for 'not too keen', or 'over the top'? And no, he's not short, not as tall as Adam, but a really nice height; he's not like... Napoleon, for example. Come and look and if you don't like him I'll make some excuse. I can say you've got a headache.'

I opened the door a fraction so that she could peep through without being spotted.

'Wow, yep, he'll do, he's not standing up though. Go and make him stand up, Kate, please, just for me, I can always wear flats, can't I? Mmm... I must say he looks rather scrumptious!'

'Gio, I said, 'come through to the kitchen. I'll put some coffee on while we wait for Annabel; she's just doing her hair.'

He stood up and put his arm around me. He was a little too friendly for my liking, but Annabel was obviously impressed because she was making a thumbs up sign from the gap between the bedroom door and the architrave.

She joined us a few moments later carrying her coat but still wearing the hat and, thankfully, minus the awful vintage boots.

'Gio, hi, I'm Annabel,' she smiled up at him, 'but you can call me Belle if you like, all my friends do.'

What...? I didn't know anyone who called her Belle, but Gio didn't need any encouragement,

'It suits you,' purred Gio, 'it is French, but I shall call you Bella, it is the Latin form and the Italian word for beautiful, a beautiful name for a beautiful woman...'

God, sleazy or WHAT!

'I'll come as well,' I said, 'I'll get my coat, and I'll tell Sofia and Adam, I know they'll want to come too.'

Annabel looked stricken, and so did Gio; he put his arm around her shoulder and led her to the door, 'Don't worry about the coffee, Bella is ready to go now and so we will leave. I want to show her this wonderful city, my city, my Venice,' he gazed into her eyes and stroked her long blond hair extensions, 'my Serenissima.'

Annabel was melting under his gaze, lost in his dark, lash-fringed eyes. I knew there was no hope; if I stopped them leaving it would just look like I was jealous. Adam saw my face and shrugged, 'Let them go,' he whispered, then the door slammed behind them and they were gone!

'Don't worry, Kate,' said Sofia, 'I suspect Annabel is more than capable of dealing with Gio. I give it a week, at most. I'm going to ask Nonna if she's happy to spend her day at home with Sibella, they aren't really up to sightseeing these days, the steps are too steep, and there are too many bridges.'

She went, and we were alone. Adam grinned, 'We always have a chaperone! There's always someone hanging around; when am I going to get you on your own, Kate?'

'We've been to the park on our own,' I replied, 'and what makes you think I want to be on my own with you? We're okay as we are; it all gets too... messy otherwise.'

'I'm prepared to risk that,' he murmured seductively, and he stepped closer and wrapped his arms around me.

'That's nice,' I murmured, 'very comforting.'

'Comforting!' spluttered Adam, 'What are you like? What do I have to do to make you interested in me?'

'I am interested in you, Adam; I just don't want to rush things. There's too much going on; I really like you, but what if you decide I'm completely mad in a week or so? In fact, I'm surprised you don't already, especially after what happened this morning in the... old kitchen,' and even saying the words reminded me that I wasn't in any way normal.

'I don't mind, really,' he said softly, 'it's not your fault; I know that. None of it is, and we'll get to the bottom of it, I promise. I won't rush you, Kate; just know that I'm here for you, no matter what.'

The front door slammed and Sofia walked in, 'Oops, sorry, I didn't mean to interrupt!' She looked embarrassed.

'Adam's just trying to make me feel better,' I explained, 'he says he doesn't think I'm completely mad.'

Adam looked down at me with his gorgeous, greeny-blue eyes that crinkled at the corners when he smiled. 'She's just a little deranged perhaps, nothing too serious; it will all sort itself out in the end. Look, why don't we go somewhere? It's all happening out there, Christmas in Venice, we shouldn't waste a minute! Are Sibella and your grandmother happy to stay here, Sofia? We can walk slowly if they want to come, and I can carry them over the bridges.'

'Yes, it is, really beautiful, but unfortunately, I won't be able to join you. I've got a last-minute booking for the upstairs apartment, two Americans; they've just arrived in Venice. They came for the day, but they like it so much that they've decided to stay over Christmas. And, no, Nonna and Sibella are happy just gossiping about the past, and how strange the world has become; and what we should all do to fix it. Go on, enjoy yourselves, there's an ice rink in Campo San Polo, do you skate?'

Do I skate? I remembered my one and only trip to the ice rink. I'd taken to it like a penguin to ice, mainly because I'd spent my childhood whizzing over the smooth London pavements on roller skates, but Tom had been knocked flat and had to dash off to accident and emergency with a fractured elbow. We never went again after that.

'Love it!' announced Adam, 'never happier than when I'm on skates.'

We strolled down to the fish market at Rialto and stood on the bridge to watch the gondoliers. They were all done up in Santa costumes, and were buzzing around the cruisers and vaporettos, like demented, brightly coloured wasps. The winter sky was as blue as a summer's day, and it was busier than ever, and bustling with tourists, who were all spending money like crazy, and conversing at the top of their voices in a multitude of languages.

'Shame no one else could come,' said Adam, but I knew he didn't mean it, and I had a sudden vision of him carrying Sibella and Nonna over the bridges, one over each shoulder. It made me laugh.

'Why are you laughing?' he asked me, 'Don't you believe me? It is a shame that no one else could come,' he spluttered with laughter, 'no, actually, I'm lying, I'm really glad! And isn't this wonderful, just you and me, in beautiful Venice, at Christmas?' He gazed down at me and I smiled back.

Wow! It was true, it was amazing! Thank you, Caterina, was this what it was all about? Was this why you brought me here, to Venice, this wonderful unique city? I felt as if nothing could spoil my new-found happiness, not even Santa could have given me a nicer present!

'Sorry,' I murmured, 'it was just the thought of you carrying two old ladies around Venice, it was so funny! I think you might have been trying a bit too hard; and not very convincingly!'

'You never know, they might have been pleased; it must be really boring being stuck indoors all the time just because your legs don't work anymore. We might be like that one day, and I'm sure I'd really appreciate it if someone offered to carry me around.'

'Well, it was very kind of you,' I said.

We crossed back and headed to Campo San Polo where they'd set up the ice rink. The streets were less crowded away from St Mark's and it was beginning to feel much colder, I snuggled close to Adam and wrapped my scarf around my face and he pulled me closer still. 'I think it might snow,' he said, 'it's definitely cold enough. Wow, that would be magical; can you imagine it, Kate? I love snow, don't you?'

I nodded, 'Yes, I love it too! It always looks so beautiful!'

Yeah, snow, when you wake up and you just know for certain, even before you look out of the window, that it's snowed in the night, because it's so silent, as if every sound has been muffled in cotton wool; and every flaw disguised by a purifying coat of whiteness; every pile of rubbish, and untended garden, each weed hidden from view, until it melts and turns to grey slush! It's still worth it though, just for that moment when the whole of your world looks perfect.

Campo San Polo was magical, like some old American movie, I almost expected someone to burst into song; Winter Wonderland, yes that would do.

Adam stopped suddenly, 'Hey, look over there; it's Annabel!'

They were here already, Annabel and Gio, sailing around the ice rink, hands clasped, and arms outstretched, partly for balance but mainly for effect. I could see Annabel's peach, fake fur coat dumped by the wall that ran around the edge, she was still wearing the hat though and she seemed to have acquired a little skating skirt that rose up showing red knickers every time she twirled. She'd also acquired a small audience of young guys and some were filming her antics on their phones; I wished I had her panache, she was so determined always to have a good time. Gio was enjoying the attention too, but neither of them had noticed us so we just watched them for a few minutes from afar and then Adam looked at me and winked, 'Shall we give it a miss?'

We left the ice rink behind us and were soon lost in a maze of alleyways, aglow with fairy lights. I was content just to wander, not caring where I was going, or who was watching us; it was sufficient that Adam was there and it seemed strange that I'd never felt this way in all the years I was with Tom. Yet I still didn't know him, not really, nothing had happened between us, apart from the odd cuddle here and there, but I still felt this odd closeness. Maybe it was a feeling of anticipation, or exciting just because it was someone different and appealing, that was it. Of course, there was no other reason, after all, what else could it be?

We wandered on until we reached a tiny bridge over a narrow canal, where a Christmas tree, festooned with silver ribbons, took up most of the bottom steps. There was a coffee shop just on the other side with a tempting display of cakes, so we crossed the bridge and went in and sat down at a secluded table by the window. Adam was gazing out at the canal, but he felt my eyes on him and he turned and looked at me questioningly.

'Sorry, didn't mean to stare,' I said, I felt guilty, but wasn't sure why, 'it's nothing, I'm just wondering if you're the new man in my life? The gypsy did warn me; you know, Julia, the Tarot reader. She said there would be one because the King of Wands was in my spread.'

'The spread?' he laughed, 'Oh, that Tarot nonsense again! What does it mean anyway? Why is he a King of Wands?'

'There are four suites, just like in any pack of cards. Of course, Annabel is the expert, reckons she's researched it all in the library, that's when she wasn't fooling around with Joe between the shelves. I think it means you're courageous, and strong, and er... thrusting.'

'Thrusting...! Thrusting...! Huh... chance would be a fine thing!'

I giggled, he looked so serious, 'Well, she also said that I should be wary of a tall, dark and handsome man, because they're all the same and just after one thing.'

'Bit of a generalisation, isn't it, and quite sexist actually. We're not all like that; plus, I'm not tall, dark and handsome, that sounds more like Gio!'

'Gio's not as tall as you, and you are very attractive, just not dark. Anyway, he's not my type at all; he's more like the other one that Julia mentioned, the one that couldn't be trusted.'

We sat in comfortable silence for a while, watching the grey water of the canal through steamed up windows, then, 'Adam,' I said, 'do you mind if I ask you something?'

He grinned, 'Sounds ominous, perhaps I'll order the coffee first, or would you like a hot chocolate?'

'Yes, chocolate please, I don't really like coffee here, it's too strong.'

'Right, well actually, I'm not that interesting, but what do you want to know?'

'Well, I've told you all about Tom and... you know... Lorna.'

'Yes, I know; how did Annabel describe her? Er... she's got a face like a horse?'

'A Norse, actually!'

'Oh yes, a Norse, I remember!'

A pretty waitress came over to take our order. She fluttered her eyelashes at Adam and seemed transfixed by his blue eyes, but he didn't seem to notice at all, even when she glanced back at him seductively from behind the bar.

'It's that!' I said, but he looked baffled.

'What?'

'That waitress, she obviously fancies you! Women find you attractive, and you're thirty years old, for goodness sake, so how is it that you haven't been snapped up already? You could easily be married with a couple of kids... you're not, are you?'

'Of course, I'm not! I'd have said. And, yes, I've had girlfriends; I'm not a monk, quite a few at university, if I'm honest...'

Quite a few!

'...but I'd grown out of it by the time I left, and they didn't come and go quite so much...'

Serial monogamist...?

'I wasn't exactly, what you'd call, a serial monogamist...'

I was right!

'because they didn't last that long.'

GULP...!

'Then, about five years ago, I met Lydia and I thought, this is it, but she left me for my friend Paul.'

'Oh, no...! That's terrible!' He was just like me; it turned out we were both a couple of rejects! And she left him for his friend, which made it loads worse.

'So, this Paul, was he a good friend of yours?' I asked.

'Yes, a good friend from uni, and it was Paula actually; Lydia left me for Paula, who now insists on being known as Paul. They've got a very successful business, something to do with computer programming, and a flat in Battersea near the...'

'Dogs home...' I added helpfully.

'No, Power Station. Nice though...'

'Dad says he's going to get a dog after Christmas, I might suggest BDH.'

'BDH?'

'Battersea Dog's Home, that's where they all end up.'

'Oh no, it's started raining, and I was hoping for a white Christmas, Annabel's fur coat will go all soggy.'

'Not a chance!' I laughed; he obviously didn't know her as well as I did, 'I bet she's cosseted in some expensive restaurant, eating foie-gras and drinking Prosecco; and Gio will be footing the bill and wishing he'd never met her! Shall we go home when it eases off?'

'Yes, let's go home, Kate, back to your Villa Alatri; but please, just stay out of the old kitchen, I don't want you going all weird on me, not again!'

Venice was just as beautiful in the rain. It reminded me of Shirl and I wondered how she was getting on with her grown up daughters. At the rate I was going, I'd likely be over sixty by the time I had adult children. Maybe Mum was right, and I should start worrying about my biological clock!

When we got back, a battered guitar box was sitting on the ground next to the lion in his bed of wilted geraniums, and two huge backpacks sheltered from the showers beneath Sibella's olive tree. The visitors had arrived! Hugh and Grace from California.

CHAPTER 20

Annabel came back around seven, just as we were trooping across the courtyard to Sibella's with a large bowl of risotto, and some home-made garlic bread that smelled delicious, and oozed with butter.

'Garlic,' she muttered, twitching her nose, 'not sure if I'll manage any though, don't want to ruin things ha-ha... and I had an absolutely huge lunch! What...? Why are you looking at me like that?'

'We guessed you would, especially when it rained. Did Gio treat you?'

'Obviously...! He's got a fantastic job, makes wads of cash; something to do with cataloguing antiques, and he's really interesting to talk to, very educated. And, anyway, I couldn't walk around in the rain in my coat,' she stroked her furry sleeve affectionately; 'it would go all soggy, I might just pop it in our room in case it rains again. Stop it! Why are you all laughing at me?'

Sibella's house was warmer than usual. Nonna had made a fire, and it crackled in the big fireplace sending splinters of burning wood onto the threadbare rug. The old ladies beamed at us, 'Have you had a good day?' asked Nonna, while Sibella nodded at us, and smiled gummily, and pattered back and forth between the kitchen and the table.

It was late when we left, and the rain was hammering down, drowning out the sound of our 'buona nottes', and covering the drenched stone lion in a silvery sheen, under the flickering fairy lights.

I lay awake for hours staring into the darkness, listening to the sound of water dripping from the gutters, and filling the canals to overflowing; St Mark's Square would be flooded by the morning. Annabel went to sleep straightaway. It was so unfair; no actually, worse than unfair, it was infuriating, to have a friend who sailed through life, seemingly without a care in the world. Nothing fazed her!

I got up, her peach, fur coat was lying on the floor where she'd dropped it, so I put it on, and feeling like a giant, fuzzy peach, staggered into the living room and turned on the lamp. Is this what a submarine feels like, I wondered, skimming silently through the watery depths while outside the universe is coming apart at the seams? Detritus from the previous evening lay all around the room, dirty glasses and a half empty bottle of Limoncello, a wet shawl that Sofia had wrapped herself in to run across the rainy courtyard, Adam's trainers, still lying damply in the middle of the floor where they landed when he kicked them off, and some cups with coffee dregs, from earlier in the day. The whole place had an air of abandonment, as if everyone had suddenly just stopped what they were doing and disappeared; like a ghost ship, with no one on board, but an uneaten meal still on the table.

I was tempted to wake Adam, or maybe just crawl into bed next to his warm body. I opened the door to the inner hall, Sofia's bedroom was only a few steps away, but even that seemed too far. It was cold and dark in the hallway, and it felt remote, as if it wasn't part of the same house, but rather a different dwelling, from a different time. I shook myself; I knew I was being ridiculous. The staircase loomed to my right, by the passageway that led down to the old kitchen, and Adam's bedroom was at the top of the stairs, the room with the window that looked out over the courtyard. I shivered and stepped back into the room, closing the door firmly behind me; no, I just wasn't brave enough to venture up those stairs, even if Adam was at the top. I went into the kitchen instead, and sat at the breakfast bar, in the half-light shining through from the sitting room lamp. A sudden noise made me jump, I could hear heavy breathing and footsteps, and...

'What are you doing in here? Come back to bed, its two o'clock in the morning! And why are you wearing my new coat?'

It was Annabel.

'Sorry, I couldn't sleep, probably drank more than I should have. I can only manage a glass or two, must be the sugar.'

'Huh, lightweight,' scoffed Annabel, 'more like the alcohol!'

'Anyway, what's your excuse?' I asked her.

'Excuse, for what...why? Have I done something wrong?'

'No, idiot; what's your excuse for getting up in the night?'

'Oh, that, sorry, I just can't sleep in these creepy old places, not on my own; it's fine when you're in there too. Actually, you know what, it's even creepier than our little flat opposite the cemetery, if that's possible.'

'I didn't think you were really scared, Annabel; not like me. You've always joked about it, so I thought you were skeptical of anything 'supernatural',' I lifted my hands and made inverted comma shapes in the air; 'you know, ghosts and ghoulies and long legged beasties, all that stuff.'

She shuddered, 'No, you're totally wrong! I'm terrified, actually; I know I joke about it, and make out it's you that's weird, but I could very possibly be worse. That's why I chickened out of the Tarot reading at the last minute, I mean, I'm fascinated by it all, but still terrified nevertheless, and,' she added mysteriously, 'it all stems from my childhood.'

I couldn't believe what I was hearing; she'd never mentioned any of this before, and we'd been best friends for the last ten years; I was almost too afraid to ask. 'Why? What happened in your childhood, Abel?'

'We lived in a very old and rambling house in the country.'

'It sounds idyllic!'

'It was, absolutely beautiful, we had trees to climb, and a little stream to paddle in; mainly me and my friends as my brothers are much younger so they wouldn't even remember the house at all. All my friends wanted to stay...'

I was getting impatient, 'Yes, yes, lovely, very... pastoral, but what happened Annabel?'

'It was traumatic...' she whispered. I leaned closer to hear her, and the walls seemed to be listening too, because the rain had stopped, and it was as silent as the proverbial tomb. 'I suppose I've never really recovered...'
She faltered, but I nodded encouragingly, urging her on, anxious for someone else to be as odd as I evidently was,

'...and it didn't actually happen to me, and maybe, if it had, it would be less frightening, and easier to deal with.'

'Yes, the fear of the unknown...'

'Exactly...! It was very late, and dark, and there was a full moon, and my mother looked out of her bedroom window and there, staring back at her, was a monk. He was standing next to the gazebo...'

'Gazebo...?'

'Yes, a pavilion, with a green copper pointed roof, not one of your cheap, wooden, pretend gazebos.'

'Yes, I know what a gazebo is; I'm just surprised you had one. Anyway, who was this monk?'

'He was the phantom monk, reputed to haunt our village, and the ancient abbey that was torn down over four hundred years ago, though some of it was still there, in our garden; a ruined stone archway and some old walls.'

224

'So, what did he do, this monk?'

'He just stood there, next to the gazebo, and stared up at her with his empty eye sockets, for what seemed like ages, then he disappeared, vanished... poof...'

'But why did she tell you? She must have known you'd be scared?'

'She didn't tell me. I liked to sit on the stairs, and that's where I was when she was telling Dad. She was hysterical, naturally; I mean you would be, wouldn't you? I was supposed to be in bed so I didn't say anything; I just went back upstairs and got under the covers. I didn't look out of the window ever again when it was dark, and I was terrified of the gazebo, still am actually, quite phobic about gazebos,'

Gawd, a bizarre phobia, even for Annabel, who is quite unusual...

'And after that, I was frightened of anything in a hood; or a cowl for that matter; and if I saw a crowd of hoodies anywhere, I had to run away.'

'But your parents live in a modern house; I've been lots of times.'

'Of course, they do, now. Mum couldn't wait to move out after the monk incident.'

'Did you ever mention it?' I asked.

'There was no need; once we'd moved, I tried to forget all about it. I put it to the back of my mind, and it's only when I'm in a really old building, like this one, that I start thinking about it and wondering about...'

'About what...?'

'...the undead, you know; your ghosts and ghoulies...'

'...and long-legged beasties and things that go bump in the night,' I murmured, finishing the rhyme for her because her eyes had glazed over and she was trembling. I shook her gently, 'Come on, Abel, let's go back to bed, there are no monks here... or hoodies,' I added, hoping fervently that Adam hadn't packed one, 'and I'll bring the Limoncello, and we'll make a New Year's Resolution when we get home; no more alcohol for a month!'

'No, six weeks at least, I don't want to lose my figure! Gio gave me a box of chocolates so let's scoff those with the booze!' she grinned, 'Hoorah, a midnight feast! We can always give up chocolate too, for a while at least, or maybe a week.'

CHAPTER 21

'Do you know what time it is? It's gone ten! I've brought you some tea, and I couldn't find the toaster so I thought you might like this instead?'

I opened a bleary eye; Adam was standing next to the bed holding a tray. I squinted up at him, 'What is it?' I asked suspiciously.

'Garlic bread, I found it in the kitchen. What's up with Abel? Why has she got a pillow over her head?'

'Oh, yeah, that's because of the monk. By the way, you haven't brought a hoodie, have you? I mean the garment, not a delinquent adolescent.'

'Eh... what? No, I'm not even going to ask...' he shook his head, and put two mugs of tea and a lump of garlic bread on the bedside table. Then he picked up the empty Limoncello bottle and peered at it, in what I thought was a rather judgmental fashion, and seizing the empty chocolate box and our smeared glasses, he slapped them on the tray and exited the room.

Annabel came out from under her pillow, 'Has he gone? Oh, pooh, what's that terrible smell? Urgh... its garlic, isn't it? Where's it coming from?'

'It's the toast alternative,' I giggled, 'but there's a mug of tea, if you want it?'

'Oh, tea, good!' she wriggled into a sitting position and I passed her a mug.

'What's the time, Kate? Gio is taking me to Murano, he wants to show me his flat, you know, the one he shares with Antonio, and he's going to borrow his boat. He's coming to get me at midday, it's SO exciting!'

I picked up my phone to look at the time, and saw there was a text from Shirl, 'Um... it's only half past ten,' I muttered, 'you've got ages!'

'What d'you mean ages? An hour and a half is nothing! Still, I'll finish my tea first, and then I'll have a shower.'

'We saw you at the ice rink yesterday; you were whizzing around with Gio, and some guys were filming you on their phones.'

'Were they? Oh, good, I don't mind at all. Actually, Gio and I are brilliant, we've got this rapport, sympatico, Gio calls it; we're almost telepathic.'

Or maybe telepathetic, I thought, but I didn't say it because she seemed so happy.

'And what about all that stuff you told me last night, you know, the phantom monk?'

Annabel got out of bed and pulled on her fur coat; it crackled with static.

'See how useful it is, it's a good thing I brought it! And yeah, the monk, I made it all up just to make you feel better about being so weird.'

'Oh, Annabel...! How could you be so... unfeeling?'

I glared at her as she walked to the door, looking like a peach-coloured, dandelion clock; then she turned back and grinned at me.

'I'm only joking, I do believe, all of it, and I am scared of monks, and gazebos, and I know that sounds kind of silly, but it's okay because there aren't many gazebos around these days, well not proper ones anyway; or monks, actually.'

She slammed the door behind her and I snuggled down under the covers to read Shirl's text message.

'How's it going, luv? I'm at Sarah's with Naomi and that Liam, the lazy git boyfriend I told you about! Bet you're having a fabulous time. How's Adam, still just friends, are we? And poor old Sibella; is she still in the land of the living? Give me a call when you're free xxx'

I didn't know where to begin. How long had we been here? Only two days, yet so much had happened already! I sent a text back,

'Hi Shirl, it's great to hear from you! Sibella is fine, she's got Nonna staying with her and they spend all day gossiping about the old days. And Adam is... even nicer than I thought he was, but we're just friends, Shirl, honestly, for now... Got to go but I could give you a call tomorrow morning? Xxx'

'Yeah, call me, I'll be here all day, so you can update me with all the goss, I could do with some excitement! Xxx'

I was shivering, the temperature had dropped again and since Annabel had reclaimed her fur coat, I wrapped a big scarf around my shoulders and went to look for Adam. I found him in the courtyard studying the old stone lion. I watched him from the doorway, he seemed engrossed and when he saw me he jumped as if I'd caught him out. 'Is it really that interesting?' I asked him.

'Yes, it is actually, I'm just wondering why it's here and not with its twin on Poveglia. It's strange; perhaps they're waiting to be reunited, just like you and Sofia.'

'Not likely to happen though, is it?' I replied, 'And it's probably illegal to nick other people's lions, and it would be really heavy to shift, you'd probably need a crane just to lift it off the ground. Maybe the other one should come here, that was the original intention.'

'Exactly, someone got this one here in the first place!'

'Yep, it was stolen by one of my ancestors!'

One of my ancestors, someone who thought it was fine to steal other people's monuments.

'And it's not really the same as me and Sofia, is it?' I added, 'They're just two stone lions, and we're distant cousins. Oh, I can't even think about it anymore, it's enough to drive the sanest person to drink!'

'All right, I get it, it's not the same at all; but Kate, you must admit, it's all very strange when you think about it. The whole thing is extraordinary, and maybe even slightly alarming.'

'Alarming...! I can assure you I'm alarmed, I keep telling everyone I'm alarmed and at last someone agrees with me. Shirl and Annabel just seem to think I'm like... like some weird and delusional eccentric, I don't think either of them is taking any of this seriously.'

'I'm sure they are; what about Sofia?'

'She's fascinated by me, who wouldn't be if someone who's your double turns up on your doorstep?'

'Well that would definitely alarm me,' said Adam.

'But she's not experiencing all the other stuff, the horrible dreams, and the time slips, and the feeling that history is repeating itself and that I'm supposed, somehow, to prevent it. What if someone tries to strangle me, like poor Caterina was strangled just on the other side of that gate?'

'It's not going to happen, Kate, I'll protect you, I'm a karate black belt.'

My mouth fell open, 'That's incredible, Adam; why haven't you mentioned it before?'

'Oops, sorry, I was only joking!'

God, why did everyone think it was so amusing to wind me up? Like I didn't have enough to cope with already!

'But I can be really hard if I want to be.'

I knew he was expecting some hilarious retort, but before I could think of something suitable I heard a voice booming across the courtyard.

'Hey, Sofia, Sofia...'

It was a moment or two before I realised he was shouting at me! I turned around; a large, balding man in knee length, khaki shorts was walking towards me.

'Hey, Sofia, me and Grace would sure like to take you to lunch; and your young friend here too, if he's free...?'

I shook my head, 'It's very kind of you, but I'm not Sofia...' He looked puzzled, as if he didn't quite believe me. 'We're cousins; I'm from the English side of the family.'

He stared at me for a long moment as if he still wasn't convinced, but then Sofia called out from the doorway, 'Grace, Hugh, I'm here, is there a problem?'

They went over to join Sofia; I could hear them laughing, and they kept glancing back at me, but eventually they disappeared up the stairs to the little apartment, and I hurried indoors to see if Annabel had vacated the shower.

'I have my own bathroom upstairs,' called Adam, 'and I'm sure there's an ensuite shower in Sofia's room that you could use. Oh, hang on, wrong part of the house, I get it.'

He was right, so long as I didn't venture through the inner hall, I felt safe. Ridiculous, I know, but no more so than Annabel and her gazebo phobia; that had to beat everything, hands down!

She went off to meet Gio soon after, and Adam and I splashed through the puddles to the Rialto market, in search of last minute gifts.

The bridges over the canals glowered in shrouds of damp mist; it turned the murky water into grey, phantom flurries, slopping noisily against the quays, and halo-ringed the Christmas lights, winking defiantly, through the gloom.

CHAPTER 22

'I'm staying here tonight! Antonio's house is gorgeous! It looks out over the Fondamenta dei Vetrai, that's like the main road, but it's a canal, and it's all strung about with blingy lights and glassy trinkets; absolutely fan-tabulous, dahling! I'm so glad you made me come here! Anyway, like I said, Antonio has met some rich American woman, she was watching his blowing techniques and she says she really impressed with his glass balls... heh... heh...! She's taken him to some posh hotel up the coast, um... could be Rimini, and we've got the entire casa to ourselves. So, ciao and buona sera, Cara mia, see you domani!'

Oh well, it was inevitable, I suppose! I sent a short text back.

'Thanks for letting me know, Abel. See you tomorrow xx ps. Glad you're learning the lingo... lol x'

Nonna and Sibella were sitting in the living room, regaling each other with memories of their younger days, which seemed to be everything up to about nineteen fifty-five, and contained all the little details of events that occurred decades before I was even alive. It filled me with a sense of melancholy, and it occurred to me that in another hundred years the Earth would be occupied by entirely new people, and the world we were so familiar with would, in effect, have vanished. It was a sobering thought. I could hear them arguing over some minor event and it made me realise how much of what we remember is down to the way we see things.

Sofia and Adam were in the kitchen chatting as they prepared the dinner. Adam was chopping vegetables for a ratatouille, and Sofia was making a pasta sauce. I made myself smile as I walked past the old ladies and into the kitchen; I didn't want to depress them too.

'What's up darlin'?' asked Adam in mock cockney.

'Nothing, I'm fine, absolutely fine,' I tried to turn my mouth up at the corners again, but it wouldn't go, at this rate I'd need a face lift before I was thirty!

They both stopped what they were doing to peer at me, then Adam opened the fridge and took out a bottle. 'Come on, cheer up; I'll make some mulled wine! Where are your pans, Sofia?'

'Are you sure you're okay, Katherine?' she asked, 'You look very pale. Is Annabel eating with us tonight?'

I shook my head, 'No, she's staying with Gio, on Murano.'

Sofia poured the mulled wine into a pan and added some extra red and a handful of cloves. 'She should be careful, there's something about him; I don't know what it is, but I just don't trust him!'

The 'Seven of Swords', the tricky fellow, calculating and devious, was that Gio, or was I jumping to conclusions? Could it be someone else?

No, not Adam, surely, or was I being too naive and trusting? Or Antonio; or perhaps it was just some reference to Tom, he certainly fitted the bill, except he was mousy rather than dark. But why didn't Sofia trust Gio?

She stirred the wine, tasted it, and added a sprinkling of powdered ginger. 'Mmm... Better,' she declared, 'delicious in fact! Kate, get some glasses out, please. Nonna, Sibella, would you like some hot wine?' Muttered sounds of approval came from the living room.

'I'll take it to them,' offered Adam, 'that's right, top it up; oil the works!'

'I wish someone would oil my works,' I said.

Adam grinned, 'I've never heard it called that before.'

Hmm... Was it me or was he really a little too keen on saucy innuendo?

'Sofia, why don't you trust Gio?' I asked her.

She frowned, 'I'm not sure, maybe because he's so good looking, and charming; and in love with himself.'

'And only after one thing...?'

'Yes, I suppose so. Actually, he reminds me a lot of my ex.'

I looked at her curiously, 'Your ex, I didn't know you had one. Stupid of me, why wouldn't you? It's just that you never mentioned one... and I went on about Tom all the time; not now though, he's gone and I feel great... released!'

'Exactly...! That's how I feel, and it's been three years now, so he rarely comes to mind.'

'The mulled wine is going down well,' said Adam, 'reckon they'll be asleep within the hour. I've got to make some phone calls, might just pop upstairs and do that now.'

'What happened with your ex?' I asked Sofia when he had gone, 'You don't have to tell me; not if you don't want to.'

She smiled, 'It's fine, I don't mind at all, not anymore, and it helps to put everything into perspective, you know, talking about it with someone who's been through the same... trauma. I suppose we were just too young when we met, barely out of school; years ago we would have got married, but everything is different now, as Nonna is always telling me. 'Oh, Sofia, you should find a nice young man and have lots of bambini', and I suppose she's right in a way, you know the old... biological clock.'

'...biological clock,' we both said it at the same time!

'Yes, well, he started running around with anyone who was happy to listen to his life story,' she laughed, 'his trials and tribulations. Women are better at that, we're good listeners usually, much too polite not to be. Anyway, one thing led to another and he departed, left me with a load of unpaid bills; and after more than six years together! As I said, we were just too young, so I can't really blame him. His name is Gino, perhaps that's why I don't trust Gio; their names are very similar.'

I went into the living room to see if Nonna or Sibella wanted a refill, but, as Adam had predicted, they were both sound asleep. Sibella was still holding her glass, but it had fallen sideways, and the contents were spilling onto the carpet so I released it gently from her grip and put it on the sideboard. The door to the inner hall was open and I could hear Adam's voice echoing down the stairs, 'Yes, stop panicking, I'll sort it; yes, as soon as I get back! Have a great Christmas, Dawn! Love to the kids, I'll see you soon.'

I closed the door silently and scurried back to the kitchen. Who was Dawn... and what kids? And why was I so jealous?

'Everything sorted?' I asked him when he came back.

'Yeah, just work,' he replied, 'they won't leave me alone, even when I'm on holiday,' he smiled at me, 'I'm indispensable you know!' '

'Yes, but it's Christmas Eve tomorrow,' said Sofia, 'they should give you a break!'

I wanted to ask him who Dawn was, but I didn't dare, if I did he'd know I'd been listening. Gawd... he might even think I was spying on him!

It was midnight when Sibella and Nonna wandered back across the courtyard. I wondered how they were still awake, these two old ladies in their nineties.

'I suppose they're making the most of the life they've got left,' I said when Adam remarked on it;

'maybe they don't want to sleep the rest their lives away.'

'They had a very long siesta this afternoon;' added Sofia, 'we're just lucky they were ready for bed at midnight.'

The house felt unnaturally still and silent when, eventually, I closed my door and climbed into my big double bed. I was hoping Annabel's creepy, eyeless monk wouldn't materialize, summoned by her recollections; or any of the strange beings who haunted my dreams, be they good or bad I just needed them to stay away. The darkness was all encompassing; I felt as if I were floating, devoid of all sensation with only the warmth and softness of the bed to remind me that I existed at all. In a panic I reached out for the bedside lamp, but it fell to the floor with a loud crash. I shuffled over to the other side and reached out into the black void for the other lamp, then, tap...tap...tap... I froze... Someone, or something, was tapping on my door!

Tap...tap... it came again, then a high-pitched voice, 'Katherine, let me in, it's dark, and I'm so cold, please let me in...'

'Adam, is that you? If it is can you stop trying to frighten me, I'm scared enough already!'

'Sorry, yes, it's only me ... pitch dark in here! Where's the light switch?'

'Mind the...'

'Ow...! My toe...'

'...lamp! It fell on the floor.'

'I know! I just found it, with my big toe! Voila! Iluminati...!'

Adam was peering down at me holding the lamp in one hand, I giggled.

'You remind me of Florence Nightingale with that lamp; and aren't the Iluminati some sort of secret society?'

'Nope, in Italian it means 'lit', I'm not entirely stupid, and shove over, I want to get in.'

'I am over; and anyway, who says I want you in here with me?'

'Oh, shut up! You know you do!'

Well, I did, I had to admit it, and it would be something to tell Shirl when I spoke to her in the morning; Adam and I were no longer 'just friends'. Wooooo... hooooo...!

CHAPTER 23

'Don't move!' I opened my eyes; Adam was staring at me in the half light, or more precisely he was staring at the pillow next to my right ear.

'Why, what is it?' I gasped.

'It's some sort of bug, huge...' whispered Adam and he leaned over to get a better look.

'Ow... your elbow's digging into my stomach, get off!'

'It looks like a big spider, yellow, with lots of legs. Oh, no! There's another one; try to keep still, they might bite!'

'What? Are they... moving? Can't you swat them with something?'

'Don't panic... just try to move over to this side of the bed and slide out.'

'Adam, if you're winding me up again... it's the end of a beautiful friendship!'

'No, I'm being perfectly serious, I really am. Oh, no, there's another one, quick, get out NOW!'

'Are you sure it's safe for me to move? I mean, they won't attack me or anything will they?' I eyed one of the long-legged creatures out of the corner of my eye. It was huge, but there was something vaguely familiar about it. I rolled quickly onto Adam's side and jumped clear, and we gazed back at the bed from a safe distance. Daylight was already filtering in, from a gap between the curtains so I inched around the bed to pull them open.

'Adam, you idiot... they're Annabel's hair extensions! They keep dropping out! Everywhere she goes she leaves a trail of yellow matted hair, it's a wonder she's got any left!' I pulled back the quilt and tufts of yellow hair flew off in all directions. 'See, they're everywhere! Yuk... to think we slept in a nest of Annabel's hair, well not actually her hair, I mean it's not real hair, is it? Gawd, I hope not... wait till I see her!'

'She can have my room. If she's got her own bed she can shed hair as much as she likes,' said Adam, 'and besides, I want to stay down here, with you.'

'Sorry Adam, not a chance; she's terrified of old houses, I just found out. She wouldn't last a minute up there on her own; she'd be too worried about the monk!'

'What monk?'

'The one in the hoodie... Oh, long story, I'll tell you later.'

'I can't wait!'

'Yes, and she's terrified of gazebos, as well.'

Sofia was already in the kitchen when we emerged from our spider-infested love nest. She was sipping coffee and nibbling on a slice of toast. 'Good morning, did you sleep well?' And she raised her eyebrows and smiled knowingly at me when Adam turned his back to pour coffee into his mug.

'Really well, actually,' I replied, 'that is, apart from the incident with the giant yellow arachnids!'

241

'Arachnids...! Now that's one English word I've never heard before.'

'Spiders,' said Adam, 'huge multi-legged spiders, they were this big!' He held out his hands to demonstrate and Sofia looked appalled.

'You must have been dreaming, there are no spiders in this house!'

'It was my fault,' said Adam, and I could see that he was trying hard not to laugh, 'they just looked like giant bugs lying on the pillow, but once we opened the blind, we realised straightaway they were just...'

'Annabel's hair extensions,' I finished his sentence because he was laughing too much, 'all over the place! Ooh... I wonder how she's getting on with Gio.'

Yes, I was wondering how she was getting on with Gio; still Annabel would cope, and she always had Joe at the library to um... fall back on!

I'd promised to ring Shirl, so I made a cup of tea and took it into our bedroom to call her.

She answered from a small, dimly-lit room that looked as if it had been attacked by an untidy glitter-fairy. A gaudily decorated Christmas tree was crammed into the corner behind her, and half-wrapped presents scattered the floor under swooping, multicoloured paper chains and a huge bunch of mistletoe. Shirl looked fantastic, her tight perm had been tamed into tiny curls all around her head, and she had bright blond highlights, reminiscent of Annabel's hair extensions. I still wasn't even dressed.

'Hey, Shirl, it's me, how are you? You look gorgeous!'

'Ooo... Facetime,' she moved her mobile to arm's length, 'there, I look even better further away! And never mind me, how's it going with Adam?'

'Well, we're still friends, but not just friends; now we're more... much more. I really like him, Shirl. He's funny, and sweet, and amazing company and he makes me feel young again.' I paused, wasn't that what Tom said about that dreadful Lorna?

'Young... are you mad? You are young; wait till you've got great, galumphing daughters, then you'll be entitled to feel old, though actually, I can't say I do! Oh, so Adam is wonderful, is he? Are you sure it's not some enormous crush, after all, you don't really know him that well, but who am I to talk? I met my old man down the pub, and look how that turned out!'

'Well, I really don't care if it is; I'm making the most of it!'

'I don't blame you, enjoy it while it lasts, that's what I recommend, I'm just jealous,' she laughed, 'don't suppose you've got one for me?'

A girl appeared on the screen next to Shirl; she had a pretty face and looked about the same age as me; one of Shirl's 'great, galumphing daughters'.

'This is Sarah, my eldest, it's her flat, but the decorations are down to Naomi and Liam and, honestly, I feel like I've been marooned in Santa's Grotto and there's no escape. Sarah is very

243

interested in all your 'goings on' and I don't mean with Adam; no, I mean your dreams, and all that stuff. She's into psychology; you know, the power of the mind.'

'Yes, I remember you told me, but I don't think it's anything to do with my mind, it's too real!' and I related what had happened in the old kitchen.

Shirl turned to her daughter, 'There, what do you make of that, Sarah? And she had witnesses, so it obviously wasn't a dream.'

Sarah stared at me under the glow of a thousand fairy lights, 'There must be an explanation,' she said, though she didn't look convinced, 'the mind is capable of far more than we realise, what about mass hysteria, for a start?'

I nodded, 'I know, and I would never have believed it either just six months ago.' 'You can't explain everything, Sarah,' added Shirl, 'life is much more complicated and mysterious than we realise. Look, Kate, we have to find out what you said to your hypnotherapist, Randolphus... whatever his name is,'

'Randi,' I said helpfully, 'we just called him Randi.'

'Yes, him, if I could only listen to that recording, the one he took off to his convention, I'm sure we'd know more. As soon as the holiday is over, I'll track him down; once we get the recording I can translate it and then we'll know exactly what you were on about.'

CHAPTER 24

'I thought we'd go out for a wander this morning,' said Sofia, 'Hugh and Grace are insisting we have lunch with them, so maybe we could join them somewhere not too far from here. They want to meet you, Katherine. They were intrigued by your story and they want to hear more.'

I must have looked worried because she added, 'of course, I only mentioned our family tree, and about the amazing coincidences; not your dreams and... you know, all the rest of it. If you don't mind, I could take the photo of Caterina and Elisabetta? It will give us something to talk about, other than Hugh and Grace, that is!'

'Will Sibella and Nonna be coming too?' I asked. It seemed a shame to leave them shut away in Sibella's draughty sitting room with just a few old armchairs and a vast table.

'I shall insist they come,' she replied, 'I'll go and see if they're up yet.'

I showered quickly and pulled on a pair of jeans and my thick black jumper then, as no one was about, I opened the door to the inner hall and called up the stairs. 'Adam,' I yelled, 'are you ready to go out?'

'On the phone,' he yelled back, 'I'll be down in a minute.'

So, he was on the phone, again, and it was Christmas Eve, and who to this time, not Dawn, surely? And who was she, this Dawn? It was no good I'd have to find out, but then he'd know I been listening. Honestly, men…! Was any of it worth the bother?

He came down just a few minutes later looking hot and flustered.

'What's up,' I asked, 'not work again, surely?'

'Just some article, they should have got it! I definitely sent an attachment, but it's gone astray, probably floating somewhere in the ether. Huh, technology, s'alright when it works. Looks like I'll have to go up north and sort it out as soon as I get back to London.'

Right, so he had to go away to 'sort it', and 'up north'!

I hated the way I'd become so suspicious. What was wrong with me? I didn't own him, so what if he had Dawn 'up north'? I wouldn't blame him if he did; after all, I was obviously 'a sandwich short of a picnic' as Dad would say, so most men would run a mile. And Tom had shaken my faith in everyone; I'd been convinced our relationship was solid, and unbreakable, and er… boring? Well yes… but solid nevertheless.

Adam was smiling at me, 'What's up snowflake?'

Snowflake, right that proved it, he really thought I was a bit… flaky.

'Come on, let's find Sofia and head out into the big wide world.' He murmured it very close to my ear and then he kissed me on the nose.

Ha, well, it was Dawn's hard luck because, for now at least, he was with ME!

A fine mist still floated above the Grand Canal, but the sun was shining through the clouds, creating a beautiful, eerie light and throwing golden, rippling shadows across the water. Sofia and I linked arms while Adam strung along behind looking slightly awkward. I felt as if I had known Sofia all my life. Everything about her was somehow familiar, and the more time we spent together the more we seemed to gel. I wondered what Mum and Dad would have said, had they seen me strolling through Venice as if I belonged there; was this where I was meant to be? Of course, I knew it was only an illusion and that really my life was elsewhere, probably in London, but for the moment I was happy to pretend. Music was everywhere, there were carol singers in traditional Venetian costume in every piazza, and masked musicians, and stringed ensembles playing Vivaldi and Puccini; and the cacophony of loud conversation and laughter from the crowds who were pushing their way through the narrow streets.

We met Grace and Hugh in the tiny, yellow restaurant near the Villa Alatri. Sibella and Nonna were already there and Hugh was ordering drinks; he stood up when we arrived and shook hands with Adam, while Grace gushed about how Sofia and I were 'surely, just like two peas in a pod'.

'How do you like Sofia's little apartment?' I enquired casually, 'It's where I stayed when I first arrived.'

'It has a rather strange atmosphere,' said Grace thoughtfully, 'as if all the history from hundreds of years has found its way there and stuck. We love it! It's the reason we came to Europe, everywhere in the States is just so new.'

"My great grandfather came from this region of Italy,' added Hugh, 'but that was many years ago and the world has changed, and not necessarily for the better.' Nonna quickly translated this sentiment for Sibella and they nodded and tutted in agreement, well Hugh had certainly made a hit with them, just so long as they didn't start talking about biological clocks. I exchanged glances with Adam and Sofia and we smiled secret smiles, and I got the feeling that Grace would happily have left them reminiscing about the old days and run off down the street to cavort with the musicians and sing loud carols. Perhaps tomorrow we'd kidnap her.

Then we showed them the photograph of Caterina and Elisabetta, and they oo-ed and ah-ed about the strangeness of it all, and what a coincidence that I should turn up the way I did. It was quite late when we left the restaurant and the sky was starting to cloud over again. My phone buzzed, it was a text from Annabel, 'Where are you all?' it asked plaintively, and there was a little emoji of a face with one tear trickling down a cheek. She was sitting on the steps outside the villa when we got back. 'Huh, about time,' she groaned, 'I've been here absolutely ages, at least an hour! Where have you all been?'

Sofia opened the gate and we went inside; then we said goodbye and thank you to Hugh and Grace and wished them a very merry Christmas as they disappeared up the staircase to their little apartment.

'Who are they anyway?' asked Annabel, 'You might have told me you were going out!'

I felt sorry for her, she looked so forlorn. 'So, what happened, Annabel? I thought you'd be late back and that Gio would bring you, it's not even four. Anyway, how did you get back?'

'Oh, Gio, don't even mention him, I never want to hear his name again, ever!'

I looked at her anxiously, 'Oh god, Abel, what did he do? Are you alright?'

'No, I'm wounded, and utterly distraught. Do you know what he did?'

I shook my head, 'No, what? That's what I'm trying to find out!'

'Antonio came back this morning. It turned out they hadn't gone to Rimini, I got that bit wrong... and she said she wanted to come back to Venice for Christmas day. She's nothing but a... a floozy! A pneumatic floozy, and they were all over her, both of them, and ignoring me completely. Honestly, Kate, I have never been SO humiliated. Well, I left them to it, I don't care!'

'So how did you get back, did you take the vaporetto?'

She smiled smugly, 'What me, the vaporetto? No, of course not! Actually, I met this really dishy fisherman, he's about nineteen and absolutely gorgeous, he brought me back; so you see, I'm a panther.'

'I think you mean a cougar, Abel.'

'No, a panther, I prefer panthers…!'

'Still, I'm pleased you're back, we weren't sure about Gio in any case.'

'Stop, I said I never want to hear his name ever again!'

'That might be difficult; he is Adam's cousin after all.'

'Yes, Kate, he is, and if I were you, I'd be very careful; it could be the whole family is like that; only after one thing!'

'Speaking of which, the bed was full of your hair extensions. Adam thought they were spiders.'

'Spiders…? My hair extensions…' she paused for a moment and then she laughed, 'You wicked girl; you couldn't wait for me to go so that Adam could move in. Well, I hope he knows it was only for last night because no way am I sleeping up there in his room, it's much too spooky.'

CHAPTER 25

The next morning, we awoke to the sound of bells from the tower in St Mark's Square. Sofia told us that they would be ringing for the whole day in celebration and that she, Nonna and Sibella would be heading off to Mass before breakfast. I was almost tempted to join them, I knew it would please Sibella, especially after the way I'd run away the last time, when she'd virtually dragged me there; but it would have been hypocritical for me to go. Instead we promised to prepare the vegetables to go with the capon that Nonna had boiled the previous day. I was a bit disappointed about the lack of roast turkey, still, when in Rome, and all that.

Mum called soon after to wish us all a happy Christmas, and I spoke to Dad as well, and Flo, and by the time I got to Greg and Mary I was just about 'happy'd' out. After that Adam called Louise, and his mother and father, and Annabel called her parents and three young brothers, and by then Mass was nearly over and we still hadn't mashed the potatoes! Life must have been SO much easier before mobile phones!

I glanced out of the window; a handsome young man was standing in the courtyard; he saw me looking and smiled.

'It's Alessio,' shrieked Annabel and she rushed to open the door, 'you know, he gave me a lift back from Murano, yesterday, in his boat! Mmmm, isn't he gorgeous?'

He was actually; movie star gorgeous, almost too good to be true. He claimed the living room, poised like a Greek god, long limbed and fleet of foot, not to mention his come-hither smile and perfect white teeth! Yes, everything else faded into blurry insignificance next to Alessio.

'Alessio, how lovely to see you!' she purred with a flutter of eyelashes and a flick of her long, blonde, but now rather sparse, hair extensions. 'Oh, this is my best friend, Kate, and her um... boyfriend Adam.'

GAWD! How did she manage it?

'I have come to give you a gift,' he murmured. Well jolly good, presents too, Greek gods bearing gifts, you might say. Huh, some people have all the luck!

He handed her a tiny, silver package and she beamed up at him, 'Come on, Alessio, let's go out, then we can talk. It's very nice of you to bring me a present.'

Adam came over and gave me a squeeze and we watched as they walked across the courtyard and down the stone steps. 'Ooo... just the two of us, for a change; we should make the most of it!' he whispered, seductively, and I was just about to surrender to his multiple charms when Sofia came up the steps supporting an old lady on each arm. All three were wearing headscarves, and looking suitably pious and holier than thou. 'Damn, foiled again!' muttered Adam.

We exchanged our gifts in front of the fire in the living room; richly patterned scarves from the Rialto market, and fragrant soaps, and chocolates. They were all fairly predictable adult presents, but I got a pair of soft, leather gloves in a lovely shade of blue and lined in purple silk, a gift from Sofia; and Adam and I gave Sofia and the old ladies beautifully ornate, Venetian papier-mache masks that were 'made in Italy', explained the vendor, 'not China, like the ones they sell in the market!'

When Annabel returned, she was wearing a pretty string of beads in green, Murano glass, that she twirled around her little finger in much the same way as she twirled Library Joe, and Gio, and Alessio and countless others.

'Alessio says they match my eyes, and he's taking me out on his boat tomorrow,' she said, and she smiled, Gio already forgotten, consigned to the dustbin of the past, 'isn't it romantic?'

I had one gift remaining; Mum had tucked it in my suitcase at the last moment and made me promise not to open it until Christmas day. It was wrapped in white tissue paper and tied with a pink ribbon, and had a little note attached that I hadn't noticed before.

'What does it say?' cried Annabel.

I read it aloud, 'This is a Biba original from 1967, it belonged to Auntie Pat and now it's yours. No one has ever worn it so maybe you can? Hope you're having a lovely Christmas with your friends in Venice. Love, Mum xxxx'

I tore off the tissue and held it up for all to see.

'It's lovely,' cried Sofia, 'look at the lace and the frilly neckline.'

'What is it?' asked Annabel.

'Bella…' murmured Nonna and Sibella.

'Yes, but what's it for?' asked Annabel again.

'It's a nightdress, isn't it obvious?' I said, and I caught Adam's eye. I could see he thought it was funny, probably imagining me tripping to the bathroom in it. Actually, tripping would be a hazard because it was really long.

'Puritan chic,' declared Annabel, 'about as sexy and enticing as Bridget Jones' big knickers!'

We were all speechless after that, so we poured some drinks and sat for a while enjoying the fire; then we carried the vegetables and boiled capon to Sibella's for lunch, along with a soft sponge, crammed with dried fruits, and Sibella's favourite, chocolate mousse, for dessert. She wanted to show us her Christmas present, delivered the day before, from one of her daughters in Milan. It was a television set with a giant screen and it dominated the room, perched as it was, on top of an antique chest of drawers. It still needed connecting and I wondered why one of her children hadn't bothered to visit her to set it up. It seemed odd to me, and not at all typical of Italian families who usually value family connections. At some point I'd have to ask Sofia about that.

Hugh and Grace came down later; Grace carried a tambourine and Hugh his battered old guitar. 'We can't have a proper Christmas without a few choruses of Silent Night,' he said, so we all trooped out into the courtyard and the air was soon filled with our raucous renditions of carols old and new.

CHAPTER 26

We left Venice the day after Boxing Day and I was really sad to go. The old ladies came out to see us off and Sibella hugged me as if she knew she'd never see me again. It brought tears to my eyes and I promised to return as soon as I was able. Then Sofia and Nonna hugged us all and came out onto the stone steps to wave as we made our way up the alley. The vaporetto arrived almost straight away, bumping up against the little quay in water that was choppy and grey, and we turned and watched as the church of San Stae disappeared into the distance.

England had the same air of despondency; the airport was almost empty for a change, and no one seemed bothered about who we were, or where we'd been. It was as if everything and everyone had suddenly slowed down, deprived of energy and momentum, like a toy when the battery is running low.

The O'Connors still hadn't returned and I didn't blame them, and it was nice to have the house to ourselves; just me and Annabel because Adam got off the tube at Kentish Town. We saw him walking along a nearly empty platform as our train pulled out of the station, the wind from the tunnel lifting his hair as he swung his bag over one shoulder and headed for the escalator.

Nothing had changed, our beautiful sprayed branches that we'd been so proud of, now looked heavy and untidy, crowding the already over-filled room with unnecessary tat; and some of our Christmas cards had fallen off the shelf onto the floor. 'Right, kettle...!' declared Annabel as I marched around turning on all the lamps, and then the television, sifting through several channels before I came to something vaguely acceptable; and when we finally slumped on the sofa, with our mugs of tea and a packet of chocolate digestives, the world suddenly seemed brighter.

'I thought your brother and his girlfriend were supposed to be staying here,' said Annabel after a while, 'you know, because Flo was embarrassed about Jim and her being an item. You don't think...' she eyed my bedroom door and raised her eyebrows questioningly just as it opened and Greg stuck his head out. 'Oh, you're back! I thought you were due tomorrow! Sorry, we were asleep; slight hangovers, old Jim's a bit radical with the cocktails.'

'Greg!' I was happy to see him, but where was I meant to sleep?

It was fine though because they set off for Mum's a couple of hours later, after cheese toasties and more tea, and I promised to go around the following day with Annabel, and Adam, assuming he wasn't heading straight up north to his other woman, my rival, the child- encumbered, Earth mother Dawn.

I was pleased to get to bed and I lay there for nearly an hour reflecting on how my life had changed. It had an added dimension, gone from being narrow, and predictable, to wildly unpredictable. It made me think of a poem I'd liked at school; 'Two roads diverged in a wood, and I, Took the one less travelled by... And that has made all the difference.'

Then I went to sleep and slept like a baby for nine hours.

CHAPTER 27

Adam arrived early the next morning; Annabel was up before me and she went down to open the front door. I could hear them talking as they clumped noisily up the stairs, so I shut myself in the bathroom to splash some water on my face.

'Ah... did you miss us already?' teased Annabel, 'poor Adam, all alone...'

'Yeah, Abel, actually I did.' Adam sat down on the sofa, I knew he had because the ancient springs pinged, 'Er... where's Kate?'

'Bathroom,' I yelled, 'be there in a tick!'

The cemetery gate was locked again at our end. Now that they were charging for entry, they needed to be sure that everyone bought a ticket, unless you had a relative in there, or two, as I did. Actually, as it turned out, I had more than two; there was Lucia Caterina di Lazio for a start, and maybe Elisabetta and her family? I'd have to find out.

We trudged wearily up the hill. A pall of lethargy still hung over north London; there was hardly any traffic and very few people on the streets. No doubt, it was the same everywhere else, everyone indoors, eating last week's turkey and watching the same inane, quiz program with some overblown reality-star, on the box.

It was just like the old days at Mum's, when Greg and I were teenagers and the house was full of noise and the fridge was always empty. As soon as Mum opened the front door, a tan coloured dachshund, with black ears, careered towards us. 'Don't let it out!' she screamed, 'It keeps trying to get away!'

Dad's dog, they'd actually done it! 'Ahhh... Battersea dogs' home?' I enquired sympathetically.

'Yeah, cute...!' murmured Adam unconvincingly when it tried to mate with his leg.

'It looks like an overstuffed German sausage!' declared Annabel as she edged around it.

Mum picked it up, 'Heavens, no, Fritz isn't ours; we're just looking after him for the woman over the road. She's away at the moment and all the kennels were full, but he thinks she's still there; very confusing for a dog, isn't it?'

Greg, Mary, Flo and Jim were sitting around the table, empty apart from a bowl of crisps and a box of Dairy Milk Chocolates, and Dad was on his favourite armchair in the corner, so they were six in all, plus the escapologist dog, but we made nine so extra chairs were gathered from around the house and we all squashed in while Mum boiled water in her super large kettle for cups of tea.

'So, Adam, what do you do?' asked Dad. I knew he was only trying to be friendly, but he might just as well have said, 'Tell me son, what are your prospects, and can you keep my daughter in the manner to which she has become accustomed?' Still Adam didn't seem to mind. 'I'm a freelance travel writer,' he said, 'Europe mainly but happy to explore further afield if necessary.'

Mum glared at Dad, and banged a bowl of walnuts and the nutcrackers down on the shelf next to him, but he just gazed back at her with a bewildered expression on his weathered face.

Greg's fiancée, Mary, with her plummy accent and big white teeth, seemed to take to Annabel immediately; she'd obviously recognised her as one of their own. Was there something I was missing; some secret sign that I wasn't aware of, like the Masonic handshake, for instance?

'Oh, where were you at school, Annabel? Yes, wonderful hacking country! I was at Highgrove, yah, all jolly nice gels... And how many horses do you have now?'

Then Flo leapt to her feet and banged her spoon on the table, 'Erm... now everyone's here, I... that is we... Jim and I, would like to make an announcement. Go on... you tell them Jim!'

Jim stood up, 'Flo and I are getting married!' he announced without preamble, 'I think she's a wonderful woman and I don't understand why she's never be snapped up before; I suppose I'm just lucky that she waited for me!'

'Hoorah for Flo and Jim,' cried Mary plummily.

Dad nearly dropped a cup of tea in his lap at the prospect of his old Auntie Flo finally tying the knot, but Mum smiled benevolently and went to find champagne glasses for the Tesco's best that she'd been keeping for New Year's Eve.

Flo smiled round at everyone, 'We're getting married in May, the little church in our village. I've chosen my dress already. Will you be my Matron of Honour, Katherine, please?'

Matron of Honour, me! Why not bridesmaid, or, at least, Maid of Honour? Did I look that old and decrepit? Weren't Matrons of Honour supposed to be married, at least?

'I'd love to, Flo,' I said through gritted teeth, 'it will be an honour to be your Matron of Honour!'

'Psst…' hissed Annabel. I looked around to see where the 'psst' was coming from. The door to the hall was ajar and an anxious eye was peering through at me, so I got up as quietly as I could and sidled towards the door to join her in the hall. 'What's up?' I asked, 'why are you out here? Mary will miss you, you know.'

'She's a bit full-on horsy, and to be honest I'm not that keen… I got kicked in the knee once when I was small…'

'For goodness sake,' I gasped in exasperation, 'what's up? Why are you out here? And why is the front door open…? Oh my GOD! You've let the dog out, haven't you?'

'Why are you two out here?' whispered Adam through the crack in the door.

'Oh, hi Adam, I've lost my earring, diamond, very expensive present from Mummy, might even be Tiffany… Please Kate, don't look at me like that, I didn't mean it; I just opened the front door to see if it was on the step and Adolf, um… Ernst… Herman…?'

She looked at me questioningly and I glared back, 'Fritz!'

'Yes, Fritz, he's scarpered, gone AWOL!'

'So why didn't you catch him?'

'He went, fast as a bullet! Whoosh... gone!'

I closed the front door behind us as quietly as I could, 'Quick, we have to get him back, before anyone notices! Come on, Adam, we'll go this way. Abel, you check down there!'

We tore up the road, looking under every hedge and in any front garden that looked vaguely promising from the point of view of a good, long sniff, but there was no sign of Fritz. We'd nearly reached the park when it started to pour, and Adam grabbed my hand and we ran to shelter under a large oak.

He put his arm around my shoulders and grinned down at me, 'No sign of the German sausage; s'pose it could be anywhere, might even be halfway to Hamburg.'

'No, Adam, not funny, Mum will have a fit if anything has happened to him. I wonder if they've missed us yet.'

'Actually, Kate, I wanted to ask you something and I haven't had the chance up till now, one way or another. My landlord wants to sell the house, so I was wondering ... you might think it's too soon, so just say if you do...' I gulped; eek, surely he wasn't going to propose, after all, we'd only known each other for a few months.

'I thought we could maybe find something together, you know, a little apartment, or even a big one if Annabel wants to come too, though preferably just you and me. You know, the other night in Venice was really special, I don't want to rush you... but it was, wasn't it?'

Oh, right, yes, a proposal of sorts, or the usual, modern day equivalent, the 'let's shack up together proposal', with the obligatory 'get-out clause'. Still, it was an attractive idea, more than attractive actually, so I smiled at him and nodded, and he picked me up and swung me round in the limited space that was available. I was quite dizzy when he put me down. The rain was splashing onto the leaves above us, but it felt snug and enclosed, like a green and limpid room. 'You've got a drip running down your nose,' laughed Adam, and he wiped it away and bent to kiss me. 'Phone,' he said, and he changed his mind about kissing me and took his mobile out of his pocket instead.

'Hi, Adam,' purred a woman's voice; he pressed it close to his ear and I struggled to hear, but the noise of the rain made it too difficult to catch her words.

'Okay, that's great; see you soon,' he said and put it back in his pocket.

'Was it Louise?' I queried, and he shook his head, 'Dawn?' I asked, and regretted it immediately, her name had just slipped out, of its own accord, you might say.

'His eyes narrowed, 'Dawn? Why did you say Dawn? Yes, well I do know a Dawn but... Hey, have you been listening to my calls?'

'Well, not on purpose, it wasn't intentional, there was a draught and I went to close the door and your voice was echoing down the stairs; Sofia's house is very um... echo-y, not many carpets I suppose that's why...'

I cringed; he obviously thought I was mad; or worse, suspicious and manipulative.

'No, it's fine,' he said, 'and you're bound to be uneasy with any relationship after the way Tom behaved, I was just the same after Lydia left. Still, you should have asked me, Kate, I could have cleared up the misunderstanding straightaway.'

I felt ashamed of myself, but I still had to ask, 'So, who is she, Adam?'

'She's my agent, with loads of experience in the travel business; she lives up in York and she's a very nice woman...'

I wasn't reassured!

'And she's in her sixties,'

Um... better, maybe...

'Well preserved though...'

What like a jar of pickled onions?

'...and she lives in an amazing house; I keep my car up there, it's just a temporary arrangement until I get somewhere to park down here. It's impossible where I live at the moment; really nice motor as well; my uncle left it to me. I'll take you out in it one day.'

I still wasn't entirely convinced, after all, what about the kids?

'Has she got any children?' I asked innocently.

'Yes, a couple, they're probably about our age though,' he paused. 'Oh, you heard that bit too, did you, when I sent love to the kids?'

'Yes, I'm sorry Adam, I didn't mean to listen; really I didn't.'

'Well there are four actually, and their names are Marilyn Monroe, Fred Astaire, Ginger Rogers and Gregory Peck. There should have been five, but poor old Charlie Chaplin didn't make it!'

I gazed at him open-mouthed.

'They're goats, you idiot. She rescued Marilyn Monroe and Fred Astaire because no one wanted them, but then Marilyn turned out to be pregnant and the others arrived. Dawn helped deliver them so now she refers to them as her kids, which I suppose they are.'

Well, it was vaguely plausible, I supposed.

'And anyway, that was Annabel on the phone to say that Fritz was sitting on the doorstep when she went back, couldn't wait to get indoors apparently.'

I sighed with relief. 'I wonder if she found her earring.'

'Let's hope so, after all, it might even be from Tiffany's...'

He took my hand and we wandered slowly down the hill.

'So, was it creepy when you slept upstairs? You know, in the Villa Alatri.'

'It was eerie, I'll admit. And there were strange sounds, almost like mumbled conversation. The trouble is, if you allow your mind to go down that track it... well it begins to imagine things, do you know what I mean? Those things that normally you'd ignore quite happily; it could easily have been just the wind in the chimneys, but I started to convince myself that... it sounds really silly...'

'No, it's not Adam, go on tell me.'

'Sometimes I'm sure I heard laughter, every now and again; and music. It's probably what I said, just my brain playing tricks, adding sounds that aren't there.'

I felt offended, after all, he knew about my dreams and my odd connection to Caterina and Elisabetta di Lazio; and he'd witnessed my strange lapses in the glass works, and in the old kitchen. 'I see, so you think it's just my brain playing tricks as well?' I murmured crossly.

'Absolutely not,' said Adam, 'I'm sorry, that was tactless of me, but I guess it's easier for me to explain it like that, the alternative is too frightening. I've never been very good at dealing with ghosts, and hauntings, any of that stuff.'

'You didn't see anything though, did you?' I asked; and for a moment, in my mind's eye, I saw the face that stared up at me from the courtyard, but he was gone in an instant before I could identify it; though why I should recognise anyone who was long dead was a mystery, and what use would it be if I could?

Adam shook his head, 'No, I didn't see anything; nothing at all.'

When we got back, no one appeared to have missed us, or if they had they weren't saying, and the dynamic Fritz was hiding under the table. Flo and Mum were waxing lyrical on the subject of wedding dresses, and Mary had trapped Annabel in the corner and was in the process of interrogating her on the subject of her family connections, and the 'English Aristocracy in the Marches'; which she told me later were the medieval borders between realms. Well, you learn something new every day! She managed to disentangle herself eventually, and after hugs and good wishes all round, we set off for home.

The gate was open and the downstairs lights were on when we got back. The O'Connors were back from their extended holiday in the Emerald Isle.

'You can stay over if you like, Adam,' I said hopefully, 'we're allowed visitors you know.'

'Yes, and don't mind me,' added Annabel, 'I can wear ear plugs if you like; I won't even know you're there.'

Adam laughed, 'Cheeky woman…! And that's very kind of you, but I won't come in. Sorry Kate, you know how it is, I've got an early start in the morning and I've got my stuff to sort out. Dawn will expect me to be ready for the off.'

'Dawn,' mouthed Annabel, 'ready for the off?' but she must have noticed my stricken expression because she added; 'I might go in and leave you to your farewells. See you in a mo, Kate.'

Adam put his arms around me and hugged me close, and I saw the curtains twitch and Eileen's face peeping out at me, probably disapprovingly.

'See you in four days' time, on New Year's Day, but I'll call, and text. I've got to go, I'm self-employed and I rely on Dawn to get me the work. All this travelling has got me behind with everything.'

'Why don't you write about it then? Christmas in Venice, it's sure to be a winner with all the Sunday papers and the colour supplements!'

'Yeah, I wish, but it's a bit of a closed shop without a decent agent.'

We said goodbye and I watched him walk away, a dark shadowy figure with an orange tinge under the amber glow of the street lights.

He turned to wave from the gloom and I waved back until he was out of sight and suddenly it was silent, just me in the dark street, all alone.

'Why are you out of breath?' asked Annabel, 'Did you run up the stairs? I saw Eileen and Mick on the way up...'

Eileen and Mick?

'...and Eileen showed me a picture of their new granddaughter, Lysette Eileen, really cute but completely bald!'

'Lots of babies are bald, Abel. Unusual name isn't it?'

'What Eileen? Yeah, quite unusual, after her I suppose.'

'No, I mean Lysette, gorgeous, but not Irish surely?'

'It's because her husband is Dutch, maybe she's named after his mother, or his sister; she met him down on the docks, Dublin Bay, I expect. So romantic...'

Honestly, how did she find out these little 'snippets'? I had to hand it to her; she'd make a brilliant double agent, 'A bel Leggup, International spy!'

'Anyway, never mind about Adam, you've still got me, and I've got a present for you! Look, Limoncello; delicious, we can pretend we're still in Italy. And four days is nothing Kate, but, just out of interest, who is this Dawn person?'

I sighed, 'She's his agent, and she's got four kids.'

'Well that's okay, as long as they're not Adam's kids; they're not, are they?'

'No, actually they really are kids, of the goat variety, there's Marilyn Monroe and Fred Astaire, hang on, I'll remember the others in a second. They're all old movie stars.'

'That's pretty remarkable for goats, you must admit. How many movies have goats in them, unless they're documentaries?'

I gazed at her in disbelief.

'I'm joking, you idiot, I know who Marilyn Monroe is, and Fred Astaire. What are the others called, have you remembered yet?'

'Yes, Gregory Peck and Ginger Rogers; poor old Charlie Chaplin didn't make it!'

'Brilliant…! Tragic about Charlie though. She sounds like a laugh, this Dawn; you'd probably get on really well.'

'What, like you and Mary, my sister-in-law to be?' I laughed, 'Why are you making that face?'

She handed me a glass of Limoncello, 'Look, I'll say only this, rather you than me! Chink-chink...'

CHAPTER 28

'I'm singing in the rain...' went my phone and I seized it joyfully. I still hadn't changed my dial tone, it reminded me of my first day in Venice, when Shirl had rescued me from loneliness and despondency, and every time I heard it, I felt uplifted and breezy. It didn't this time though. It was nearly eleven and I hadn't had so much as a 'good morning' text from Adam, and sadly it wasn't Adam this time either, but in my haste, I'd answered it without checking.

'Helloooo...' I cried happily, 'Adam, about time; what happened?'

OOPS...!

'Is that Katherine Elliot,' said a no-nonsense voice that I recognised straight away as Barb from the agency; surely, they didn't work in the school holidays, you'd think that would be one of the perks of the job!

'I'm just sorting out my stand-ins for January,' said Barb, 'and there will be lots of vacancies. It's a bad month for illness; you know influenza, coughs, colds, chickenpox, measles...'

Great, she was really selling it to me!

'We like to get everything planned before school starts again. I'm assuming you're available, no more last minute hols; or family traumas?'

It was no good, I had to go back to work or I'd run out of cash! 'Yes, I'm free, Barb, not sure for how long though.'

'That's great, we'll work with that, and I'll need to speak to your friend as well.'

Annabel was listening to my one-sided conversation and her face said it all. She was shaking her head wildly and gurning horribly.

'Um... it might be difficult,' I said, 'because she's away at the moment in... er... Barbados...'

'Lucky girl, so when's she back?'

'I'm not sure when she gets back.'

'Never...!' hissed Annabel, wrapping her fingers round her throat and making choking noises. I struggled not to laugh.

'Is someone there with you?' asked Barb suspiciously.

'No, it's just me; and the cat...' I frowned at Annabel.

'Look Barb, I've got to tell you,' I paused and took a deep breath, 'I'm not going back to St Job's, and from now on I'm not teaching anyone over the age of eleven, actually, make that eight; and... only North London, in this area. There are loads of schools around here so if you want me on your books, well, those are my conditions.'

'No problem, you should have said before. You've just always been so capable and obliging, up till now.'

Adam hadn't called by midday or by three, or eight, or any time in between according to my phone; and I'd called him at least ten times.

'He could be in some remote area where there's no reception,' suggested Annabel, 'the Yorkshire

Dales maybe, I think it's still quite primitive up there...'

Well, it was a possibility.

'...so stop moping! Let's go down the pub, there's karaoke!'

The Royal Oak public house was full to overflowing; people were obviously desperate to get out again, freed from their self-imposed exile. Mick and Eileen O'Connor were there, tucked away in a corner with a couple of red-faced guys who were downing pints of Guinness. They called us over to join them and Mick fought his way through the crowd at the bar to buy our drinks. Someone was singing 'I'll take you home again Kathleen' into a karaoke machine, cheered along by a large and noisy Irish contingent, who all seemed to know each other. Then a band arrived with a couple of fiddlers playing Irish jigs, and a pretty dark-haired girl who sang nostalgic Irish melodies, and by the time the 'last orders' bell was rung there was such an atmosphere of bonhomie that it was hard to feel depressed. Annabel took Mick's arm and they danced along the street together, both a little worse for wear, while Eileen and I strolled behind and she told me all about how wonderful it was being a grandmother, and how they couldn't wait to sell up and return to Ireland.

Adam didn't call the next day either, and even Annabel got tired of jollying me along. She was meeting Library Joe in a nightclub to 'ring in the

New Year', no doubt surrounded by drunks throwing up, and girls collapsing in the street.

'You have to come,' she implored, 'it's no good hanging around waiting for someone to call and thinking the worst! Adam could have lost his phone. You've got to lighten up, I'll ask Joe to bring a friend; he knows some really fit guys from his gym... yum... You can borrow my red dress.'

By the evening, with still no word, she'd almost convinced me. After all, I reasoned, he could have used Dawn's phone, and I knew she had a phone because I'd heard him speaking to her on it. I wasn't sure if I wanted to borrow Annabel's red dress though, I was a bit particular about who saw my underwear, but I got my little black dress out of the wardrobe and hung it on a hook on my bedroom door, then I lay down on the bed and stared at it, trying to decide whether or not to put it on. Maybe I was giving up on Adam too readily; I mean, there was sure to be an explanation, wasn't there? I could still go out; it wouldn't mean that I was on the prowl for a bit of action, or a one-night stand, would it?

'You're coming, hooray...' screamed Annabel when I emerged a few minutes later, 'and you look amazing. Joe's friend will be well impressed!'

'It's not for Joe's friend, it's for me,' I said, 'and I'm only coming out because I know Adam wouldn't want me to be miserable on New Year's Eve, would he?'

'No, he wouldn't, of course he wouldn't. Er... do you want to borrow some heels? I'm going to wear my Portobello boots and you'll look really short if you wear those… flats!' She squeezed through the door into her box room and I heard her rummaging through one of her drawers. 'Here you go, they're Manolo Blahniks and incredibly comfortable, and they're not high, only three inches. Red, so they'll liven up that black dress, aren't they gorgeous? And you can borrow my sparkly throw-over, if you like?'

It was nearly nine o'clock when we went out, and it took me a good five minutes to get down the stairs. 'Don't think I can do it, Abel…' I screamed after I tripped and only just managed to catch the banister in time, 'I'm going to break something, my neck probably!'

'Rubbish…!' she yelled up at me from the bottom of the chasm that was the stairs, 'You'll get used to it and don't you dare take them off, you just need to practice!'

Still, I made it down eventually and Eileen and Mick came out and told us how wonderful we looked, and we wished them a Happy New Year and I staggered out onto the path like a drunk in drag. What was I thinking? I wouldn't even make it to the tube station at this rate!

Someone was coming up the road.

'God, its Adam,' cried Annabel, 'look, you won't have to come out after all. Good thing if you ask me, wouldn't fancy your chances on the escalator!'

Adam? I couldn't believe it; rescued from certain death from a plunge down the escalator at Archway Station! Adam! WOW, my hero!

I threw myself at him as he turned into the gate, then I took off the dreaded Manolo Blahniks and we ran upstairs! It was sheer bliss having him back, but I still needed to know why he hadn't been in touch.

'Well, Adam, did you forget me completely?' I asked, and I smiled sweetly so that he thought I didn't mind that much, not really, even though I did; but to be honest, I didn't want to frighten him off.

'I'm so sorry darling,' he murmured softly, 'I lost my phone, and I don't know any of my numbers, so I couldn't even use Dawn's. It's ridiculous, I rely on it totally, for contacts, emails, everything... but I won't in future, that's for sure.'

I knew there was an explanation, obviously. How could I ever have thought otherwise?

CHAPTER 29

It was freezing when we woke up so it was lucky I had someone to share my bed. I snuggled up close to Adam for a cuddle, but he was still fast asleep so I got up and I put on my thermal top and thick dressing gown, just to go to the bathroom. If anything, it was even colder in there, I almost expected to see icicles hanging off the taps, or a polar bear sitting in the bath. One of those big, furry, white ones with a benign expression! Gawd, I really had to lay off the Limoncello! When I came out, Adam was curled up on the sofa wrapped in a blanket, 'You'd better tell your mate Mick the heating's kaput,' he groaned, 'of course, it might just be the thermostat that needs tweaking.'

A thermostat that needed tweaking! Why did I always end up with men who were totally incompetent when it came to simple house maintenance? What I needed was a Jim; Flo had got that right.

'Look, tell you what, I've got a couple of plug-in fan heaters at my place, I might go over and get them. I'll jog so it won't take long.'

I sniggered, 'Well, they'll warm one bit at least, so I'll look forward to that.'

'Morning, Mick, Happy New Year!' he shouted as he ran past a startled Mr. O'Connor on the stairs, 'Oh, and did you know the heating's kaput?'

'Sure, I were just on my way t' fix it. F'sure, tis the fecking termostat...!'

At least, I think that was what he said, his accent had become somewhat stronger since our night out with his Irish rebel compatriots in the Royal Oak.

There was no sign of Annabel; she hadn't come in during the night and I wondered briefly if she was okay. No, she'd be fine, she was a survivor, wasn't she?

I was getting dressed when my phone sang its merry ditty. It was a woman's voice, and she was crying so hard that I couldn't make out who it was to begin with, but it was Sofia, not Annabel.

'Sofia, what's wrong, what's happened?' I gasped, but she continued to cry softly and when, at last, she managed to answer, her words were punctuated by heart-wrenching sobs.

'Kate, it's… Sibella…she's dead, the police have been; they think she was… murdered… I went to Verona, to take Nonna home… and when I came back this morning… her door was open… and she was just lying there, on the floor.'

Murdered? Sibella, how was that possible? And why Sibella, she was the sweetest old lady, she would never hurt a soul. I fell backwards onto the bed as the blood drained from my head and I thought for a moment that I was going to faint. I didn't know what to say, and then I began to cry too. 'We'll come back Sofia,' I murmured between sobs, 'Adam and me, we'll help in any way we can. You can't stay there alone, what if someone came back… for you?'

She calmed a little then, 'I have to stay, at least until the police have taken statements from myself, and the neighbours. She lived here all her life, so everyone knew her. Don't worry; they'll look out for me. I just needed to tell you, I know how attached you'd become.'

'We'll come,' I assured her, 'as soon as we possibly can. And I'm so sorry Sofia; she was wonderful and so kind to me when she found me in the courtyard...' tears poured down my cheeks as I recalled her kindness that night. I didn't know what else to say; my heart was racing, and my inadequate words just stuck in my throat.

I was bereft. Who would murder an old woman, and why? I was still there when Annabel got back. She came into my room carrying her vintage boots and complaining about the blisters on her feet, and about how the house was, in her opinion, 'colder than a penguin's bum!'

'What the hell is wrong?' she demanded when she saw my tear-stained face, 'it's that Adam again, isn't it? The bastard, wait till I see him!'

'Sibella's dead,' I murmured, and I began to sob again, 'they think she might have been murdered.'

She sat down on the bed next to me and began to wail, and we were still there when Adam returned with a fan heater in each hand.

'God, you two, I know it's cold but there's no need to carry on like that. Look, I'll plug these in; you'll be warm as toast before you can say Happy New Year.'

'It's not happy, Adam,' I gasped, 'not happy at all; Sibella's dead!' And he slumped on the bed too while I repeated everything that Sofia had told me, which wasn't much. 'It's… such a shock,' he said at last, 'we'll get over there. She's going to need help sorting everything out!'

Annabel mopped her eyes on my quilt cover, 'I'm coming too, so don't try to stop me!'

'Of course, you can come, Abel,' I murmured, 'I want you to come, you're my best friend… we need you…'

Adam switched on his laptop, 'Day after tomorrow; how does that sound?' I'll have to call Dawn and put everything on hold for a week or so.'

A week, how would that be enough? Still, it would do for a start; and I'd have to call Barb and explain why I wasn't available, though she'd never believe me, would she?

We bought our plane tickets on line; we'd be leaving on the third of January and arriving in Venice at four in the afternoon; my third trip in as many months.

Adam stayed again, I needed him there. I couldn't cope on my own, nor could Annabel, or, I suspect, could he, we were all in such a state of shock.

The heating was still off when we went to bed so I put on my long, white nightie with my thick cardigan over the top and a pair of woolly socks; not a good look, but I didn't care. I resembled someone's ancient granny; perhaps I could wear my long nightie when we went to Flo's wedding, in my role as Matron of Honour?

CHAPTER 30

I was aware how cold I was before I opened my eyes. It bit into me, chilling my blood, and numbing my aching fingers, as gusts of wind lifted my hair and froze my neck and ears. 'Adam...' I murmured, and I reached out for him, but he wasn't there, he'd gone, again!

I lifted my hands to rub away the tears that were streaming down my cheeks, and when I opened my eyes, I understood why I was so cold. The beautiful, marble angel stood before me, her features marred by her resentful expression, her arm raised and her finger pointing accusingly; Lucia Caterina di Lazio. The moonlight glinted on her, outlining her body and her outstretched arm, with an eerie glow, and she seemed to turn her head slightly to look down on me. I wanted to scream, but I was paralysed with fear, and who would hear me anyway in the midst of this endless forest of tombstones. Why did no one notice when I climbed out of bed, and went down the stairs and out into the night? And Adam, why didn't he stop me? Did he even know that I'd gone? I looked down at my feet; my woolly socks were muddy and torn, and brambles poked through them; sticking into my wet skin, and clinging, leech-like, to the lace on the hem of Auntie Pat's ruined nightdress.

The moon disappeared behind a cloud and, for a moment or two, I was plunged into terrifying darkness; then the sky cleared and my eyes were drawn to a small gravestone on the other side of the path. GIOVANNI VICENZA, it said, and underneath his name, in an elaborate Victorian script, were the words, 'Vengeance is mine'.

A sudden noise made me turn; it was Adam, Adam Vicenza! I staggered backwards, scrabbling frantically through the tangled undergrowth.

'Stop...!' he said, 'Kate, stop, for goodness sake, what are you doing out here? You'll catch your death!'

'Stay away from me!' I yelled; my voice sounded insane, irrational. A sudden terrible thought came into my head, 'Where have you been for the last three days, Adam? Did you kill Sibella? Is that what this is all about?'

He reached out for me as I lay sprawled amongst the brambles and weeds, and I recoiled. 'Have you gone completely mad?' he asked, 'Why would I want to kill Sibella?'

'For the necklace; just like him, Giovanni Vicenza...' He lunged at me then, and held my arms as I tried to fight him off, but he was too strong for me.

'Enough, enough, stop now...' He seized my wrists and pulled me to my feet, 'You know that none of this makes any sense, I couldn't kill anyone; nothing would be worth that. God, Kate, look at the state of you, your feet are torn to shreds!'

He was right, of course, I knew he wouldn't kill anyone, but Sibella's death was more than I could cope with; it had tipped me over when I was already teetering on the edge.

I fell against him and he lifted me up, holding me close as he staggered over the uneven ground and down the steep hill, watched silently by a thousand unseeing eyes. The gate at the bottom was open just enough for us to squeeze through, an oversight that had allowed me to enter in the first place; coincidence, or fate? I was past caring.

The light was on, and Annabel was awake, when we climbed back up the stairs. Adam put me down as soon as the front door closed behind us; he just couldn't carry me any further. I ached all over, and my feet felt as if they were on fire; I struggled to reach the top, but Annabel was there waiting and she helped me to the sofa.

'What the hell were you doing?' she asked crossly, but Adam shook his head, and she knelt down beside me and took my hand when I began to cry noisily. 'I'm sorry, Kate, but we were worried, and it's really lucky that Adam was here, and that he woke up when he did. You could have died from hypothermia!'

I dried my eyes on my sleeve, 'Thank you, Adam!' I said, 'but how did you know where I'd gone? Just because I wasn't in bed, why did you assume I was wandering around in the cemetery? I don't think my first thought would have been, 'Oh Adam's not in bed, he must be having a late-night stroll through a graveyard'.'

He stroked my hair and tried to smile. 'I noticed your side of the bed was empty, the sheet was cold, and the room was freezing, even colder than you'd expect with the heating off. Then I realised that all the doors were open, and there was a gale blowing up the stairs, so I ran down into the street, and there you were, in the cemetery and halfway up the hill. Honestly, you looked like a ghost in that white night-gown and you seemed to know exactly where you were heading. I ran back up for my coat and shoes, and then I chased after you. You'd turned off when I reached the top and you were walking down a narrow path. It was overgrown with weeds, and I knew then that you were sleep walking because there were sharp stones and thorns, yet nothing seemed to stop you, you just kept on walking.'

Annabel shuddered, 'It sounds like something out of some Gothic horror movie! You poor thing, you must have been terrified when you woke up and found yourself there. Quick, get her a drink, Adam!'

He heated some hot milk, with a large measure of whisky, and I sipped it while they removed what was left of my socks, exclaiming all the while about the state of me. I was still chilled to the bone and shaking with shock, and my feet were caked with mud; worst of all, I felt overwhelmed with exhaustion, and guilt from the things I'd said to Adam. Then Annabel went for a bowl of hot, soapy water and they washed my muddy feet, gently, but firmly, and smothered them in antiseptic cream till I reeked. My nightdress was only fit for the bin, and after all those years languishing in Auntie Pat's linen drawer.

'I'm so sorry,' I repeated at regular intervals, until it started to sound monotonous, even to me.

'Stop apologising, for goodness sake,' moaned Annabel as she brushed the leaves out of my hair, 'I've had enough, I'm going back to bed; we'll talk about it in the morning!'

I was amazed that Adam wanted to get into bed with me, after the horrible things I'd said, but he did, and surprisingly I went straight to sleep. In spite of all that had happened, I felt that something had been resolved, as if, maybe, everything was coming to an end, though heavens alone knew what kind of an end it would be.

CHAPTER 31

I was alone when I woke up and I could hear whispered conversation from the other side of the door; Adam and Annabel, they were discussing me, I was certain of that. They were probably deciding how best to deal with their delusional friend. It was a good thing Bedlam was no longer an option or I'd be there, wrapped in a strait jacket and howling at the moon.

They brought me breakfast on a tray, and then sat on the end of the bed in silence while I nibbled unenthusiastically on a piece of toast.

'Do you remember the angel,' I asked them, 'the one over the grave of Lucia? I told you about it before.'

Adam nodded, 'Yes, I remember. You found it when Shirl came to visit; it upset you then as well.'

I saw Annabel glance at Adam and she raised her eyebrows, but he ignored her. 'Go on, Kate,' he said, 'what about the angel?'

'I didn't notice before because it was during the day, but last night, when the moon came out from behind the clouds, the light streamed down her arm illuminating a headstone just across the path. It sounds insane, but I'm sure she's pointing to the gravestone of the man who murdered Caterina!'

Annabel stared at me like I'd gone mad, but I was starting to get used to it, 'It's a bit far-fetched, Kate! Why would he be there?'

'I don't know, but it can't be coincidence, and I just need to explain to Adam why I shouted at him.' I glanced at him and tears ran down my cheeks, 'I'm really sorry Adam, but I wasn't in a rational state of mind!' Irrational state of mind; was that another term for insanity?

'Er… right, so who is in there?' asked Annabel.

'Giovanni Vicenza…' I whispered it quietly, hoping to somehow reduce its potency.

'Adam, did you know he was there?' she asked him.

He rubbed his eyes; he looked tired. 'No, not until last night, I mean, I'd heard we had distant family buried there. I told Kate that, ages ago, when we first met, well it feels like ages…' he stopped and smiled at me, 'actually it was only November. Anyway, why would it have any bearing on my behaviour, even if we are related? Maybe, it's a completely different family, it might be quite a common name,' he added, though he looked doubtful.

'Odd, isn't it, Adam? Especially as Kate is a direct descendant of Lucia on her father's side. And, don't forget she was warned by that Tarot reader, you know, Julia, with the posh house.'

Yes, Julia, who said that something was unresolved in my past, and that I should beware of deception; not to mention Death, the horrible Grim Reaper. And now Sibella was dead, murdered; was I supposed to somehow prevent that?

'It's that necklace, isn't it?' said Adam suddenly, 'Someone killed Caterina because of it, and now history is repeating itself; but I can assure you it's nothing to do with me, even if we do share the same name. It's all ancient history, no one even knows about any of that now. Sibella lived a long while, but she was an exception, most of her contemporaries are gone. We know, the three of us, and Nonna, of course, and Sofia, that's five, no one else though.'

'Don't forget Shirl!' I added.

He laughed, 'Yes, Shirl, part of the Manchester mafia, renowned dealers in ancient priceless artefacts, yep, must have been her, without a doubt!'

The colour drained from Annabel's face, 'I might have mentioned it to Gio, in passing, but I'm sure he isn't the type to kill anyone; I mean, he has his faults, but… murder… and, of course, whew… he's a Barletta, isn't he? Not a Vicenza at all, is he Adam?'

'No, he's not a Vicenza, but he would have been, if my aunt hadn't married a Barletta. She took her husband's name; her maiden name was Vicenza!'

Shirl would have said 'gobsmacked', because that's what we were. And I suddenly knew whose face it was that stared up at me from the courtyard! It was, undeniably, Gio's, with his seductive smile, and come-to-bed eyes! Gio, who had shown such interest when I told them I was staying at the Villa Alatri, and Gio who had told Annabel that his job was cataloguing antique items. Maybe he'd known about it all along and it wasn't her fault at all, though she'd obviously decided it was.

'Oh, God… what have I done?' she gasped, 'It's because of me that Sibella was murdered; me and my big mouth, and… and vanity. I thought he was interested in me, but all the time he was just fishing for information.'

'Did you mention Sibella?' I asked her, 'Or give any impression that she knew where it was hidden?'

'Possibly, that is I might have, I just repeated the story she told you, about the lion on Poveglia, and that Sibella thought the murderer believed the necklace was hidden somewhere in the Villa Alatri. I didn't say she knew where though. Do you really think it was Gio? Oh no! What about Sofia? We should warn her!'

I called Shirl as soon as I was up. The gas fitters were there too, fiddling with the radiators while Adam followed them around muttering about thermostats. I knew she would be upset about Sibella, even though they'd only met the once, so I shut myself in the bathroom so that we could talk without interruption.

'Poor old thing, what a way to go, after such a long life,' murmured Shirl, 'I hope she didn't suffer too much. When is the funeral?'

'Not yet, the police are investigating, and there's the coroner's report, but we're going to Venice tomorrow, me, Adam and Annabel, we have to help Sofia. She's terribly shocked; we all are, shocked and distraught!'

It was comforting to talk to Shirl, she was so down-to-earth, yet open minded and... and... 'Shirl,' I said, 'something very frightening happened to me last night, maybe you can make some sense of it? I woke up and I was in the cemetery. Somehow, I'd managed to sleepwalk there, in just my socks and nightdress, and, when I opened my eyes, I was standing in front of the angel. Do you remember her? We found her when you came to visit me. She had an angry expression, not serene, like you'd expect an angel to be, and her arm was raised, and she was pointing at something, or maybe, someone.' There was silence at the other end, and I paused, wondering if she was still there, I wouldn't have blamed her if she wasn't, after the way I'd been ranting.

'I'm still here, Kate,' she said eventually, 'I'm just trying to take it all in. Can I call you back? I need to think.'

'Hellooo... can I get in the bathroom any time soon?' It was Annabel, hopping around on one leg like a five-year-old. She pushed past me slamming the door behind her, 'Sorry, can't wait... won't be a mo...'

'Heating's back on,' she told me with a grin, when she emerged, 'might order a pizza, any preferences?'

Well, at least Annabel seemed to be back on form.

I couldn't wait for Shirl to call back. She'd insisted she was psychic and open minded, well, you'd need to be, wouldn't you? And there had to be a reason for it all, didn't there? Maybe Shirl could help me to make sense of things.

We ate our pizzas and watched TV for a while, then Annabel went off to meet Joe, and Adam spent an age on his phone talking to Dawn. I still wasn't convinced she was sixty, and as for her family of goats with their quaint names, well, I'd believe that when I met them. And, I'd have to call Barb at the agency, to make my excuses, again! Oh, why was everything so complicated?

It was gone three when Shirl called back, 'I'm really sorry, Kate, I've been trying to contact your Randolphus Lebedev Popov!'

Gawd, I'd forgotten about him!

'He's still away, as far as I can work out; must be a long conference, he could be up to anything! Is there a Mrs. Popov? Anyway, was saying, if I can pin him down, I might get a copy of that recording and I can translate it. I'm certain the answer to all of this lies buried in your subconscious. Most of all, luv, don't let anyone try to convince you that you're responsible in any way. Too much has happened, and it's clear to me that you were destined to meet Sofia; she is living proof that your lives are irrevocably entwined. I'm certain that you've lived before, that you are Caterina, and that you were murdered for this necklace. It seems trite to called it a necklace because I believe it's a valuable artifact, that even now is of great importance; maybe even important enough to kill for. Perhaps we'll keep that to ourselves for the moment, and bear in mind that whoever killed Sibella is unaware that fate is leading him too, every step of the way.'

It reminded me of something Adam had said to me that day in the park; that life was all down to cause and effect. He said there was nothing supernatural about fate, it was just science, and if it was all stored on a giant computer there would be no surprises because we'd know everything in advance.

Shirl continued, she was on a roll and seemed to be enjoying every minute; I wished I was!

'That necklace could date to the twelfth century, not a trinket, but something of great value that was stolen and brought back to Venice. Many deaths could have resulted from its theft. There are lots of similar examples; the Black Orlov diamond for instance, reputed to be one of the eyes of a statue of Brahma, stolen from a temple in Southern India; and said to curse anyone who possesses it.'

'Where does all this leave me, Shirl? I don't want the wretched thing if it means I'll be cursed!' Was I even having this conversation? Seriously…!

'Perhaps you have to find it and give it up. We don't know who it was stolen from so you can't return it; a museum is probably your best bet, but we might know more when I've tracked down old Randi Popov.'

What…! And why me…?

We were feeling thoroughly depressed when we left for the airport, early the next morning. Even Annabel had abandoned her yellow puffer jacket and her furry peach, dandelion coat, and was wearing a somber, navy coat and leather gloves; and her hair extensions had finally relinquished their hold, so she was back to her respectable blond bob.

I was all in black, a reflection of my mood; black coat, black jeans, black hair, and my faithful black beanie, funereal, to say the least.

Nothing in England had recovered from what was rapidly becoming a two-week holiday. It was bleak mid-winter, the bleakest, and the lethargy persisted.

CHAPTER 32

It was early evening when we stepped off the vaporetto at San Stae. The crowds were gone from the wintry alleyways and squares, and some of the magic had disappeared too. The sky was overcast, and a wintry chill numbed my cheeks and nipped my fingers, but I knew St Mark's would be as busy as ever; a tourist bustle that never ceased.

We'd called Sofia earlier and told her of our suspicions concerning Gio, but she'd assured us that we had no need to worry, and that she would be busy all day as there was so much to organise. Plus, she had her work to catch up on, a welcome distraction, even though she was finding it hard to concentrate. She'd already contacted Sibella's children, the son in Rome, and two daughters in Milan, and they'd promised to be there for the funeral, and most probably before to divvy out her possessions. I couldn't wait to see Sofia, but an overwhelming sense of despair clasped my heart in a tight grip every time I thought of Sibella, frantically sweeping dust from the courtyard.

The gate was open when we reached the stone steps. I could see the lion in his bed of frost-bitten geraniums looking back at me, and I thought I heard him growl, 'Oh not you, again…' but it was just the sound of the wind churning up the leaves.

'Something's not right here,' said Adam, and he hesitated on the bottom step and pulled me back, 'this gate is never left open! Maybe we should call the police, they'll come; it's a murder scene, isn't it, what if someone is still here?'

'Sofia!' I screamed, and I pushed him aside and ran up the steps, past the disapproving lion, and into the dark hallway, 'Sofia,' I screamed again, 'where are you?'

Adam and Annabel raced in behind me and Adam switched on the lights. I peeped around the door into the living room, it was deserted, but nothing seemed to be out of place, or missing – only Sofia. We searched the house, flinging open doors and calling her name, but our cries just echoed back at us from chill, silent rooms. The heating had gone off and I was shivering with cold as well as fear. 'She should be here,' I cried, 'she was expecting us! Perhaps she's hiding at Sibella's, something could have frightened her.'

We tore back across the courtyard, where we'd sung carols with Hugh and Grace just the week before, when the world was, almost, perfect. A yellow tape hung loosely across Sibella's open door, in a half-hearted attempt to discourage intruders; it wouldn't have prevented anyone from entering, but there was an air of desolation and I knew instantly that no one was there. Sibella's new television had been moved into the hall, and it sat in its giant box just inside the doorway, surrounded by a pile of leaves blown in through the open door onto the wooden floor. She would have been horrified by such a violation, and I felt an irrational need to find her broom and sweep them back into the courtyard where they belonged.

'Gio has taken her,' said Annabel, and Adam flinched.

'Oh, for God's sake…! I've had enough of this; he's my cousin and, yeah, he's a pain in the neck, but a murderer, impossible! It's all just supposition, stirred up by this Shirl woman, and that weird hypnotist. He could have planted all that… rubbish in your mind, Kate! Alright, I admit there's a lot of bizarre stuff going on, but we can't jump to conclusions. What happened to 'innocent till proven guilty'…'

My phone rang, it seemed disrespectful somehow, and incongruous, as if we'd suddenly been jolted back into the modern world.

'…and for God's sake, change that ring tone because it's doing my head in!'

'It's Sofia!' I gasped, 'Where are you? We're here but the house is empty, deserted!'

When she answered her voice was so soft that I could barely hear her, 'I'm on Poveglia, Gio brought me here; he said he would hurt Nonna if I didn't come with him. He took Antonio's boat; he's gone mad, Kate! I managed to get away, but he's searching for me and… I'm so scared. I've got to go now, he might have heard me; just get help, come and get me, please… I managed to hide my phone down my boot, but the reception comes and goes… and the battery won't last much longer…'

'Well?' asked Annabel, 'Gio's got her, hasn't he?' She glared at Adam, 'Huh, so innocent till proven guilty, really? I knew he was no good the minute I set eyes on him!'

298

I glared at them both; 'Look, sorry Adam, I know he's your cousin, but he's stolen Antonio's boat and taken Sofia to Poveglia. She's managed to get away from him, but he's searching for her now! We have to call the police, you do it; they'll take more notice of you, and your Italian is much better than mine; here use my phone.'

'No, Kate...' he said quietly, 'it's me who should be apologising. Just because you're related to someone it doesn't mean you know them. In fact, you can live in the same house and still not really know someone.'

Well I could vouch for that!

'Shut up!' yelled Annabel, 'what the hell are you two going on about? Adam, call the police before he finds her. Tell them that Gio has taken Sibella to Poveglia, and that you think he's connected to an ongoing investigation into a murder; they'll have to take you seriously!'

'Okay, I'll give it a go, but don't expect too much, they probably won't even understand what I'm saying!'

We waited impatiently while he spoke to the police. He was right, his Italian was pretty basic, hardly better than mine, and we could only hear one side of the conversion which didn't help! 'She's thirty, er... trenta,' he explained, 'and no, she's not his girlfriend; he kidnapped her. Yes, and he's taken her to Poveglia; her name is Sofia Lazio, and her neighbour was murdered! Sibella...'

He turned to me, 'What's Sibella's last name; anyone know?'

We shook our heads, either we'd never known, or we couldn't remember.

'I'm Adam Vicenza... yes, Vicenza... Yes, I'm English; does anyone there speak English?'

He shrugged, 'They rang off! They didn't believe me; acted like it was some kind of joke, and they wanted to know why anyone would take a girlfriend to Poveglia. Then when I said she was thirty they nearly had hysterics, and said I've got to call them tomorrow if I'm still worried! At least, I think that's what they said! What do we do now? Poveglia is only ten minutes across the lagoon, but how are we going to get there, I don't fancy swimming it, do you?'

Annabel smiled, 'I could call my friend, Alessio; he's got a boat and I'm sure he'll help us if I ask him, he's very obliging.'

Alessio arrived almost straight away, and he looked as gorgeous as ever! 'Where is your beautiful long hair,' he asked as soon as he saw her, but she just kissed him on both cheeks and gazed up at him beseechingly. 'We need to go to Poveglia; Gio's got Sofia, and Adam reckons it's only ten minutes across the lagoon.'

Alessio expression turned from enthusiasm to abject fear.

'I don't go to Poveglia, no one goes to Poveglia. It is bad luck; we cast our nets there sometimes, but never step ashore. It is the island of the dead, of fantasmi.... ghosts.'

'Oh… man up, Alessio,' scolded Annabel teasingly, 'you don't have to come ashore, can't you just leave us there?'

'Mi dispiace, bella, I can't leave you on Poveglia,' he shuddered, but she wasn't giving up, though I was rapidly going off the idea myself. If it had been anyone but Sofia, I'd be agreeing with him, and telling her to shut up and wait till morning.

'We can call, and you could come back for us if there's a problem. Oh, please, Alessio, for me, please…' she batted her eyelashes, 'please, Alessio…'

It worked, his face softened. 'Very well, but only to the jetty, it's already dark, it's dangerous, and not only because of the ghosts. The ground is unstable and full of the dead; and there are wild dogs and, perhaps, vampires…'

Vampires…! And now she'd persuaded him, there was no going back now!

Alessio's fishing boat was tiny compared to Antonio's and the black water seemed far too close for my liking, but soon the Bell Tower of Poveglia loomed like a giant shadow just ahead of us and Alessio slowed the engine.

'We're here!' he whispered, so as not to wake the ghosts, 'See the tower, the evil Doctor Paulo fell to his death from the top, though many believe that he was pushed.'

He turned to look at us and his eyes were wide with fright, 'Are you sure?' he asked, 'Please, come back to Venice with me.'

It was an appealing idea; we were turning into a narrow channel and I could see Antonio's boat moored just ahead of us, but I knew Sofia was somewhere on the island expecting us to come for her, so I said, 'Thank you, Alessio, but we're here now so just leave us, it will be fine.'

He tied up the boat and we climbed out. 'Are you sure you want to come with us, Abel?' I asked her, 'I don't mind if you go back.'

'No, I'm game,' she replied.

'So, I've heard!' muttered Adam, rather unnecessarily I thought, given the circumstances.

Alessio reversed his tiny fishing boat and headed out of the narrow channel.

'Be careful, cara mia, and call me when you want to return…' he turned to blow her a kiss; and then, with a wave, he was gone; just a faint speck of light, disappearing across the lagoon. Only the glow from nearby islands illuminated the overgrown paths; Poveglia, what the hell were we doing here, in the dark, in this godforsaken jungle of stunted trees and contorted stone?

Annabel took my arm, 'We must stay together! You can feel it, can't you, the presence of death and… misery…'

'It's all in your mind,' said Adam, 'anyway, the dead can't hurt you. Just stay close; we'll find somewhere reasonably safe and then call Sofia. Gio could be out there and we don't want to lead him to her. Look, there's a big building over there, let's head that way, we'll feel safer if we've got four walls around us.'

I stopped in my tracks, 'It's the asylum; I know it is! It's... horrible...!'

'Oh, come on, Kate, it might not be; and even if it once was, it's not an asylum anymore, and we're here now so we've got no choice.'

'We could go the other way...' I faltered; I knew I was being cowardly, but I couldn't help it, 'and we can't see a thing; what if we fall over, or break something, we'll be sitting ducks. I've got a torch on my phone; I'm going to switch it on.'

'But what if he sees us?' said Annabel, 'What if he's watching us now?'

'No, she's right,' he whispered, 'we can't risk any injuries, give it to me, I can check the path ahead and switch off as we go, just keep your voices down. Oh, bloody hell... reception's gone, let's hope it comes back or we've got a problem! Come on, I'll lead if you like.'

The building stood before us, a forbidding and menacing, grey outline against the sky; remnants of glass, in the broken and barred windows, reflected the moon in pale circles of light that glared out at us, like demon eyes boring through the darkness. The door was open and swinging on creaking hinges; it beckoned; a gaping maw ready to swallow us one by one.

'Stop, Adam, please, we can't go in there,' I grabbed his arm in an attempt to pull him back, 'it's definitely the asylum; look, there are bars on the windows!'

'Oh no... You've made me drop the light, Kate... where is it? I can't find it; it's gone off!'

'Smells gross round here,' muttered Annabel, 'I reckon those wild dogs have been here before us! Wow, look, it flashed, it's down there, you've got a text from Sofia. Great, we must have reception! It says she's in the asylum, so let's hope we're in the right place.'

We stumbled blindly across the grass and through the entrance into a long, narrow corridor leading to a barred door at the very end. Adam pushed it open and went through, and I was just about to follow him when I noticed that someone was missing.

'Where's Annabel?' I whispered, 'She was behind me just now. Stop, we've got to find her!' And I turned and ran back down the corridor; it seemed longer, and narrower, than it had when we came in, and darker too because Adam had the torch. And, where was he? Hadn't he heard me?

I found her on the step outside, she was reading a message. 'Oh, hi, Kate,' she said, like we'd just mislaid one another at Sainsbury's.

'Honestly Abel, you scared the life out of me. I thought you were behind us!'

'Sorry, I didn't fancy it, my claustrophobia was kicking in, and it was too dark in there, not to mention, airless as a tomb. I felt like I was wrapped up in a... in a black shroud. Plus, I just got a really lovely text from Library Joe; he is so sweet, I think I like him best of all!'

Black shroud...? And she'd come back to read a text!

I stared at her, could it be that she'd been possessed by someone even more flaky than she was? She smiled, 'Look, he says he can't wait to see me!'

'You'd better not let on to Alessio that you like Joe best,' I said, 'at least, not until he's picked us up and we're safely back in the land of the living!'

She peered around into the darkness and giggled, 'Yes, I see what you mean! But I like Alessio too; actually, he's rather delic.'

Well, I couldn't argue with that.

'And, you really don't need me to come in there with you; just get Sofia and bring her out, and then we'll go.'

'You can't stay here, Abel; what about the death and the misery?'

'No, I don't care about that; it's all just superstition. Adam's right, the dead can't hurt me!'

I couldn't believe what I was hearing, 'But what about Gio? You know; kidnapper, and possible murderer?'

'Oops, I forgot about him, right, you lead; I suppose I'll have to follow. Wait a mo though, I've got another text!'

I frowned impatiently, 'Well, who's it from this time, Mick Jagger?'

'He's a bit old for me, Kate! No, it's from Google Earth, and it says... 'Beware...! Do not dig, the ground contains human remains.' Oh, FECK...! Lead on, I'm right behind you, I'll close my eyes; let's get this over and done with!'

'Adam…' I called, but there was no reply. Why hadn't he come back to find us? The door at the end of the corridor was closed and I pushed against it, it seemed to be stuck. Suddenly it shot open and there, on the other side, was Gio. He smiled at me and his eyes glinted under the glow of a lamp that hung from a hook in the ceiling. It swung slowly in the cold air, a gentle arc illuminating the room in a sinister relay of light and shadow; then the door slammed shut behind me and I was confronted by a scene from a horror movie. Steel trolleys and gurneys stood at odd angles, they vibrated slightly with a metallic murmur, their straps quivering in the draught from the broken panes. 'Next patient, please!' they murmured.

Adam lay on the floor; blood streamed from a gash on his head, and for a moment I wondered if he was still alive. Sofia was leaning against the wall, bound and tightly gagged; she looked back at me with frightened eyes.

Gio crouched next to her, 'Look, it's the other one; it's your twin, Sofia. Aren't you pleased to see her?' His voice sounded strange, and I noticed he was holding a knife with a long blade that shone silver in the half-light.

The other one…? Did he say 'one'? I glanced behind me for Annabel, but she wasn't there and I breathed a sigh of relief.

'What's going on, Gio?' I asked him. 'Why are you doing this?' He looked confused, as if he wasn't entirely sure himself; then he got to his feet and I cringed as he came nearer until he was standing so close that I could feel his breath on my face.

'I didn't kill the old woman; she died, in front of me, she just dropped like a ...'

'Stone...?'

'No, an old rag doll, or a feather; there was nothing of her!'

'So you just frightened her to death?'

'I didn't kill her; I only wanted information! I'm not a murderer!'

'Then you should have got help,' tears poured down my face, 'she might have lived! Anyway, that doesn't explain why you're here!'

'She sent me here! This is her fault, not mine... She said it was buried here, on Poveglia.'

'Oh, you mean the necklace?'

He moved even closer until our noses were almost touching, 'What are you talking about? A necklace...? You make it sound like a... string of beads. It's far more than that! It's a piece of art that has survived for six hundred years, possibly longer; an artefact beyond material value; but you'd never understand! I went back to the villa to explain and she... she accused me of killing this woman, this... Sibella.'

'But you did kill her,' I said, 'you did kill Sibella. How could you do it? She was just a poor, lonely, old woman!'

Adam's eyes flickered, and he looked up at me as if he couldn't believe I was really there. 'Kate, what is this? What the hell's going on?' He struggled to sit up and I pushed Gio aside and ran to him.

Something stirred in the trees just outside the window, a rustling, like wind in the long grass, and the sound of whistling, hollow and melancholy. Gio dropped the knife and backed slowly towards the door; I saw terror in his eyes as a fine mist began to rise from the damp floor, slowly filling the room until I could barely see across it. The gurneys increased their chatter, jumping and clattering, moving in a maniacal jig, to and fro... then, out of the mist, came something darker and, denser, it moved stealthily, and I could feel its malevolence as it gathered speed...

CHAPTER 33

'Then what happened?' asked Annabel.

I rubbed my eyes; they were red and sore from fatigue.

'We saw a black shape, it appeared out of the mist so actually it's quite hard to describe, but the next thing we knew, it sounds ridiculous, but... this gurney, you know, one of those metal stretchers on wheels, well it came shooting out of nowhere, just as if someone was pushing it, and it gained speed, faster, and faster, and then it hit Gio in the back of his legs and he shot up into the air and landed on top of it.'

'Yep, you're right, it does sound ridiculous.' She turned to Adam, 'What about you Adam? Did you see what it was?'

'Not really, I'd just come round and my head was pouring blood. I was trying to work out what was going on when this thing shot past me and hit the end window with such force that it went straight through. The wooden frames were rotten, so they just shattered, and splinters of wood and glass shot everywhere. Anyway, Gio kept going and we heard him screaming, then he must have hit a tree, or something, because everything went quiet, just like that, one moment all was screaming chaos, and the next, it was silent.'

'Silent as the grave,' murmured Annabel.

I nodded, 'As silent as the grave, and we heard nothing after that, so we made a run for it in case he came back, and you and Alessio were waiting for us with his boat, thank God!'

'Yes, clever of me, I thought. I ran off when you pushed open that door. I got a quick glimpse of Sofia all tied up, and that weird swinging light and that was it, I scarpered! Luckily Alessio had come back because he was worried, bless… and he was down at the mooring and he called the police and persuaded them to come. They still weren't convinced that it wasn't all a huge joke. Apparently, people are always roaming around on Poveglia trying to film a real ghost so that they can upload it.'

We were back at Sofia's. She had already gone to bed and we were sitting in front of the fire eating toast and downing cups of tea. Well, Annabel and I were; Adam had a large brandy, a friendly spirit, he said, as opposed to the other variety. I didn't feel as if I'd ever be able to sleep peacefully again, and I still wasn't sure what I was supposed to do about any of it. Maybe Shirl could make some sense of what had happened; I'd call her in the morning.

Adam finished his drink and stood up, 'I'm going to bed now. I suppose you two are staying down here while I'm alone up there, dreaming of pale skeletal arms stretching out of the sodden earth to pull me down into the swampy depths… I just hope Gio's ghost doesn't turn up and climb in with me.' And he laughed, but I could tell he almost believed it.

'The vanishing house party,' said Annabel when he'd gone.

'How do you mean?' I asked.

'It's only the two of us now.'

'Not really, Adam and Sofia haven't vanished, they're just in bed!'

'Whatever…still… my life will never be the same, and it's your fault, Kate! If it hadn't been for your macabre dreams, and coming here, not to mention your weird Tarot reading, plus, living opposite that appalling cemetery, my life would be fine, untouched by any of this creepy stuff!'

'It was your Tarot reading, Abel; you just made me do it!'

'No, it was obviously for you, anyone could see that, given the facts. Plus, it was you that made me enter the competition in the first place, still, I suppose I've met some interesting people because of it. Think how boring our lives would be otherwise!'

We stared at each other across the room and then we collapsed into fits of giggles at how absurd everything was.

'Limoncello…?' I queried, 'I think there's some in the fridge.'

'Absolutely, why not, we don't have to get up in the morning. You get it, and I'll shove another log on the fire.'

I was exhausted, but I knew I'd never sleep if I went to bed, so we sat for a while staring into the fire. The warmth of the room was making me drowsy and my eyelids were starting to droop when Annabel suddenly announced, 'Actually, he wasn't that bad, you know.'

I came to with a jump, 'What... who?' I asked.

'Gio, of course; he wasn't that bad. Oh, I know he did this macho, Casanova thing but I think it was because people seemed to expect it of him. He was nice to me, and obviously very passionate about his cataloguing.'

'About his cataloguing..?'

'Yes, he was really into old relics. Haha... probably explains his attraction to the floozy,' she grinned, 'no really, he was a bit of an expert and, of course, I fell right into his trap, giving him all that info about Caterina's necklace.'

'That turned out to be some really ancient relic, a missing item of great repute; like the Black Orlov diamond, according to Shirl.'

'Shirl is a bit of a contradiction, isn't she? She's obviously very intelligent, but she still believes all this psychic stuff. Perhaps she's your Queen of Cups and not your mum?'

'No, I'm sure Mum is my Queen of Cups, but Shirl is there somewhere. Maybe I'll be able to work it out in the end, when this is all over.'

I stood up to stretch, but she hadn't finished, and she was looking gloomy so I sat down again.

'What's up?' I asked her.

'It's just that I feel so guilty taking your room, like I'm keeping you and Adam apart, and I know it's selfish of me but the idea of having to sleep up there... on my own...'

'Well, first of all,' I said, 'it's not my room at all, it's the one Sofia keeps for Nonna when she comes to stay, it's near the loo and the kitchen, in case she wants to get up in the night. It's just that for the last year or so she's been staying over at Sibella's to keep her company, and to gossip about old times…' I stopped because my bottom lip was trembling, and a large wet tear was running down my face, 'and I only finished up in it because I was too pathetic to sleep upstairs on my own; far too many years being part of a couple and not standing on my own feet; and… Oh no…! I've just thought; Nonna will need it back; she won't want to stay in Sibella's house anymore, will she, not now she's gone?'

'And her children will want to stay there if they come for the funeral. Oh, I hope they come, Kate, because it will be awful if they don't, but where will we go.'

'We'll go upstairs, to the flat. I don't know why we didn't think of it before, except I suppose Grace and Hugh were there over Christmas. It's perfect, Adam and I can have the bedroom and you can have the sofa in the living room. We'll move up there tomorrow so Sofia can get things ready for Nonna. Now come on, bed… it's our last night together, dahling!'

CHAPTER 34

We went to the police station the following morning. It was about ten minutes away and situated in what was once the convent of Santa Chiara in the Piazzala Roma.

'Why did you go to Poveglia?' asked the Ispettore, 'We've searched the island and your friend isn't there. Maybe he fell in the lagoon? He could have become tangled in the nets and weeds, or he may have hit his head when he fell. Either way, he is probably dead, drowned; food for the fishes,' and he grinned at us showing two rows of shark-like, white teeth. 'Or he could just come back,' he shrugged, 'people are reported missing all the time and they seldom are! Do not return to Poveglia, it is a dangerous place, there are wild dogs, and you are trespassing on private property.'

'Helpful,' remarked Adam, when we were back outside, 'it was as if he just wanted to get rid of us, reduce his caseload. And fish food; huh, a bit rude if you ask me.'

'It's because they don't believe that Gio murdered Sibella,' said Sofia, 'they just think I had a fight with my boyfriend and I'm trying to make trouble for him... put the blame on him as revenge for something. I wonder how well they searched; and what if he does come back?'

I put my arm around her. I felt angry; why wouldn't they even consider the possibility that Gio had killed Sibella? He could at least have been a bit more sensitive, he must have known how upset she was, but could it be possible that Gio was right when he insisted that Sibella had died of fright? We wouldn't know until the official report arrived from the coroner, but maybe the police had a pretty good idea already.

Adam agreed that it was a good idea to move upstairs, and when we told Sofia she said she would telephone Nonna straight away and arrange to collect her. It made me wonder if she might have come before if her room had been free, and I felt slightly guilty about keeping her away. We packed our things as soon as we got back and carried everything upstairs to the tiny flat.

'Yeah, I like it!' said Adam approvingly, 'it's a bit small after downstairs, but it does the job.'

We dumped our cases on the bed and went to find Annabel. She was staring at the sofa with a dismayed expression. 'My legs are much too long to fit comfortably on that,' she muttered, '...and there aren't any pillows!'

'The important thing is that you're just a few metres away from us,' I said, 'so if you get scared in the night you can yell, and we'll rescue you.'

Adam laughed, 'Yeah, I might do, just don't come and find us!'

'Don't you have to phone Dawn, or something?' I asked him, 'I'll help Annabel sort out her bed.'

'Yeah, I can take a hint; look gone!' and he was!

'I've decided I like it,' declared Annabel, 'it's cute, and it's got a friendlier feel to it than the rest of the place, probably because it's smaller, more compact. I said I'd call Joe this morning, so toodle pip...'

And I was dismissed, which was just as well as I had to speak to Shirl, expert on all things supernatural; or 'a bit of a contradiction', if you agreed with Annabel.

'I knew it!' she crowed, when I told her what had happened on Poveglia.

'What do you know, Shirl?' was my baffled reply.

'Well, it's obvious, isn't it? This necklace of Caterina's has an intrinsic worth far greater than the value of a few diamonds. Okay, so centuries ago it was probably pillaged because it was a nice bit of bling, you know, some gold and a few sparkly gems; can't tell you what exactly because we haven't seen it yet...'

'Hang on, Shirl; what do you mean 'yet'? Can't we just 'draw a line', you know, assume that it's gone now and put an end to all this...'

'It will never end, not until it's been brought back into the light. Until then we'll never really understand its importance; perhaps it needs to be returned, somehow.

What we know for certain, is that it's the reason you went to Venice in the first place. We have to accept that this world is far stranger than we realise and we'll never know the truth. Such arrogance, all these scientists working flat out to discover why we're here and so on; and religious lunatics waging wars because they think they've got all the answers, and for what? I'd say that was arrogance, wouldn't you?'

EEK! I was sorry I'd asked! And 'brought back into the light'! What was that all about? Was she expecting me to scale some statue, just to pop a shiny emerald into the empty socket of a green-eyed yellow idol, somewhere to the north of Kathmandu?

'If you think I'm going back to Poveglia with a spade, Shirl, you're mistaken!' I said somewhat impatiently, 'No way am I setting foot on that island, ever again!'

'I don't think you'd find it if you did; it's more likely Sibella was trying to mislead him, unless she was getting all her stories mixed up; or perhaps she really didn't know where it was hidden. She was very old, Kate, and maybe Gio was right and she did die of shock. Anyway, aside from all that, I'm trying to catch up with your elusive Mr. Popov. He still isn't back from his erm... conference. And there is a Mrs. Popov, I spoke to her yesterday; she says he's always finding reasons to disappear. Seems he's quite a Svengali; she reckons he's got a wife in Zagreb, and probably lots of little Popovs as well.'

'What? You mean he's a bigamist? And a Svengali...?'

She laughed, 'Yeah, quite possibly; a con man, a manipulator of women; you must have frightened the life out of him when you went into a trance and started speaking Italian.'

'Well bigamist or not, I must say I found him quite convincing!'

'We'll give him the benefit of the doubt, shall we, luv? She says he's due back any time, so we'll keep on trying.'

Sofia went to Verona the next day. She had some translation work to deliver to the university before meeting Nonna, so we agreed to stay behind and guard against intruders; including Gio, assuming he had survived his wild gurney ride, and the pale and skeletal arms rising from the sodden earth, pulling him down to the depths, or the inspector's voracious fish. It didn't sound to me like he had much of a chance, one way or another! Poor Gio, I was starting to feel quite sorry for him!

The villa was gradually being re-populated. Nonna was back with Sofia and ensconced in her room next to the kitchen, and we were upstairs in the little flat. Then, a few days later, the police turned up and removed the yellow tape from the doorway and, to our surprise, informed us that it was no longer a crime scene. Almost as soon as they'd gone two elderly ladies arrived, Sibella's daughters from Milan; Maria and Emilia, who both spoke good English, and were accompanied by two gruff old men, one round and fat, and the other tall and cadaverous. They took over Sibella's house on the other side of the courtyard and began to dispose of her clothes, and other possessions, with a ruthless abandon.

Sofia cooked vast pan-loads of pasta to feed the increased numbers, who all descended on us regularly at five in the afternoon, looking for sustenance and remarking, non-stop, about how similar Sofia and I were and discussing the likelihood of it happening after so many years.

Maria told me that they had often tried to persuade Sibella to come to Milan to live with her and her husband, Giuseppe, and their three children, but she'd always refused, preferring to stay in Venice. 'She lived here all her life,' she explained, 'and in this villa; it was almost as if she'd become a part of it, like a snail, or a hermit crab, rejecting the real world because of the way it had changed. I'm afraid we gave up in the end.'

'She remembered Venice the way it was,' added Emilia, 'not a living museum, but a prosperous city. It might seem strange to you, but can you imagine Venice without tourists, and without electricity, and all our modern conveniences? No, no one can, not anymore, but when Sibella and Nonna were small it was an entirely different place. Before electricity it would have been very dark.'

'Si, il Codega,' murmured Maria, 'the one who carried a lantern through the streets, bringing light into the darkness. As for the canals, these days the water is changed and filtered regularly, but then there was the smell, an all-pervading miasma, that rose up from the water because everything went into the canals and then slowly out into the lagoon.

319

It was probably full of dead dogs, and waste and sewage...'

We were all transfixed, and Nonna's eyes were sparkling and she was nodding, no doubt recalling her childhood in the Villa Alatri.

'It sounds just like Poveglia!' said Annabel, 'disgusting! And a health hazard, no wonder they got the plague; so good thing it's changed if you ask me.'

Sofia laughed, 'Yes, I'm with you Annabel, it's a good thing it has changed! More pasta anyone...?'

A few days later, the police inspector called round to see Sofia; his visit was brief, and she was shaking with anger when he left.

'What did he say, Sofia?' I asked her when she'd begun to calm down.

'He says that no one is responsible for Sibella's death, she died of a stroke that could have happened at any time! There was nothing at all to indicate that she'd been threatened by an intruder, and no visible sign of violence. He said a loud noise would have been sufficient to kill her, given that she was so old and feeble, and her body was in such a fragile state, and we can bury her now. And, can you believe it? He said that, 'he hoped I'd cleared up the misunderstanding with my boyfriend after the incident on Poveglia'!'

CHAPTER 35

We saw her off on a day when the sky was overcast and full of snow.

The little church in Campo San Giacomo dell Orio, where she regularly took mass, was full of respectful mourners, including a pew full of little old ladies, at least as old as Sibella had been. They sat in a black-clad cluster murmuring inaudibly in the dialect beloved of Sibella; a literally dying breed, the real Venetians, just a small percentage of the inhabitants of Venice who lived and died there, as opposed to the transient majority, 'i turisti'.

Paolo, Sibella's son from Rome, had arrived the previous evening, accompanied by his partner, a distinguished looking gentleman in his late fifties. They looked very similar too, small and slender, and almost completely bald, with tiny domed heads and large noses. Both wore expensive suits and cried copiously into large white handkerchiefs, throughout the service. The two remaining sons had obviously decided that their mother's death didn't warrant the cost of the flight from Australia and instead had elected to send a series of floral tributes, consisting of three large hearts entwined with fragrant white lilies.

It was snowing heavily when we left the church. It covered the square and the bare trees in a thick blanket of white, and gusted in whirling flurries that wetted my cheeks, and stung my eyes. I watched for a moment, as giant snowflakes swirled and landed feather-like in the grey water of the canal, forming tiny circular ripples on the surface before fading away to nothing. We walked slowly back to the Villa Alatri for mulled wine and, at my request, a chocolate cake, which I knew would have pleased Sibella because she loved chocolate. Her coffin would later be loaded onto a funeral boat and taken to the cemetery island of San Michele, a privilege reserved only for true Venetians, accompanied by her remaining Italian children.

'I'm done here!' announced Sofia, when Nonna had gone to her room for some peace and quiet, and Sibella's aged offspring had retired to their disinfected, and refurbished, rooms on the other side of the courtyard. 'There's nothing to keep me here anymore so I've decided to sell up and move to Verona. The owners of one of the big tour companies have been pursuing me for the last year, at least. They want to turn the place into apartments; soon no one at all will live in Venice, it will be nothing but a giant museum and then it will sink!'

'You could do that yourself,' said Adam, 'you'd be a millionaire in no time. Everyone wants to visit Venice before it sinks!'

'How long is it before… you know… before that happens?' asked Annabel, 'And can't they do something to stop it?'

I knew the answer because Shirl had told me! God, was that only in November?

'It's the cruise ships, they send out huge bow waves soaking everything and weakening all the foundations.'

Sofia looked tired and miserable, she tried to yawn, but it turned into a sigh. 'It's not only that, Kate. The Adriatic is rising, and the east coast of Italy is starting to slope down into the sea; there's no hope.'

'Oh well, look on the bright side;' said Adam cheerfully, and I glared at him wondering what he was going to say next; 'at least we came in time. And Sofia, you've got another house in Verona.'

I glared some more, 'Adam...! Honestly, men!' I muttered.

Sofia grinned at me. 'No, you're right, Adam, I'm very fortunate, one of the lucky ones. Anyway, it's time the Lazio family said goodbye to this crumbling edifice, before it falls down!'

'But what about the buried treasure,' asked Annabel, 'Caterina's necklace, the priceless relic? What did Gio call it, 'an artefact of great intrinsic value'? Speaking of which, where do you think he's got to?'

She was right! Gio's disappearance had been forgotten in the midst of everything else.

Adam rolled his eyes, 'I told you; dragged down into the mire, remember? Those pale skeletal arms reaching for him... or the sharks...'

Sharks...?

'...the ones he mentioned, that Ispettore, the bloke from the polizia,' he added, when he saw our puzzled expressions.

I laughed, 'Oh, you mean the voracious fish?'
But I didn't believe any of it, and neither did
Adam, nor Sofia, nor Annabel, not really. Just like
Arnold Schwarzenegger, he'd be back...

CHAPTER 36

'Sotto leone, Caterina, sotto leone...' The voice was clear, melodious even, almost as if we were sitting next to each other; Sibella, but a younger, brighter Sibella, happy and full of life. I was back in the painted room, with the marble washstand and the red velvet armchair, and the all-pervading fragrance of roses and oranges, and patchouli. I opened my eyes, Sibella was standing next to me and she took my hand, pulling me towards the window. I drew back expecting to see Gio's face peering up at me, but he wasn't there, only the lion in his bed of bright red flowers.

'Kate, what are you doing up? It's half past three in the morning, for heaven's sake! And why are you standing there staring at the wall?'

I shook my head; it was dark, and cold, and Sibella had gone. 'Adam, I'm sorry, I was looking out of the window at the lion, and Sibella was here and... there was a window on this side of the room before they changed everything.'

'You were sleepwalking again. Go back to bed, I'll bring you a hot drink, you're freezing!'

I followed him into the kitchen. 'Don't wake Annabel,' I whispered. Her door was ajar, so I shut it quietly. 'Adam, I know where Caterina buried the necklace. It's under the stone lion, Sibella just told me; she was here, and she took me to the window. The room was how it used to be; and, Adam, she looked amazing, a beautiful young woman, and there was this incredible fragrance, just like before!'

'Oh, that fragrance; the reason you went to that weird organic place and came back with all those strange smelling oils. Are you sure it wasn't the smell of the canals? That was pretty overpowering, by all accounts.'

'I was afraid. I thought Gio would be out there, or his face anyway, staring up at me, but it was just the lion.'

'Look, Kate, there's no way that anything could be buried under that lion. It's the first place Gio would have searched!'

'It's been waiting for me, Adam. I know it's been waiting for me!'

'Tomorrow, we'll look, okay? Come back to bed now. I'll bring you some hot chocolate; it will help you sleep.'

I was already asleep when he came back. I knew because when I woke up there was a mug of rather unsavoury looking, brown liquid, on the shelf next to the bed. Adam was still asleep so I got up and tiptoed down the stairs and out into the courtyard. The snow had stopped, though the sky was still laden, and icicles hung from the gutters, dripping onto the white patina that covered the ground.

'Idiot, you'll catch your death out here,' exclaimed a voice behind me, and Annabel ran out and grabbed my hand pulling me back inside.

'Your mum's on the phone, you left it in the kitchen, it woke me up. She wants to know if we're managing.' We went back upstairs, I was shivering and my feet were tingling.

'Your toes have gone blue. It's probably the early stages of frostbite!' she added with a grin.

'Who's got frostbite?' asked Mum anxiously.

'No one, Mum, we're all fine, thank you; though it was a bit grim yesterday, with the funeral and so on. But now the police are saying that Sibella died as the result of a stroke, so I suppose the good news is that she wasn't murdered.'

'Yes, not quite so bad, not as violent, even if the result is still the same... So, when are you coming home dear?'

It wasn't until she said goodbye and I'd rung off that I realised she knew nothing about Sofia being kidnapped, and the so called, 'incident', on Poveglia. And, when were we 'going home'? That was something I hadn't even considered, but she was right, we did have to go home. I needed to get back to work before I ran out of money completely or I wouldn't even be able to pay the rent. And Adam had put everything on hold; what would Dawn say? We'd been so busy living some kind of alternative existence that we'd almost forgotten about the other.

Adam was still snoring. 'Don't know how you put up with that racket, does he always do that?' queried Annabel, and she handed me a mug of weak tea and two slices of slightly burnt toast, smeared with butter, 'Go and wake him!'

'How do I know if he always does that, I haven't had the chance to find out, have I? And I

327

can't wake him, it would be mean; we were up half the night.'

'Oh, too much information,' she covered her ears with her hands, but I dragged them away. 'I was sleepwalking. Gawd, Abel, you've got a one-track mind!'

'Yeah, well, I might be lying in the gutter but I'm looking up at the stars...'

Blimey... Oscar Wilde now; could it be that she'd actually been reading at the library, when all the time I thought she was pursuing Joe around the book shelves. I must have misjudged her!

'Come on, Kate; let's go out in the snow before anyone else is up.'

We dressed quickly, and went slipping and sliding down the steps and along the deserted streets, shrieking like children.

The Grand Canal was transformed. Snow coated the bridges and the ranks of gondolas, like frosting on a cake, reflecting the morning sun, and running in sparkling rivulets where it had begun to melt. It dripped into the canal, a melodious bell-like orchestra of drips, like pebbles dropped in a drain, and a faint grey mist rose in curls from the grey water.

Adam was up when we got back. 'Where were you two?' he asked, 'I thought it was quiet, no wonder I slept late. Shirl called, she's been trying to contact you. You forgot to take your mobile!'

'Randi!' cried Annabel, 'Quick call her; she's caught up with Randi!'

'Oh... the hypnotist,' Adam winked at me, 'I thought I was being accused of something.'

'Shhhh...' I said, 'I'm going to call Shirl!'

'Sotto Leone,' said Shirl, 'it means under the lion, so tell Annabel that it's nothing to do with anyone by the name of Otto,' she laughed, 'or, for that matter anything to do with any otters!'

'You're on loud speaker, Shirl, you tell her, she's here; next to me.'

'I thought it was a bit peculiar,' murmured Annabel, 'I mean, how many otters do you get around here? What about the 'opera', Shirl?'

'Sopra, of course, just as I thought; but you were rambling a bit, Kate; and Popov didn't get all of it. I reckon he only started to record halfway through, when things were starting to sound interesting; probably thought it might be worth a bit. But, basically, you were shouting because you were terrified of someone, frightened out of your wits, in fact, and when you looked down into the courtyard from the room above, well there he was, looking up at you! The artefact, or necklace, or whatever you care to call it, is buried under the stone lion, 'sotto leone', Annabel's 'Otto', but at least she got the lion part right!'

'Sotto leone... Sotto leone...' I murmured, and the sound was as intoxicating as a softly whispered mantra. I descended the stairs, and wandered trance-like into the courtyard to where the stone lion stood in his bed of dead geraniums. I gazed at him, and our eyes met; 'it's time' they seemed to say, as I bent down and began to part the snow with my hands, paying little heed to the cold, or the hardness of the earth. I looked up and in my mind's eye I could see Sibella smiling at me, and nodding encouragingly, as she had so often in life. A small girl, with long black hair, stood next to her, it was my sister, Elisabetta, and she smiled too. I didn't notice the onlookers; Nonna and Sofia, Adam and Annabel, and Sibella's aging progeny, as I delved under the feet of the lion until I came upon a wooden box, like a tiny coffin, with a rusted metal clasp.

'She's found it, Shirl!' said Annabel into my phone, 'we'll call you back, luv!'

'Is that it?' she cried when we lifted the lid, 'it's not much to write home about, is it?'

Nonna lifted it out of the box and held it up to the light, 'It's just how my mother described it;' she said, 'the gold is probably very pure, and these stones are diamonds and sapphires, and these are rubies; it's beautiful and very ancient. It was probably stolen from a tomb. We shouldn't keep it any longer than we have to, it will bring bad luck. Our family has suffered enough already, but now you've found it Katherine, we can be rid of it for good.'

CHAPTER 37

We left the next day and I was pleased that our lives would, very soon, return to normal. I felt lighter, as if a burden had been lifted from my shoulders; one that I hadn't even known was there.

The necklace had gone too, collected the afternoon before, by two incredulous ladies from the museum. 'Yes, they'd known of its existence from ancient documents, but had given up all hope for ever finding it.'

As Shirl suspected, it was much older than twelfth century, hundreds of years older, but its exact provenance was still to be decided.

They smiled knowingly when they told us that they knew Gio, 'Oh yes, very charming,' they said, 'and so attractive, but he had disappeared, though where he'd gone was a mystery.'

It was strange being back in England, almost as if we'd been away for much longer.

The O'Connor's had gone off to Dublin again, so the house was silent and the heating was off. A letter was sitting on the hall table; it was addressed to Annabel Leggat in an italic scrawl. She picked it up and scrutinised it, 'Huh don't recognise the writing, but at least they got my name right...' she muttered, as she tore it open and pulled out an official looking letter on thick blue paper. 'I don't believe it!' she gasped, 'I've got a job! Look, it's in a tiny, private school for littlies, starting straight away. Mummy said she'd have a word with the headmistress; they belong to the same golf club. Great, I can say goodbye to that horrible graveyard, and I won't be in your way, and Adam can move in, and the box room can be a study again. I'll really miss you though!'

Well, it seemed as everything was changing, or coming to an end. 'That's lovely, Annabel,' I said generously, 'it sounds like a great job, just what you need. We'll miss you too, and you're not in the way, not at all. And you can come back whenever you like!'

Annabel's 'Mummy' turned up the next morning and they loaded her possessions into a huge Range Rover that carried a distinct whiff of dogs. We hugged, and then, just like that, she was gone and I felt miserable, not helped by Adam's announcement that he had to go back to Yorkshire to see Dawn, and all her little kiddies.

He put his arms around me, 'Why don't you come with me Kate? You don't want to be here on your own, do you?'

No, I did not! Although, maybe, I wouldn't be taking anymore nocturnal strolls through the gravestones, because that was all behind me, wasn't it?

He popped off to Kentish Town to pick up the rest of his belongings; it looked like I had a new flat mate, except this one wouldn't need the box room, though Annabel's bed and chest of drawers still languished there; until 'Daddy' was available to collect them.

I was all alone again, and I wondered if I should visit Mum and Dad to get them up to speed with everything that had happened, but there was something else I had to do first.

I crossed the road to the cemetery. The gate was slightly ajar, so I squeezed through and wandered up the long hill between the gravestones; no one was about, at least, no one living. I was outnumbered by the dead and for some reason the idea amused me. I turned left down the now familiar pathway; it was overgrown with weeds and wet grass, and criss-crossed with brambles, and I marvelled at how I could have found my way here, in the dark, with only a pair of woolly socks on my feet. And, suddenly, there she was, the marble angel. She stared down at me, but her face had changed somehow because now she looked serene, content even, and her mouth turned up at the corners, almost as if she was smiling at me. I picked a sprig of laurel and placed it in her outstretched hand, 'Lucia Caterina di Lazio,' I murmured, and I smiled back at her; then I parted the grass where the stone met the wet earth, 'Resting in Peace' it said, and I knew she was.

EPILOGUE

Merry, Merry Month of May

Adam and I found a lovely flat opposite the woods, near Muswell Hill, so now we can peer out into wooded glades instead of the creepy old cemetery, and it's got a tiny garden and a little off-road parking space, so he was able to bring his car down from Yorkshire. She's very ancient, and off white; that's the car, not Dawn. I met her too, and was relieved to discover that she is reassuringly mature as well; and the all the little kids, Marilyn, Fred, Ginger and Gregory, are gorgeous!

Auntie Flo and Jim are getting married next month, and so are Greg and Mary. They brought the wedding forward because Mary is pregnant, so at least I'll have a nephew or niece, and Mum hasn't mentioned biological clocks for ages because she's too busy buying up babygros and romper suits from Mothercare.

Actually, we've had three wedding invites because one came from Tom and frumpy Lorna, and little baby Genevieve, along with a note that said, 'he hoped we could still be friends'! Ha...! Well that's one invitation I won't be accepting!

I'm 'Chief Matron of Honour' for Flo and Jim's wedding, but I don't mind anymore because she's taking me to Harrods for a posh frock, so eat your heart out, Annabel!

Anyway, I got an interesting update from Flo, whose in-depth research had produced a photocopied article from a newspaper, circa eighteen eighty, regarding the death of Lucia Caterina, and entitled, in true Victorian fashion,

A STORY THAT WILL CHILL YOU TO THE BONE

Stranger than fiction is the tale of a grieving mother, Lucia Caterina di Lazio, recently deceased, and her beloved daughter, Caterina, who passed into the Realm of Spirit, aged just seventeen, an innocent victim of Giovanni Vicenza of Venice. His mortal remains rest in limbo beneath the sodden earth of the cemetery at Highgate, for across the narrow pathway is the marble statue of a vengeful angel, now the tomb of Lucia, mother of the murdered girl, who purchased both plots on his death, vowing to deny him absolution until she is content that her daughter's soul is at peace...

MORBID OR WHAT...? And yes, it certainly did chill me to the bone!

On a lighter note, Mum and Dad got their dog! He's some sort of terrier mix, and they didn't have to go to BDH in the end because he just turned up on their doorstep one morning, completely unannounced. They've called him Prince; not that he looks in any way royal, but because his ears stick out rather fetchingly. I asked if Camilla would be joining him soon, but they said that one animal was quite enough to cope with, what with the walks, and the dog biscuits.

Best of all, I'm no longer working for the agency, HOORAY!!! I followed Annabel's example and found a job in a sweet, little school just a bus ride away; I'm teaching seven-year olds and it's wonderful! Annabel is still with Joe, he got a transfer to the library in Gloucester, and he already seems to be a part of their family. I just hope he knows what he's getting himself into!

Sofia sold the Villa Alatri to the tour company and she's living with Nonna in Verona, which could be the start of a limerick, 'There once was a lady called Nonna, Who had a large house in Verona', you get the gist; it probably needs a bit of work though so maybe when I've got more time... We'll visit them in the summer, and I'll get to see the chandelier that caused my fainting fit on Murano. I'm certain now that all that weirdness is behind me. Julia told me that there was something in my past that needed to be sorted, and I'm pretty sure that it has been; and since we got back from Venice my life has been completely normal, whatever that is. Of course, you just never know what will happen tomorrow, or the day after, and actually, I don't think we ever have any choice, we only think we do, but we don't, not really.

'Looks like everything she said was right though,' said Annabel, when she came down to see us in the new flat, 'you know, Julia, the fortune teller from the end of the pier? And very posh, you've got to hand it to her; she's done really well for herself, and she knew what she was talking about. And all that stuff about meetings and partings... You know, 'The Lovers', well that was right for a start. You'd parted from Tom and then you met Adam...'

'Yes, my 'King of Wands'...'

'...and I suppose I'd never have met Joe either, if I hadn't been doing all that Tarot research in the library. Der... we thought the Major Arcana was a friend of hers! Actually, they're pretty grim aren't they? All those weird pictures of the 'Moon' and the 'Hanged Man' and so on...'

'Oh yes, Grim... he was there too... poor old Sibella! She might have lived a few more years if Gio hadn't frightened the life out of her, though I'm not sure she wanted that. Maybe her time had come.'

'Yes, poor old Sibella!' sighed Annabel, 'And what about Gio? I suppose he must have been the 'tricky fellow' she mentioned; quite attractive though wasn't he? I wonder what became of him...'

'Oo... I meant to tell you, Adam found out where he was. Gio's mother wrote to him; she said he'd turned up somewhere near Naples! It was completely out of the blue, and she hadn't heard about any of the other stuff; actually, she hadn't even realised he'd left Venice. He's still searching for ancient artefacts, but this time all completely legit.'

'Gosh, Kate, you mean he survived?'

'Yes, just about; not sure it did him much good though. Can you imagine being stuck on Poveglia?' I felt queasy just thinking about it, 'Still, he deserved it! Antonio went back for his boat a couple of days later. He'd been off with your floozy, so he hadn't noticed it was gone.'

She smiled, 'Good of Antonio to be so nice about it! Julia did warn you though, didn't she?'

'Yes, I suppose she did, but it was all going to happen anyway; just fate, I suppose, leading me down some totally unexpected and random, winding path! Can't complain though, can we? After all, it led us to Adam and Joe, and Sofia, and beautiful Serenissima, and loads of people we'd never have met otherwise. It was destiny, and even if we know what's going to happen, well, it seems that we still can't change it.'

'Yes, you're absolutely right! Destiny...' murmured Annabel, '...already written in the stars! Shall I put the kettle on, Kate? Or I could open that bottle of Prosecco I brought with me...Yes; let's do that, mmm... cheers, dahling, chink-chink...! Got any nibbles...?'

THE BEE'S KNEES
and
OTHER SPIRITS

Adam is off to Mongolia, but a yurt, albeit a designer yurt, doesn't appeal to Kate. Instead, she opts for a staycation at Hiddleback Hall, currently occupied by Annabel's great uncle, and the ghost of the gardener, who fell from the encroaching clifftop in suspicious circumstances. Fortunately, they're not too far from their local tavern, and the landlord, Clive, who makes fabulous cocktails, including Annabel's Bee's Knees.

Now available on Amazon Books

Also, by this author:

Joni
The Dead Man in the Tree

Writers always need readers, so if you've enjoyed 'The Gypsy Warned You!' please recommend it to your friends and post a comment on the Amazon website.

Amazon Author's Page:

amazon.com/author/carolprior

Website: carolpriorbooks.com

Carol Prior Books – on Facebook and Instagram

Printed in Great Britain
by Amazon